Asunder transforms the rea
to the streets of New Yo
atrocities of fascism to the
twists and turns of this fictional story are well dramatized from start to finish! Spellbinding and captivating. A must-read!

--Susan Quinn, CGA,
Visions from Handwriting

Janet Sierzant's Asunder is a heart-wrenching love story set against the backdrop of the Second World War. The main protagonists are well-developed characters. Antoinette comes across as sympathetic, and it's easy to fall in love with the handsome Domenico. This novel's complex, interesting, and believable emotional tension is overwhelming because it comes from the main protagonists' interaction and outside forces they can't control. However, it is their emotional journeys that direct the plot. This is an enthralling novel with numerous twists and turns and a completely unexpected ending. It is a captivating story that will hook readers from the moment Antoinette and Domenico meet in Milan up to the last page of the book. Highly recommended.

--Maria Victoria Beltran,
Readers Favorite

In Asunder: Forgotten Love by Janet Sierzant, the author has taken a very sensitive subject and period in time and written a most intriguing, heartfelt, and lovely romance that anyone can associate with in current times. The reader's attention is captured from the first sentence and remains riveted until the last page is read. Along with tears, signs, laughter, and hope, the reader will become part of the cast of characters in the book.

--Bernadette Longu,
Readers' Favorite

Asunder

Forgotten Love

Janet Sierzant

Asunder

ISBN: 978-1-970153-33-0
Library of Congress Control Number: 2023902282
Distribution: Ingram Book Company

Please excuse any typos. Between the auto spell, my cats running across the keyboard, and an occasional glass of wine, it happens.

LA
Maison
La Maison Publishing
Vero Beach, Florida
The Hibiscus City
lamaisonpublishing@gmail.com

Take a Risk!
Climber Higher

Chapter 1

1932

Antoinette stood in front of the mirror, the scissors in midair. Her long wavy hair hung down past her shoulders. She closed her eyes to envision the look she wanted. Her father would surely disapprove, but if she learned one lesson growing up in a Fascist home, it was not to conform. Suppressing her inhibitions, she opened her eyes and began clipping until all her long tresses lay at her feet.

Gaetano knocked on her bedroom door. "Hurry, Antoinette, our Prime Minister, Mussolini, is about to make his speech."

"Oh, Papa. You know I don't care about politics."

"This is important. The broadcast is live from the Duomo in Milan. You should know the political climate since you'll attend school there."

"All right, I'm coming."

She joined her parents and grandparents in the living room. Gaetano was adjusting the antenna on the radio. He looked up, and his face reddened.

"What did you do to your hair?"

"All the girls wear their hair short now, Papa."

"Hair is the crowning glory of a woman," he said. "Why would you want to look like everyone else?"

"I think it looks cute," her mother said.

"It's not befitting a Fascist lady. Il Duce would disapprove."

"He's dragging women back to the past, Papa. I want to be stylish like the women in Milan."

Mussolini's booming voice burst into the room.

"Black Shirts of Milan! I intend to lay down the position of fascist Italy with unions who disrupt our society with strikes."

The crowd roared.

"The rule of law," Mussolini continued. *"That's what we need in this country."*

"He sounds like a dictator, Papa."

"Nonsense. Italy cannot prosper if workers strike every week. "The trains run on time thanks to Mussolini, and I still have a job. The Instituto Marangoni costs a great deal of money. Unless you plan to pay for it, you'll be happy I'm working."

"His achievements so far are miraculous," Grandpa said. "The man has single-handedly put the railroad employees back to work. Mussolini has modernized the entire transportation industry." He grabbed a tissue and had a coughing fit. "Sorry, I can't seem to shake this bug."

"I think it's more than a cold," Grandma said, smoothing her hair. Grandma was a stout woman with strong opinions.

"I don't like it! You need to see a doctor."

"Nonsense. I'll be fine."

Grandma was about to argue, but Mussolini's voice drowned her out.

"Fascism is opposed to that form of democracy which equates a nation to the majority."

"Mussolini is the only man capable of bringing order to this chaos, Gaetano said. "He will provide stability to our country."

"Mark my words, Son," Grandma argued. "He will divide our country."

"Shush," Grandpa said. "I'm missing his speech."

"The fascist state is not apathetic to religious phenomena," Mussolini shouted. "Nor does it maintain an attitude of indifference to Roman Catholicism, the religion of Italians."

The crowds raised their voices in approval.

"I wonder if he's truly religious," Grandma said.

"If the Church thought he was a bad man, Mother, I'm sure they'd speak out," Gaetano said. "He agrees with the teachings of the Pope."

"It's true," Josephina said, agreeing with her husband. "He was married in the church and baptized his children there."

Antoinette's mother accepted her place in the patriarchal family. She dressed in traditional matronly attire of long skirts and tailored blouses. The only hint of femininity was the lace on her embroidered apron.

"Grandma's right," Antoinette said. "My teacher told us he only did that to get the church's support.

He's trying to make amends with the Catholic Church after declaring himself an atheist as a socialist youth."

"Doesn't your teacher realize what he's done for education?"

"Maria Montessori is no longer at the school. He drove her out because they believed her teaching method was too democratic."

"Well, if that's what it takes to put this country on track, I'll be the first on our street to wear the black shirt."

"If Mussolini had his way, Papa, he'd force everyone to be a fascist."

"I'm having second thoughts about letting you go away to school. I don't want my daughter to get Socialist ideas. Maybe you should stay here in Florence and find a suitable husband."

"Husband? I don't want to be a housewife. My life would be so dull!" She turned to her mother. "Sorry, Mama. I don't mean…." Antoinette stood up to leave.

"Where are you going?" Gaetano asked. "It's not over."

"This is all very interesting, but I'm meeting my friends at the Teatro Niccolini. I can't be late."

"I hope it isn't one of these liberal plays from the west."

"Don't worry so much. It's a Parisian play."

"Hmm. All right but come straight home after."

"I will, Papa," she said, kissing his forehead and hugging her mother.

"Good night, Grandma. Good night, Grandpa."

"Take a sweater, Dear," her mother said. "It's chilly in the theater."

Antoinette obediently went to her room to get a sweater.

"She's been taking too many liberties lately," Gaetano said.

"She isn't a baby anymore," Josephina said. "She will be on her own in Milan. You must trust her."

He shook his head. "In my day, women married and stayed home to raise children. They could hardly dream of getting a university education, much less a profession."

"Antoinette isn't like other women."

"No, she's stubborn and…."

"Just like her father?" Josephina interrupted.

Before Antoinette closed the door behind her, she heard Mussolini's call to action.

"Raise your banners and your arms to the sun. Salute the fascist march!"

Chapter 2

Antoinette's beauty stood out among the ordinary ladies of Florence. She inherited her mother's high cheekbones and ample bosom, which made her self-conscious. Her brown eyes turned amber when they caught the light just so. The world lay before her as she prepared to leave her hometown.

She awoke earlier than usual and jumped out of bed. Her new orange summer dress hung on the doorframe. It was one of the many she had designed and sewn with the help of her grandmother. It had a shorter hemline and emphasized her figure.

Most textile firms under Mussolini were now controlled by government officials who required fashion to meet the criteria of the new fascist regime. Antoinette looked up to stylists considered dissidents, such as Salvatore Ferragamo and Elsa Schiaparelli. She had dreams of following in their footsteps.

Slipping into her dress, she admired herself in the mirror. She followed the scent of bacon frying in the kitchen, where her family ate breakfast.

Her father dropped his fork. "You're not wearing that dress," he shouted.

"But Papa. I designed it, especially for my journey to Milan."

"It's too short. No daughter of mine will flaunt her legs for all of Italy to see. You change right now, or else you're not going anywhere."

"Do as your father says," Josephine said. She hugged her daughter and whispered in her ear. "Change into something more to your father's liking. It will smooth his ruffled feathers."

Antoinette went to her room and changed into a navy-blue skirt and matching blazer that rested just below her hips. It had a single button in the front, and the sleeves were embellished with intricate scrollwork, making it look militant. She folded her sundress into the suitcase with the rest of her creations.

"That's much better," Gaetano said when she returned to the kitchen. Too excited to eat, she nibbled on a piece of Italian bread smeared with her grandmother's homemade jam.

After breakfast, Gaetano carried her baggage to the car and climbed behind the wheel. She hugged her mother, promising to come home for a visit whenever she could.

Gaetano lectured her the entire way to the Santa Maria Novella train station.

"Be very careful. Milan is not like our small village. The people there are too liberal. Their minds are too democratic. It is a major city with crime, and many people will try to take advantage of you, especially men. Watch out for them. They only want one thing, and it isn't marriage."

"I'm going to Milan to study, Papa, not to find a husband."

"You know, I'm leaving for Rome next week," Gaetano said. "I want to make sure you're safe."

"Rome? Why are you going there?"

"I'm joining the Black Shirts to support Mussolini."

"I hope you're not joining the Italian Army."

"Don't be silly. No one wants an old man like me as a soldier. I'm going to work on the train system."

Antoinette kissed her father's cheeks and clung to him before she boarded the train. She couldn't shake the feeling that something bad might happen to him.

"Be safe, Papa."

*****

Antoinette sat by a window and watched the open fields go by. Three hours later, they abruptly ended, replaced by high-rise buildings as she entered the city.

She stepped from the train to the sound of whistles blowing, and people rushed to take connections. She looked around, trying to get her bearings. Following the crowd, she pushed and shoved her way off the platform to the exit.

Outside, she found the bus to *Via Pietro Verri*. Her best friend, Gabriella, was already in Milan. They'd known each other since grade school. Together, they signed a lease to share an apartment close to the university. Antoinette wanted to be a fashion designer, and Gabriella dreamed of being a model. She had come to Milan a week earlier to be in a fashion show planned for Christmas.

Antoinette searched the crowds, looking for a familiar face. As she began to panic, she spotted her friend.

"I'm so relieved to see you," Antoinette said. "This place is a madhouse."

"Yes, Milan is a busy hub, and I'm afraid you came at the height of tourist season."

"How far is the apartment?"

"It's only a few blocks, but your luggage looks heavy. Maybe we should take a cab." She flagged a driver sitting in his vehicle in front of the station, and he loaded Antoinette's baggage in the trunk.

"I can't wait to hear about your strange tales and adventures, Gabriella."

"I have so much to tell you. The boys here aren't as stuffy as the ones back home. They have lots of parties." Gabriella was self-confident and, at times, too trusting in boys. "There are so many already, and a party tomorrow night for us to go to."

Gabriella helped her with the bags. Giggling and excited, Antoinette unpacked as her friend told her what was happening around town.

"The fashion show is tomorrow. One of the girls quit. I can get you in if you're interested."

"It sounds like fun," Antoinette said, "but I'm not sure I can walk down a runway in heels. I'll probably trip and fall into the audience."

Gabriella laughed. "That would get you some attention, I'm sure." She rummaged through the closet and pulled out a pair of high-heeled shoes. "You can practice. Trust me. It's like riding a bicycle. Once you get your balance, you'll be fine."

Antoinette looked doubtfully at the shoes.

"It pays well," Gabriella said. "You might even meet someone important to help your career as a designer. It's all about who you know. And it doesn't hurt to meet an attractive man or two."

"All right, I'll do it. I'll fill in for the model tomorrow."

They giggled like schoolgirls.

"We're worse than a couple of starry-eyed teenagers," Gabriella said.

Chapter 3

Antoinette put all her best designs in her valise and zipped it up.

"Why are you bringing your drawings?" Gabriella asked.

"I know it's silly, but you never know. I could get an opportunity to show them to the designer. I don't want to miss my chance."

Gabriella laughed. "It's going to be hectic. You'll be lucky if the designer knows a real person exists under his creations."

They walked to the *Palazzo Serbelloni* and entered the stage door to sign in.

Gabriella introduced Antoinette to Ethan, the fashion designer.

Although he was busy, he paused to kiss her hand.

"Thank you for filling in," he said. "I couldn't have chosen a lovelier woman to display my collection."

Ethan, a handsome man of twenty-two, was only five-foot-eight inches but stood perfectly straight, making him seem taller. His eyes were baby blue, and his hair was the color of corn silk. He was stylish, with a laid-back attitude. The other designers barked orders to their models, threatening to take their stilettos and send them home. The stress levels were high, but Ethan remained calm and confident.

The staff was running in every direction, setting up for the show. The last to arrive was a handsome man in his late twenties wearing a button-down shirt and tailored black slacks.

"Hi, Domenico," the models greeted him in a musical chorus crowded around him. Milan was full of young girls looking for romance. Apparently, Domenico was a catch.

Unaffected by the beautiful women around him, he headed toward the platform to set up. Antoinette watched him pass. She was instantly attracted to his black hair and warm brown eyes.

"That's Domenico," Gabriella whispered. "He's the main photographer—popular with the ladies. He has an appetite for gorgeous women and fast cars."

"He's the most handsome man I've ever seen."

"Buongiorno girls. You are all looking lovely today. Before the show, I'll take your picture. The dressing room is on the left." He pointed. "You'll find your name on the garment you'll wear on the runway. Please come to the podium when I call you. You'll have one hour to rehearse. The catwalk is slippery, so you must practice in the stilettos."

They giggled and moved as one behind the stage to a well-lit room with racks, dresses, and accessories to get dressed.

Antoinette zipped up the long silk gown. It was the color of rubies and emphasized her complexion.

When she stepped out of the dressing room, she saw a white sheet stretched across the wall, illuminated by a giant spotlight.

Ethan gestured to the spot in front of the camera and directed her under the lights.

Domenico caught sight of her as she moved gracefully onto the platform. Struck by her beauty, he gazed into her amber eyes. His stare was intense. Time seemed to slow down. She waited for him to break the contact, but he did not look away or drop his eyes. Held in his gaze, she had a strange feeling, like they already knew each other.

"Domenico," Ethan said. "How do you want her to pose?"

Jolted back to reality, Domenico dropped his gaze and concentrated on his camera. After the shoot, he stood mesmerized for a moment.

"Are you finished?" Ethan asked impatiently. "Or are you just going to stand there staring at her?"

"I wasn't staring."

"Of course, you were. "

"No, I was.... Yes. I'm ready for the next girl." He reached out to help Antoinette down from the platform.

"Do you have plans tonight, Senorita? I would love to get to know you better."

"I'm sorry. I'm busy tonight. Perhaps another time."

He smiled. "Yes, another time."

Chapter 4

Gabriella was already dressed for the party when Antoinette came home. She wore a form-fitting blue dress. Although she was thin, the low cut accentuated her meager cleavage.

"What did you think about Ethan?" Gabriella asked.

"He seems nice, but…." Domenico flashed through her mind. "Ethan is nice, but Domenico has my eye."

"Domenico? Don't get your hopes up."

"I don't have any expectations. I only think he's interesting. Besides, he stared at me all day. Didn't you notice?"

"Forget it, Antoinette. He has an appetite for gorgeous women and the opportunity to meet many of them in his field of work. They all have a crush on him."

Antoinette looked wounded by her friend's warning.

"Don't take it personally," Gabriella said. "He's just unattainable."

"Perhaps."

"You're beautiful, Antoinette. I'm sure you can find someone more suitable. Take Ethan, for example. He's quite taken with you.

Antoinette's eyes opened wide. "Maybe he'll hire me to work at his shop."

"You know seamstresses start at the bottom."

"Yes, but if I could work my way and become a designer. I'm not looking for a romantic relationship." I hope he doesn't get the wrong idea.

Antoinette wriggled into a honey-colored dress with a scalloped neckline. It didn't look like much on the hanger, although on her body, it came alive.

"Wow," Gabriella said. "That's some dress. You look stunning. Now all you need is a little makeup."

Antoinette sighed. "I didn't bring any with me. My father never allows me to wear makeup."

"You can borrow mine. Just a little mascara and lipstick will make all the difference." Gabriella dug through her cosmetic bag. She applied a little brown powder on Antoinette's lids, highlighting her amber eyes.

"Perfect," she said and gave Antoinette a mirror.

"Wow. You should be a makeup artist."

"Hmm. I'll think about it if I don't make it as a model. I've thought about being a cosmetologist."

"Is your boyfriend coming to the party with us?"

"I'm not sure. He had something to do and might meet me there."

"If he shows up, I'll be alone. I hope I don't feel out of place."

"Don't be silly. Ethan and his sister Rachel will be there, along with many of the models you met at the show. You'll be fine."

They walked arm in arm to the party around the corner from the college. They heard the music as they approached.

Ethan sat next to a blonde on the couch while his sister chatted with her fiancé.

"Hello again." He stood up and kissed her hand. "I'm so glad you came this evening."

To her amazement, he seemed to be interested in her.

His eyes grazed over her. "I love your dress. The details are unusual."

"Thank you. I designed it myself."

"I'm very impressed."

My dream is to train in a couture house here in Milan."

"With talent like yours, that shouldn't be a problem. Gabriella says you're from Florence. How are you liking Milan?"

"I've only been here for a week now. I'm not used to the culture."

He laughed. "I'm sure it's quite different from Florence. It takes time, but you'll adjust to our fast-paced lives."

"Yes, things seem to move rather quickly here, but I love being in the center of the fashion capital."

As the party heated, everyone was drinking and dancing. Antoinette lost track of her friend Gabrielle but noticed her arguing with her boyfriend, who staggered at the bar.

Antoinette looked up just as Domenico entered the room. She couldn't look away from Domenico. Smiling, she studied his face, noting his complexion was paler than hers against his dark beard. He needed a haircut, but the wild locks in front of his eyes made him look sweet.

Her smile faded as another woman rushed over and linked her arm to his. Antoinette felt a lump in her throat.

The woman was stunning with long straight black hair and a dainty figure. Domenico didn't pull away.

"Perhaps we can have dinner sometime next week when things return to normal."

Ethan was still talking, but she didn't hear a word he said.

"Antoinette?" Ethan's voice snapped her back. She took her gaze away from Domenico and fixed it on Ethan.

"Dinner? I'd love to. I'm sorry. I need to find the powder room."

"It's at the end of the hall."

"Thank you." Antoinette moved through the crowd. Her eyes met Domenico's. He smiled, but there was no sense of longing like before. His blank expression pained her more than anything else. She found the restroom but had to wait until the person inside came out and brushed past her in the narrow hall. Antoinette closed the door behind her and leaned against it. She placed her hands on the sink and glanced in the mirror. *What does she have that I don't?* She splashed cold water on her hot cheeks and returned to the living room to find Gabriella.

"Can we leave soon?"

"Sure. My boyfriend has had too much to drink. He's acting like a jerk."

Antoinette said goodbye to Ethan and left with Gabriella. She was relieved that she didn't have to watch Domenico and his date any longer. Once they were outside, she drew in the night air.

"Domenico was there," she said. "Did you see him?"

"Yes, and that Asian bombshell glued to his side, too."

"Do you think they're an item?"

Gabriella huffed. "Even if they aren't, you'd never be happy with him."

"I may never get the chance to find out."

"You and Ethan seemed to be hitting it off. I think he really likes you."

"I told Ethan I'd go to dinner with him."

"That's great. Stick with Ethan. He's a sure thing."

Chapter 5

Ethan parked in front of Antoinette's apartment and took the elevator to the second floor. He smoothed his shirt, raked his fingers through his hair, and knocked lightly on the door.

"Come in, Ethan," Gabriella said.

"Hi, Gabriella. I didn't know that you shared an apartment with Antoinette."

"We're childhood friends. I'll let her know you're here."

"Can I get you something to drink?"

"Thank you, I'm fine. I'll sit on the couch and wait."

She stuck her head inside the bedroom and whispered to Antoinette.

Turning to Ethan, she smiled. "Antoinette is almost ready." She sat next to him. "The show is going well, don't you think?" she said.

"Yes, indeed. I already have orders from two major department stores in London and one from New York."

"New York? That's exciting."

When Antoinette came out of the bedroom, Ethan gasped.

"You look fantastic. Gabriella has told me you want to be a designer. Is this one of your designs?"

"Yes. I made this one a few years ago. I'm afraid it's outdated."

"Not at all. You look spectacular."

"Thank you. My grandmother worked at a textile mill and brought home discarded fabrics. She taught me how to sew and take old clothes apart to make new ones. Sometimes, I stayed up all night sewing."

"I'd love to see your sketches. Maybe you can show them to me."

"I don't usually let anyone see them."

"Oh, come on. I won't steal your designs."

"I wasn't worried about that." Realizing he was joking, she pulled out her portfolio and showed him her sketches.

"These are quite good," he said, flipping through the drawings.

"I can use a good seamstress with an eye for fashion. Would you consider working for me?"

"I would love that."

"Great. You can start Monday if you like." He offered his arm. "Shall we go?"

"Have a splendid evening, you two," Gabriella said with a sly smile.

Antoinette rolled her eyes. "By Gabby."

Ethan opened the car door for Antoinette, and she slid into the passenger side of his Fiat. When they arrived at the restaurant, he pulled in front and handed his keys to the valet. The staff went out of their way to greet him when they entered.

"Wow. You must be a celebrity."

"I come here a lot," he whispered. "The food is terrific, and the service is impeccable."

The hostess showed them to their table. Ethan caught the sommelier's attention, and he came right over.

"Good to see you again, Mr. Rubenstein," he said. "A nice Rosso today, sir?"

"Yes, indeed. The thirty-two."

"Certainly, sir," the sommelier said.

Antoinette smiled and fanned her face. "I've never been here before. I see they have chocolate mousse on the menu."

"We'll order that for dessert. But first, may I suggest the lobster for our main course?"

"Lobster? Oh, that's so expensive."

"Please don't worry about the price," Ethan said. "I'm lucky enough to afford some modest comforts, like eating good food in my favorite restaurants. My whole family has managed to live a good life."

"What did your father do for a living?"

"He was an alchemist. He wanted me to follow in his footsteps, but I had no interest in chemistry. I preferred to hang around my mother's shop."

"What did she do?"

"My mother was a seamstress. She hated readymade clothes and considered them ugly. That gave her the idea to buy patterns from an emerging couture house. She began making her own clothes, and all the women in town noticed her unique style. They begged her to make them a dress or skirt. My mother had difficulty refusing, and soon new orders flowed daily. Her home business expanded, and the house was filled with bolts of fabrics and boxes of notions. It was more than she could handle.

"My father protested and moved her into a shop around the corner from our house. Elegant ladies came from all over Milan for new outfits. The shop prospered, and she spent long hours in the shop."

"I guess you didn't see much of her at home if she was always in the shop."

Instead of going home after school, I went there to help my mother thread the needles because my eyesight was better. She liked that I took an interest in her business and always had a snack waiting for me after school. I was a favorite in a sea of women as I scurried around picking up pins that had dropped under the machines. They always fussed over me, and I became addicted to their praise. I loved the feel of the fabrics. I'd study the patterns pinned to the materials and watch as the seamstresses carefully traced them in white chalk. It amazed me to see the garments take shape.

"Is that the reason you became a designer?"

"I believe so. As I grew older and nimbler with my fingers, the girls would let me sew tiny pearls onto the bodice of wedding dresses. They thought the job was tedious, but I didn't mind."

"Did they let you use the sewing machines?"

"Not until I was twelve. I gathered scraps of material that fell to the floor to make Rachel clothes for her dolls. That worried my father. 'Playing with dolls is for sissies. Why don't you go out and play like normal boys?'"

"'I'm not playing with dolls,'" I'd say. "'I want to learn how to make clothes.'"

"'Leave the boy alone,'" my mother would say.

"It sounds like you had a close relationship with your mother. What about your father?"

"My father worked long hours, too, and did everything to ensure his family was cared for, but he was a solitary man. He didn't show emotion very often. I don't remember him telling me he loved me, although I knew he did. My sister Rachel and I went to the best schools. She later studied medicine which made my father happy. Alas, I was a disappointment. My Father wanted me to go into the medical field. He didn't think textiles would provide a decent living."

"Did Rachel become a doctor?"

"No, she never finished her degree. She decided she wanted to be a singer. It's a long story. Enough about me. I want to know about you."

"I want to be honest. My family has strong fascist beliefs. It's not always popular."

"These are scary times," Ethan said. "I'm hearing stories that are disturbing and hard to believe."

"Do you think Italy will go to war?"

"That's unlikely. Ethan grinned. "Italians are lovers, not fighters." His smile faded. "That's also what makes the situation concerning. Germany could easily overpower us if Hitler spotted an ounce of weakness in Mussolini. Hitler seems hell-bent on acquiring more land. Right now, he has Czechoslovakia in his sights. If he…."

The background music was interrupted by two German soldiers who demanded a table. Their uniforms had an air corps decal embroidered on their sleeves. Both had short-cropped hair, one light brown and the other white-blond.

"Mi dispiace," the maître d' said. "There is no room."

The soldier with blond hair stepped forward and grabbed him by his collar. "Do you know who I am?"

Antoinette turned her attention toward the commotion.

"Nazis," Ethan whispered.

"There seems to be more and more of them lately."

"Yes, especially now that Il Duce has initiated cooperative talks with Germany.

Flustered, the maître d' looked around the restaurant to see if anyone had finished their meals.

"That couple is almost done. I may be able to seat you. Give me a moment."

Realizing the maître d' was gazing at Ethan and Antoinette, the men walked over to their table. "I believe you are finished with your meal," one said.

Antoinette smiled. "We haven't had our mousse yet."

The Nazi laughed in a manner that wasn't pleasant. "Oh, excuse me. My mistake." His eyes turned vicious, and he laughed again. This time it was an ugly sound. "This is an Italian restaurant, lady!"

Antoinette set her jaw and narrowed her eyes. "And we are Italians."

The blonde soldier turned to Ethan. "This is a Jew if I ever saw one."

Ethan stood. "Let them have the table, Antoinette. We'll have dessert at the café."

Antoinette wouldn't back down. She glared at the men. "You don't have the right to treat people this way. Please sit down, Ethan. We're not leaving."

"If you don't want your Jew boy to get his head bashed in, you might reconsider," said the soldier. The other man stepped behind Ethan and hooked an arm around his neck.

The maître d,' four servers, and two cooks quickly encircled the table. "Stop!" The maître d' shouted, pointing a gun at the men. "This is a respectable restaurant."

The soldier released Ethan, who dropped back into his chair.

"We wouldn't eat here if it was the last place in Milan." He turned for the door with the other soldier close behind him. "Jew Lovers!" he shouted and spat on the floor. "All of you!"

The staff returned to work, and the patrons returned to their meals as the music resumed.

Chapter 6

Ethan and his sister Rachel worked together in the family business. Antoinette hadn't talked with Rachel during the party, but she was anxious to know her better. She arrived early on Monday morning and went to the office.

"Hello, Antoinette," Rachel said. "Ethan isn't here, but I've been expecting you. This is Jakub Kaminski. He is the floor supervisor."

"Nice to meet you, miss," he said in an unmistakably Polish accent.

"Come," Rachel said. I'll show you around."

Antoinette followed her to the main production room, where forty women worked at sewing machines. They were singing and laughing over the clatter of the bobbins.

"I'm so happy you'll be working with us," Rachel said as she showed Antoinette to her workstation. "The pattern you'll be working with is for a day dress.

Antoinette ran her finger along the edges of the pattern pinned to a delicate soft fabric with a slight shimmer. "I love the clean lines of this dress."

"Yes, it originated in Japan. Ethan had it duplicated. I'll check on you later to see if you need anything."

Cutting and sewing the dresses seemed never-ending as she produced one after another.

What made it pleasurable was Rachel. Despite the heat and humidity, she always wore a smile. She was continuously singing. Antoinette recalled Ethan saying that Rachel had wanted to be a singer.

During the lunch break, Rachel sat next to Antoinette in the dining room. It was a sunny room at the back of the shop lined with windows.

"How's it going so far?" she asked.

"Great. Ethan's designs are easy to follow."

"That's because he believes in simplicity. My brother has an instinct for what looks good on women. It took a while before his designs were accepted. French designers govern the world of couture. They don't take to outsiders, especially unknown talent from Italy."

"Paris has always been the world's fashion capital," Antoinette said, "but Italy has the advantage. We produce beautiful, high-quality fabrics. French designers rely on our silk production."

"You seem to know a lot about the industry," Rachel said. "Where did you learn it?"

"My grandmother was an excellent seamstress. I pored through her magazines and cut-out pictures of fashionable women. She took me to all the shows to see the newest designers on the south side of the Arno river. One of my favorite couturiers is Emilio Pucci. He's from one of Florence's oldest noble families. I love his contemporary designs."

"Then, you have a lot in common with my brother."

"Ethan told me you went to medical school."

"It wasn't my idea, but I didn't want to disappoint my father. I was the obedient child, the diligent one who studied and always did what I was told, while Ethan was a rebel."

" A rebel? How so?"

He neglected his studies and spent his class time filling notebooks with sketches of women's dresses. Sometimes, we'd cut classes and go to the cinema. Ethan wasn't as interested in the film as he was in what the sultry actresses were wearing.

I was the only one who understood him. When our father took away his allowance, I'd give him most of my weekly allowance so he could buy fashion magazines. He was sent to a military lycée. But no matter what he did, my father couldn't take his love of design from him."

"Ethan told me he worked with your mother."

"Yes, once he was old enough to drive, she'd send him to Rome to deliver finished garments and hunt for new fabrics. Ethan wanted the chance to work on his designs, but our mother thought they were too avant-garde. He worked on her until she finally gave him her blessing. He single-handedly turned the factory into a bustling center for design with state-of-the-art sewing machines."

"Didn't he have an interest in girls?"

"Oh yes. All my friends loved him. I think he has dated every one of them."

"Did he fall in love?"

"There was one girl. He would have died for her. I thought they would eventually get married, but…."

"What happened?"

"She was a Gentile. Our father put his foot down and forbade it."

Ethan came up behind them. "Are you giving away all my secrets?" he teased Rachel.

His demeanor was reliable and kind, and his conversation leaned toward humor which made her like him more.

*****

After lunch, Ethan came to Antoinette's station.

"I see my sister has you working already." "I think she likes you as much as I do."

He examined the pattern that lay on the table. "This is one of my favorite designs. I'm glad Rachel put you on it."

"It's very stylish," she said. "Do you have many orders for it?"

"Yes. One of the largest retailers in Paris has ordered a thousand dresses in various sizes and colors. Soon everyone in France will wear my designs."

Rachel walked over and wrapped her arms around his waist.

"I guess Parisians have a passion for gunny sacks," she kidded.

"Oh, you think so?" he replied and spun around, tickling her until she was in hysterics.

Antoinette loved the way they cracked jokes with each other. Growing up as an only child, she'd wished for a sister.

Ethan was impressed by Antoinette's ability to work with a dress. She was so skilled she didn't need a pattern and could cut cloth for a dress by marking the edges with pins. Ethan encouraged his seamstresses to try new things and welcomed her ideas.

Chapter 7

A model called in sick on the show's last day, so Antoinette returned. Ethan came back to the dressing room, which bustled with preparations. There was barely enough room to move. Brushes and tubes of makeup littered the vanity. The girls giggled and chatted in front of the bright klieg lights as they applied lotion to their arms to make them shine under the runway lights. Makeup artists and hairdressers scurried around creating final looks under the supervision of designers. They had their eye on Antoinette, but Ethan beat them to it.

Last-minute preparations and alterations were made by seamstresses—tucking, sewing, and pinning garments to fit the models perfectly. Each model had to be choreographed to specific music to set the tone for over twenty outfits.

"The girl who didn't show up was supposed to model the last dress," he said. He pulled the shroud off a mannequin, revealing a stunning wedding dress.

The other girls stopped what they were doing and looked at Antoinette, envious that Ethan would choose an unknown model to end the show.

When the lights went up on Ethan's collection, the models descended a double staircase to a glass walkway. The camera bulbs flashed as each girl walked down the runway. Antoinette waited in the wings for her turn, her face covered by a veil. When it was her turn, Ethan instructed her to walk up the runway slowly, then back and raise her veil. She looked at the sea of people in the audience and thought she would be sick. In the corner of her eye, Antoinette noticed Domenico. She could hear her heart beating, even louder than the crowd's murmur, as she passed. Focusing on the long, she hoped she could make it to the end without fainting.

Domenico's camera snapped, recording her every move. As she turned to go back, he paused with a puzzled expression. Antoinette lost sight of him as the flash bulbs blinded her. Once she returned to the top of the runway, she took her place in the center and lifted her veil. There was an audible hush.

Ethan stepped onto the runway, and the audience gave him a standing ovation. The excitement rose to a fever pitch. Then, one by one, the models ascended the stairs and disappeared.

Ethan complimented them. Backstage, a banquet was set with champagne and hors d'oeuvres. After the girls had changed, they came out of the dressing room and surrounded Domenico. A pang of jealousy spurred inside Antoinette. Suddenly, their eyes met.

Domenico abandoned the other girls and headed toward her.

"I'm not sure I could function another day unless I see you," he whispered. "Meet me by the fountain after the show."

Antoinette considered his invitation. "All right," she said and smiled coquettishly.

*****

The sky was cloudy and grey with the promise of snow. Antoinette could see her breath in the crisp air and pulled her coat tighter across her chest. Her heart thumped when she saw Domenico standing at the fountain. He had changed into something casual, and she thought he looked good.

"Hello, Antoinette. I was worried you wouldn't come when I didn't see you here."

"I had to go home and wash off the theatrical makeup. The makeup artist layered it on pretty thick for the show."

"You look more beautiful without it." He took her arm, and they walked across the street. A burst of steam escaped the espresso machine in a nearby café, sending the rich aroma into the street.

"This is one of my favorite places. Do you like coffee?"

"I love the smell of it, but I prefer tea."

Domenico laughed. "That's not very Italian. Are you sure you're not English?"

Antoinette smiled. "I'll have coffee."

"Great. Let's find a cozy table in the back, away from the street noise."

"All the tables seem to be taken," she said.

"Look," Domenico said. "That couple is leaving." He grabbed her arm and pulled Antoinette toward the table. They sat down before the waiter could clear the dishes, and he looked a little annoyed. Still, he smiled and gave them the menu.

"We'll have two espressos," Domenico said.

"Will that be *all*, sir?"

"Perhaps dolce."

"I'll send the dessert cart to your table," he said in a huff.

"He doesn't look happy," Antoinette said.

"Don't worry. I'll leave a good tip."

The piazza was humming with people. Captivated with each other, the rest of the city seemed to disappear.

"Tell me about your family," she said.

"My father and his brothers made a success of an olive farm in Campania."

"Isn't that between two volcanos, Mount Vesuvius and Campi Flegrei?" she asked. "They say that one of those volcanoes is ready to erupt."

Domenico laughed. "They've been predicting that for years. It could happen, but the locals tend to ignore the possibility."

"Do you have a large family?"

"I have a brother, but we're not very close."

"It must have been fun growing up on a farm?"

"Yes, it was a good life, but things are changing."

"I've never been to the southern part are Italy. What's it like there?"

"It's beautiful along the Amalfi Coast. My family has a home in the Gulf of Sorrento. It's hot in the summer, but there's a frequent breeze from the strait. The beach is beautiful, with crystal blue waters and soft white sand. You'd love it."

"Except for trips to my aunt's vineyard in Montepulciano, I've never left Florence. The nearest beach is Viareggio, but it's an hour away by train."

"Florence! The center of so much art and culture. You're so lucky. What made you come to Milan? To be a model?"

"No, I want to be a fashion designer. That's what I'm studying."

"Be careful. Unsavory types prey on young girls with the promise of glamor in the fashion industry."

"Ethan Rubenstein has hired me to work at his studio. He was the designer for the last show."

"I know Ethan well. He is well-known in Milan. He just won an award for being the top designer in Italy. He's a good man. Maybe you know Jakub Kaminski. I believe he works there too."

"I met him briefly. He's Ethan's assistant."

"Yes, another admirable man. You'll learn a lot at Ethan's shop. It's a terrific opportunity."

"Yes. I plan to learn quickly, and maybe I'll get to sew my designs."

"I admire your passion," he said.

"And I admire yours. It isn't easy to be a photographer. You have to capture your subjects at their best."

Domenico grinned, lines appearing at the corners of his mouth and eyes. "Photographing beautiful women is not my passion. I'd rather take photos of more significant subjects."

"How did you become a fashion photographer?"

"It wasn't my plan, but….

"What happened?"

"I was offered a good job here in Milan working for The People of Italy. It became the main newspaper of the fascist movement."

"Isn't that a good thing?"

Domenico looked puzzled. "I think Mussolini is taking the country in the wrong direction."

"Some Italians believe Benito Mussolini has been great for our country."

Domenico weaved his fingers through his hair. "Enough talk about politics. I'd rather talk about more pleasant things, like how beautiful you are when the sunset is reflected in your eyes."

Antoinette blushed as their knees came together under the table, sending a jolt to her heart.

A line was forming outside the café. People were circling for open tables like buzzards. The waiter began clearing the table, impatient for them to leave. Domenico paid the check and left a large tip.

"*Grazie, grazie,*" he said, changing his demeanor.

They both giggled as they walked down the street.

Chapter 8

Antoinette dressed for her second date with Ethan. All she could think about was Domenico. He was six years older, but she didn't care. That only made him more magnetic. She hadn't heard from him in more than two weeks and imagined he had gone back to the Asian girl from the party.

She was quiet during dinner, but if Ethan noticed, he said nothing.

"I want you to see where I live," he said enthusiastically.

She nodded absentmindedly.

"Great. I'll pay the check and take you to see my house."

Her jaw dropped when he drove to a sprawling mansion in the heart of town. There was a large iron across the driveway.

"You live here?"

"Yes, it's pretty big for a lonely bachelor, but a friend from China closed his textile company and went back east. He put it up for sale, and well, I had the money."

Ethan opened the gate and drove through.

After giving her a tour of the house, he led her to the living room.

"Have a seat. I'll put on some music." Ethan placed a Lillian Roth Holiday record on the Victrola. Antoinette closed her eyes and let herself disappear into the music.

"Do you like champagne?"

"My aunt in Montepulciano let me have a sip once when my father wasn't looking, but I don't remember what it tastes like."

"Then, you're in for a treat. "In your honor, I would like to open this Veuve Cliquot Champagne, which I have been keeping for an appropriate occasion."

Ethan opened a bottle that was chilling in a bucket of ice.

Antoinette jumped when the cork hit the ceiling.

"I guess I'm a little jumpy this evening."

Ethan chuckled. He poured two glasses and settled next to her on the sofa. Antoinette tasted the champagne, keeping the glass in front of her mouth and taking small sips. Outside the large picture windows, she could see the massive grounds lying beneath the moonlight. Ethan put his glass down and moved closer.

"This is good," she said.

Ethan took her drink, set it with his on the end table, and pulled her to him. His fingers whispered up and down her spine.

"I love this song."

"Can I have this dance?" He said, taking her hand.

"Yes," she said, happy to change the tension.

As Ethan swayed against her, she felt his hardening groin and pulled away.

"I'm sorry. I don't want you to feel uncomfortable."

"I'm a little tired."

"It's been a long day, and we both have work in the morning. We have plenty of time to dance. If you like, I can take you home."

"Yes, I'll have to call it an early evening. Thank you for understanding."

Ethan drove her back to her apartment. He shut the engine at the curb and reached over to kiss her on the lips, but she turned her head. The kiss landed on her cheek.

"I'll be leaving this week for a conference," he said. "I look forward to seeing you again when I return."

"Good night, Ethan. I had a lovely evening." Antoinette hurried out of the car before he could reply, and she didn't look back.

Chapter 9

The next day, Antoinette could hear Rachel singing even before she opened the door to the shop.

"You sing so beautifully. Did you have singing lessons growing up?"

"No, I always sang, but I didn't take it seriously until college. My father pushed me to attend medical school, but I wanted to sing after winning a talent show. I finally got the courage to confront our father and dropped out. I gave my poor father a great deal of heartache."

"What did he say?"

"He was furious. Education is important to him. He believes Jews get more respect in professions such as medicine or law. The sight of blood always makes me ill, and I've never been interested in being a lawyer."

"Do you know Domenico Defino?"

"He's the fashion photographer from our last show," Rachel said. "He's worked for Ethan before. Nice looking man, isn't he?"

"Yes. I haven't seen Domenico around town lately."

"I think he went back to Campania. He has a large family there."

"Oh," she said, her lower lip protruding in a pout.

"Sounds like you may have a thing for him."

"Oh, no," Antoinette said, shaking her head. "I was just wondering."

Rachel gave her a knowing look. "If you say so. Although, I know infatuation when I see it."

"How did you meet David?" Antoinette asked, changing the subject.

Rachel smiled. "I met him at the Synagogue. He was in my bible study class. My father was so happy when we were engaged. It was the one thing I did right as far as he was concerned.

"Do the two of you have plans to marry?"

"The way things are right now, I'm not sure."

"The way things are?"

Rachel started to say something, then looked away. "Don't mind me. I worry too much."

*****

After work, Antoinette went to some places she had been with Domenico. She went by the café where she and Domenico had their first date and scanned the tables. He had told her it was a favorite place to sit and unwind with espresso in the afternoon. There was no sign of him, so she continued to the market, passing the fountain where lovers kissed and threw coins into the water. She sighed and continued to the market.

Arms full of groceries, she pushed through the exit without looking. Flustered, she lost her grip on the bags, spilling oranges and tomatoes onto the ground. Domenico helped her pick up the fruit. She found herself face-to-face with Domenico. Their eyes met, and she froze. He smiled.

"I'm sorry if I startled you."

"It was my fault," she said. I guess I was daydreaming."

Domenico laughed. "You do that a lot, don't you?" He offered his hand to lift her to her feet. "I'm glad we ran into each other. I just returned from Campania. I've been thinking about you lately."

"Really?" she said with a rush of pleasure.

"Maybe we can get together for another stroll around the city."

"I'd like that."

"Wonderful. Let's meet at the fountain tomorrow. I should be caught up with work by then. How about five?"

"I get off work around four. That will give me time to go home and change. Well, these bags are getting heavy. I'd better get home before I drop them again."

"Here, let me help you." He took both packages from her. "Let me walk you home. That will save your arms, and I'd enjoy keeping you in my company."

Antoinette laughed. "Seems like I'm surrounded by honorable men."

Chapter 10

The next afternoon, Antoinette walked to the *Fontana Delle Quattro Stagioni* in the center of Piazza Giulio Cesare to meet Domenico. The streets were busy with holiday shoppers, and the air filled with the aroma of roasting chestnuts. Halfway there, she stopped to look in a store window. A man rang a bell in front of a department store to attract donations for the less fortunate. On the corner, a gypsy peddled flowers. Their delicious scent perfumed the air. Antoinette looked up at the sky, gray and heavy with clouds. It might have promised snow if the temperature was a few degrees lower, but it only threatened rain.

Domenico was standing in front of the fountain, surrounded by the four Vicenza statues. He was holding a bouquet of gardenias from the same stand she had passed.

"These flowers reminded me of you."

"Oh, how lovely." She buried her face in the flowers, intoxicated by their scent and his thoughtfulness.

Domenico smiled. "Yes, but their beauty pales next to you. You're all I thought about today."

Antoinette blushed.

"Are you warm enough to take a walk?"

Although shivering, she nodded. "Yes, I'd love to."

They talked and joked, strolling around the Piazza. Neither noticed the daylight fading.

A flash of lightning lit up the sky, turning night into day for a moment, followed by a crack of thunder. Rain pounded down, and they ran for cover under a store awning. Trapped by the storm, they huddled together, their faces close together. She could smell the espresso on his breath. A surge sizzled through her body at the thought of him kissing her. She wanted him to and looked up, expecting to feel his lips meet hers. The attraction was there—she felt it.

"Maybe we should go to the movies," he said hesitantly. "Then we can get a bite to eat."

"Oh, can we see Lost Horizon? I love Jane Wyatt."

"Yes, Frank Capra is the director. I've wanted to see it too. He's the greatest director in America."

They took a cab to the Teatro Alla Scala, and Domenico bought two tickets.

Before the movie, the cinema showed a newsreel. Propaganda filled the screen as Il Duce boasted of Italy's position on the world stage.

"What a bunch of hooey!" Domenico said, guiding her toward a seat at the back of the theater.

"Don't you like to know about the events in our country? This is a valuable service for those who aren't fortunate enough to own a radio."

"They feed you only what they want you to know. Fools eat it up with a spoon."

She was about to argue, but the lights went down. The major feature began, and conversation in the theater quieted to a murmur.

The movie was about a hijacked British plane flying over the mountains of Tibet.

Lost in the film's romance, Domenico caressed the silky skin on her arm.

Antoinette did not pull away.

Ultimately, the characters in the film found inner peace, love, and a sense of purpose in Shangri-La, where the inhabitants enjoyed unheard-of longevity. Antoinette was taken by it.

"Do you think there is such a place like that?"

"If there is such a place, I'm sure there aren't any Germans."

Antoinette sighed. "I don't care about Germans. I wish I could live in Shangri-La."

The next round of propaganda flashed on the screen.

"Damned black shirts!"

Antoinette felt a surge of anger. "My father is a black shirt!" She said it proudly. He's on his way to Rome to participate in Mussolini's new government."

Domenico's face froze. "The Black Shirts are thugs and murderers."

"That's not true." She raised her voice to equal his. "They're fighting for a better Italy."

"Haven't you heard the stories coming out of Rome? The Black Shirts attack anyone who goes against them."

"Yes, but there are only a handful of offenders. Il Duce arrested them. He'll put a stop to that."

"That's because it gave him bad press. Il Duce is the one who incited them. He only cares about himself and power."

Antoinette recalled her teacher saying Benito Mussolini had a reason for everything he did. It was to further his power and influence.

"They even bombed the voting polls. Mussolini wants to bring down the Socialist party and replace it with fascists. He wants to control the elections and has threatened the voters who oppose him. If that happens, there won't be a choice."

Her face reddened. "My father isn't a Nazi. Well, my father is a good man. I'm sure he'd never do anything to hurt Italy."

"I'm sure he wouldn't intentionally, but I'm afraid he's being used and might be in danger if he finds out the truth."

The voices of the state followed them as they left the theater. The rain had stopped, the thunderstorm had passed, and there was a break in the clouds. He stroked her hair to calm her, but she pulled away.

"I'm sorry," Domenico said. "I get passionate when I talk about politics."

"I think it's better to be passionate about photography," she said.

"You're right. Let's not talk about this subject."

"Look, it's a full moon tonight," Domenico said. You look so lovely in the moonlight. Let's walk along the Naviglio River and fall in love."

Antoinette's face softened. Still angry, she tried to deny her feelings because she still wanted to be with him.

They strolled across the bridge and stopped in the middle.

"You can kiss me if you want," she said.

"More than you can imagine."

He kissed the nape of her neck softly, making her purr.

Forgetting their differences, she turned to Domenico, hungry for his kiss.

His lips met hers. Antoinette felt dizzy with love, as if she were on a cliff's edge. The feeling both scared and excited her.

"I really should get back to the apartment," she said. "I have fashion history class in the morning."

He nodded. "And I, too, have an early appointment at La Rinascente."

"Wasn't that the men's department store that closed due to a fire?"

"Yes, it was originally owned by the Bocconi Brothers, but they sold it before the fire. It's been rebuilt, bigger and better than ever."

They walked the rest of the way in silence. Domenico playfully bumped her shoulders several times, making her smile.

"I hope to see you again," he said, smiling.

Antoinette didn't reply. She had a lot to think about before seeing him again.

"I hope you're not still mad at me."

"No. Although I inherited my father's disposition to anger, I tend to forgive easily."

"Well, then. May I kiss you good night?"

She smiled and closed her eyes, breathing in his scent. His kiss was more forceful and lingered as if he wasn't sure he would get to taste her lips again.

Antoinette reluctantly pulled away. "I hope to see you again soon."

"I would like that," he said and waited for her to be safe inside.

Lying in her bed that night, she thought of Domenico and Ethan. Both men were handsome and kind. Domenico's dark hair and intense looks were hard to ignore, but his political persuasions were a problem. Gnawing-doubts surfaced about her father's beloved Fascist party. They touched on her feelings about Mussolini.

Chapter 11

Milan bustled with creativity. Artists, writers, and numerous specialized workers in the fashion industry were busy with their craft during the day. But in the evenings, they savored their leisure time around the fountain, laughing and talking in the square. By nighttime, diners filled the cafés with customers, eating and drinking.

Domenico introduced her to the party scene in Milan, taking her to the insiders' meeting places where influential people gathered to make connections. The favored locations constantly changed, but Domenico always knew where to go. At these places, glamorous girls sought his attention. As they dined, his friends came to the table to meet Antoinette. Girls waved to him from across the restaurant. When they realized he was with a woman, jealousy burned in their eyes.

"You could be with any woman in Milan," she said. "Why did you choose me?"

"I don't want any other woman. I only want you."

She blushed.

"Let's sit near the fountain," Domenico said after dinner. "I hear live music, and it's a beautiful evening. We should take advantage of it because there's a cold front coming in tomorrow."

Antoinette rummaged through her purse.

"What are you looking for?"

" A coin to throw in the fountain. "I want to make a wish."

Domenico dug into his pocket and retrieved two coins.

Antoinette turned her back to the fountain and closed her eyes. Then tossed the coin over her shoulder, but not far enough.

"Here you go. Try again." He handed her the second coin.

"Don't you want to make a wish?"

"My wish already came true."

They gazed into each other's eyes, flirting and teasing. Antoinette laughed so much that her cheeks hurt. As they walked around the city's outskirts, they discovered an old house on the edge of town. Both could see its beauty beyond the decaying shingles and happily discussed how they would renovate it.

The sun sunk below the clouds.

"It looks like we get snow," he said.

"How can you tell?"

"I can taste it on my tongue."

She laughed and stuck out hers. "It is starting to get cooler. I should get back to my apartment. I have an early class in the morning."

Domenico walked her back to her apartment and kissed her.

"Will I see you tomorrow?" he asked.

"Yes, if you like."

"Same time at the fountain. I'll spend the whole day at work tomorrow anticipating."

"Dream of me tonight," she said.

She looked up and saw her friend Gabriella peering out the window.

When Antoinette entered the apartment, Gabriella gave her a disapproving look and shook her head. "I feel bad for you."

Antoinette raised her brow and looked at her friend cynically.

"Why?"

"Because you look like a lovesick fool."

"I can't help it. I'm falling in love."

"What about Ethan?" She peppered her with questions. I thought you were seeing each other."

"Yes, but I can't decide."

"Ethan is a master of couture. The two of you have more in common."

"My heart and head tell me different things."

"You better keep your feet on the ground," Gabriella warned. "You're taking a big risk."

Antoinette's stomach quivered. "I know, I know. Domenico has many pretty girls chasing him. But he doesn't seem interested in anyone except me."

"Actually, the truth is, I envy you. At least you have passion. Theodore is more of an intellectual."

"Why? Because he's a teacher?"

"Perhaps. Teddy is a sweet talker. He's always using similes to tell me how he feels about me. 'Your eyes are like two deep pools of water, and I can drown in them, or your teeth are as white as the pearls in the ocean.'

His eloquence is a substitute for taking me in his arms. He never follows through."

"So why do you keep seeing him?"

Gabriella shrugged. "Maybe I'm waiting for someone better to come along."

"What would your dream man be like?"

"Oh, I don't know—maybe he'll have strong muscles and a crooked smile that melts my heart on the spot."

"Domenico does that for me."

"He's good-looking and smart. But to be honest, I think you would be better off with Ethan. He's a better catch. He can afford to buy you anything you desire."

Antoinette shrugged her shoulders.

"I don't care about money. Domenico makes simple pleasures seem like luxuries."

Gabriella laughed. "You're hopeless."

"Hopelessly in love," Antoinette said.

Chapter 12

The Christmas season in Milan was magical. The streets filled with the sounds of people rushing home with their last-minute gifts.

The song Adeste Fideles flowed from church services. It echoed off the brick walls lining the street, beckoning the faithful to celebrate the birth of Jesus. The bishop believed Mussolini had ulterior motives but rejoiced in the reunification of church and state. The white papal banner flew alongside Italy's orange, green, and white flag.

Domenico and Antoinette walked around the Piazza, their fingers laced together. Amid the celebrations, no one seemed to notice the effects of Hitler's master plan.

"They didn't even have to fire a gun," Domenico said bitterly.

"Let's not think about that," Antoinette said. "It's Christmas Eve." She linked her arm with his. "I wonder if Gabriella arrived safely back in Florence. She went home to be with her family. She's been having a hard time lately with her boyfriend and feeling homesick."

"I'm sorry to hear that, but you shouldn't be alone on Christmas. Come home with me tonight," he said. "I want to cook Christmas Eve dinner for you."

"Alright. I would like to see where you live."

"Great. Let's go shopping. I'll buy a bottle of wine. What would you like to eat?"

"Fish, of course. It wouldn't be Christmas without the bounty of the sea. I'm sure my mother is preparing seven fish tonight. It is a tradition in our family. But I'd be happy with a Neapolitan specialty."

"That would be Zuppa di Pesce alla Napoletana. I have pasta in my cupboard, but we'll need to buy the seafood. Hmm. I'll need scallops, shrimp, clams, mussels, squid, and monkfish."

"Monkfish?"

"Yes. Coda di Rospo. The toad of the sea."

"Toad? That doesn't sound very appetizing."

Domenico laughed. "It's a flatfish that resides on the seabed and is quite delicious."

"Altogether, that's six fishes. If we add one more, we can combine our Christmas traditions."

"Maybe octopus or codfish. We'll see what's available."

They headed for the Mercato Ittico. When they entered, the shopkeeper had his back turned toward them. "We're closed," he said over his shoulder. "Don't you know—a blizzard is coming?"

"*Per favore Signor,*" Domenico said. "I promised my girl I'd make her Zuppa di Pesce. I'm sure you want to get home to your family, but we won't take up much of your time."

He turned around, his eyes widening. "Domenico Defino?"

"Well, if it isn't.... Leonardo! This old fish Mugler is from Naples," Domenico said to Antoinette. "He's a good friend of my father."

Leo laughed. "You were in short pants the last time I saw you."

"It's been quite some time since then," Domenico said. I'm all grown up, and I have a girlfriend. I'd like you to meet Antoinette from Florence."

"Pleased to meet you, Antoinette," he said, wiping his hands on his apron. "That's a lovely name." He took her hand and kissed it. "Domenico, where did you find such exquisite beauty?"

"She's studying fashion here in Milan."

"That's the dream that brings people from all over Italy."

Leo looked at Domenico apprehensively. "How is the family?"

"They're doing their best, considering the turmoil in our country."

"War is on the horizon," Leo said. "I feel it in my soul."

"Not if we in the south can help it," Domenico said. "But that is for another day. Today, we celebrate Christ."

"What can I do for you to make that happen?"

"We need seven fishes to make a delicious cioppino. Do you have any Monkfish?"

"No, not this week, but I have some nice cod."

"That will do," Domenico said.

Antoinette looked relieved.

Leo smiled at Antoinette. "You're going to let this guy cook for you?" He laughed and pulled out various fresh fish from the glass case, wrapping them in a newspaper.

"This is the freshest seafood in Milan. Don't cook it too long."

"I know how to cook Zuppa di Pesce, Leo. I'm from Campania too."

"Ha! You think being born in Sorrento makes you an expert?" He handed him the brown paper bag of seafood, and Domenico fumbled for his wallet.

Leo shook his head and raised his hand in a halting motion. "No. Your money's no good here."

"These are hard times. You should get paid for your fish."

"The fish is a gift for two Christmas doves. Buon Natale."

"*Grazie.*"

"Please give my regards to your father and his brothers the next time you see them."

"I will. Buon Natale, Leo."

As Domenico and Antoinette walked through the city streets, the snowfall steadily increased, making it difficult to see in front of them.

"How much farther?" she asked, blinded by the snow.

"Not too far. Another two blocks. My place is by the creek at the edge of town."

Arriving at his apartment, Domenico unlocked the door and led her to the kitchen.

"It's a bit chilly in here," Antoinette said.

"I'll start a fire, and we'll be warm in no time," he said, placing the groceries on the counter.

As he loaded logs into the fireplace, his arms bulged under the weight of the wood.

After the fire burned brightly, they returned to the kitchen, and he rolled up his sleeves. Domenico washed the clams and mussels in the sink while she deveined the shrimp and chopped the garlic. He unwrapped the cod, scallops, lobster, and squid.

Antoinette scrunched up her nose. "That looks and smells awful!"

He picked up a tentacle and pretended it was talking. "You can't make a cioppino without squid," he said in a falsetto voice.

He sautéed the garlic in olive oil and added tomatoes to start the sauce, then he seasoned the fish and placed it in the pot.

"It shouldn't take long," he said, putting water on the pasta stove. Domenico set the table and lit a candle.

"Would you like some wine?"

"Yes, I'd love some."

He opened a bottle and poured two glasses.

Antoinette took a slow sip and allowed the pungent fruit to explode on her tongue before swallowing. "This is an excellent wine. My aunt and uncle have a vineyard in Montepulciano. When I was a young child, my uncle would let me have a sip. He said it was medicinal.

While the cioppino cooked, they talked about their families, careful not to mention politics.

They ate dinner in the flickering candlelight. Domenico was everything she had ever dreamed of in a man. Caught up in the romance, Antoinette closed her eyes and savored every moment. There was no other place on earth that she would rather be.

After dinner, they took their wine to the living room. Domenico noticed she was shivering, so he pulled a quilt from the sofa and draped it over her shoulders. He added another log, and the flames licked the new wood, hungry for more fuel. A log snapped, sending sparks up the chimney. Domenico adjusted the damper and put a screen in front of the opening.

When he returned to Antoinette, he filled her glass and sat next to her. She nestled against him and sipped her wine, unsure if she tingled because of the alcohol or if this was the power of love.

It was getting late. Outside, the storm blew in full fury.

"I'm afraid you're stuck here for the night."

"No," she cried, suddenly coming out of her reverie. "I can't stay here. What will people think? I must go home."

Domenico sighed. "If you must leave, I'll walk you home."

The wind had whipped the snow into drifts creating a winter wonderland. The heavy snowfall camouflaged everything under a heavy blanket of white. Struggling through the snow, Domenico cleared a path.

The snow fell lightly around them as they arrived at her apartment, and the world was muffled.

Domenico opened his coat and pulled her close to warm her. Their bodies fit together perfectly. When they kissed, her frozen feet seemed to melt on the spot. The midnight bells of the church rang out.

"Buon Natale, darling," Domenico said, releasing her from his grasp.

Antoinette reluctantly said good night and stepped inside. Before she could use her key, Gabriella opened the door.

"Where have you been?" she scolded. "I've been worried sick that you."

were lost in the blizzard."

"I thought you left to spend Christmas with your family."

"The roads were closed. I couldn't leave."

"I'm sorry to worry you. I was with Domenico. He cooked dinner for me."

"Domenico?" She broke down and cried.

"What's wrong?"

"I don't know," she replied with frustration. This thing with Ted isn't going anywhere. Something is missing."

"I thought you guys were getting along."

"We are. But…."

"But what?"

"I think Teddy is seeing another girl."

Chapter 13

As the last of the snow melted, tiny green sprouts poked through the earth with the promise of new life.

"I have good news," Rachel said. "Ethan agreed to let you design some dresses for the spring debut. It's a great opportunity to get your name out there."

"Really? I can't believe it."

"I'm surprised he hasn't told you."

Antoinette's smile turned down. "Actually, I've been avoiding him."

"Why?"

"I sense that Ethan wants more from me than my designs."

"What's wrong with that? I think you two make a cute couple."

Domenico flashed through Antoinette's mind.

"I'm very fond of Ethan."

"But you're not in love with him."

"Well, not exactly. I like and respect Ethan, but I don't have romantic feelings for him."

Sensing discord, Rachel stood back. "What are your intentions?"

"Why? Do you think I will hurt him?"

"Frankly, yes. I know my brother. He sees what he wants to see, but I sense you have feelings for someone else. Is it Domenico?"

"I, um, yes, my feelings for Domenico are…."

"That's unfortunate. I think Ethan's planning to propose to you."

"Where did you get that idea?"

"Don't play with my brother's emotions, Antoinette. You must tell him before he makes a fool of himself."

"You're right. I don't want to hurt your brother. I'll tell him as soon as he returns from the conference."

*****

Ethan trusted Antoinette and didn't question why she was late, rushing in just before the show.

"I've missed you while I was gone," he said, lifting her and twirling her around the room.

She smiled. She didn't want to upset Ethan by saying she was in love with someone else. It needed to be discussed, but not until after the show.

"You did a great job with the dress," he said. "I'll let you choose the model to wear it down the runway."

Antoinette already knew she would choose her roommate. Gabrielle was thrilled.

The show was a success. Ethan's eyes held a glimmer of triumph and insisted that Antoinette join him on the runway to thunderous applause.

The after-party was elegant at a private restaurant along the shores of the Po River.

Ethan presented Antoinette as his girl throughout the evening. Then he swept her away shortly after dinner. It was a great night for a walk. The moon was full and illuminated the water.

As they strolled along the river, the stretch of white lights along the city looked like low stars. It all seemed so romantic—two lovers strolling along the river, except they weren't lovers.

Ethan reached for her hand. "I'm so happy you came into my life. I can't wait to see what our future holds." He kissed her hand tenderly and reached into his pocket.

She pulled away. "I'm afraid you have the wrong idea. I'm seeing Domenico and, well, I…."

It took a moment for him to understand. The light in his eyes diminished. He cleared his throat and found his voice.

"I just assumed because…."

She gripped his hand and looked at him with tears in her eyes. He looked so sad, so defeated.

"I'm sorry. "I should have told you sooner. I never wanted to hurt you."

When they returned to the party, Rachel ran up to them. "Don't forget. Everyone is coming to my place for drinks later."

"Don't wait on me," Ethan said. "I have a few calls to make. I don't know when I'll return."

Antoinette reached out to him, but he turned his back and left.

"Ethan!" she called, but he didn't respond. She watched him walk away into the darkness.

"What's gotten into him?" Rachel said.

*****

By Spring, Domenico and Antoinette were inseparable. They rode bicycles and had picnics in the park.

As they pushed their bikes uphill, they noticed a group of men by the roadside. They didn't look like Italian soldiers.

"I wonder where they came from," Domenico said.

"They look like Germans. But why would German soldiers be here in Milan?"

"I heard Mussolini was forming an alliance with Hitler. I don't think he understands how ruthless the Germans can be."

Out of breath, they reached the top of the hill. Antoinette puffed out her bottom lip and blew a strand of hair off her forehead as they pedaled to the shade of the Pines at the edge of the woods. The air smelled fresh and green.

"Let's eat," Domenico said. "Then we can go for a swim. There's a water hole a little farther from here. It's secluded. No one will know we're there."

"Won't the water be too cold?"

"Probably, but it'll be refreshing." He unfolded the blanket from his basket and laid it on the soft, dry pine needles covering the ground.

"I'll get the sandwiches." Antoinette retrieved the food she had prepared for them that morning. The soldiers had moved on, so the world was quiet except for the birds above them.

"Listen to the quiet," Domenico said.

The two of them were in a universe by themselves for a moment.

"I think I'm falling in love with you," he said.

She looked away.

"Does that scare you?"

Domenico entwined his fingers with hers. He touched his forehead to hers, and they kissed.

They wandered around aimlessly, absorbed by the love growing between them.

"Look, the figs are ripening on the trees." Domenico reached up and plucked one off a branch. He inhaled its sweetness and then offered it to Antoinette. She took one bite, and he kissed her lips.

"So sweet!" he grinned.

"The fruit?"

"No, your lips."

Antoinette laughed. "You're such a romantic. I can't believe people warned me not to get involved with you."

Domenico looked wounded. "Me? Why?"

"You have a reputation as a ladies' man."

"It's the women who come after me. I'm actually timid."

"I believe you," she said, wrapping her arms around his waist and kissing him.

"I'm going to miss you."

"Miss me? Why?"

"I have to go back home to Sorrento."

"Is everything alright?"

"I'm not sure. It has to do with political changes. My cousins have called an emergency meeting of the family. I may be gone for a while."

"I'll miss you, too."

*****

Gabriella's suitcases were in the living room when she entered the apartment.

"What's going on? Are you leaving?"

"I'm going home to Florence."

"Has something happened?"

"Yes, Teddy happened."

"But Teddy loves you."

"I'm not sure he does. I know he has another girl. I've left messages for him, but he hasn't called back. I'm tired of chasing him."

"Please don't go. I'll miss you terribly."

"I've made up my mind. I'm sorry, Antoinette, but you'll be fine. You have Domenico. I presume that's who you were with all weekend."

"Yes, we were at the lake house, but he's leaving too."

"You had a phone call. It was your mother. She wants you to call home as soon as possible."

She recalled her premonition. "Is it my father? Did something happen to him?"

"She didn't say."

The news of her grandfather's death came as a shock. She recalled the cough he had before she left for Milan. Tears streamed down her face as she packed her bags to take the next train home for the funeral.

Chapter 14

Antoinette's grandfather was laid out in his coffin. She could smell death even before she entered the living room. She inched to the front where her mother and grandmother were standing. Josephina had her arm around Grandma. They seemed to be holding each other up.

"Mama," she said and rushed up to the front of the room. She hugged Josephina. "How is Grandma?"

"I think she's in shock. She hasn't even cried."

She looked around for her father, but he wasn't there. "Where's Papa?"

"He's on his way back from Rome. I hope he gets here before the priest arrives."

Finally, he came through the door wearing his Black shirt attire.

Antoinette was torn between happiness seeing him and the policies he represented. She waited until after the funeral to discuss the matter.

"Papa. Rumors have been spreading."

"Remember your fascist roots. Don't let politics sway you. Fascism is cultural in its mission."

"Il Duce is even taking land from the rightful owners around Naples to produce wheat for the soldiers."

"By creating drainage for farms, public health was improved. It reduced malaria."

"Fascist propaganda!"

"Watch what you say. As a leader in the PNF, I will not go against my beliefs."

"It seems as if you won't oppose Mussolini on anything."

*****

Antoinette had second thoughts about going back to Milan. Her father had to return to Rome, and she wanted to be close to her mother.

"Maybe I should quit school and stay with you," she told her mother.

"Nonsense. You have made a life in Milan that I could only dream of. I'm very proud of you."

"But I don't want you to be alone. I've decided to take a leave from my job and studies."

"I thought you were seeing someone special."

"All right, but my family is more important to me. Domenico would find another girl, I'm sure."

"All the same. I think you should take a few days and pray about it."

Antoinette went to the church to light a candle. She kneeled in front of the Virgin Mary and prayed. Votive candles flickered in the alcoves on both sides of the aisles in the church.

Feeling a presence behind her, she turned and saw Domenico.

"What are you doing here?"

"When I heard you're grandfather passed, I wanted to console you, but you had already left for Florence."

She smiled through her tears. "Thank you."

His arms cradled her as she leaned against him and wept silently. She pressed her face into his shoulder, and he stroked her hair.

"Please come back to Milan," he said. "I don't want to lose you."

Antoinette agreed.

Chapter 15

Working on a new design for a dress, she tried not to think about Domenico, although she found it was impossible. Her mind wouldn't let go of his face, voice, or scent. Trying to focus on her task, she drew a simple shift with a hemline above the knee. Her inspiration was a white dress with a green overlay.

There was a knock on the door. Antoinette put down her pencil and went to see who it was. The sight of Domenico on the other side made her race.

"Grab your bathing suit. We're going swimming."

"But I have to work."

"Nonsense. The weather is beautiful. The sun is warm, and the lake is calling to us."

"What lake?"

"Lake Como."

"That's an hour away. How are we going to get there?"

"I would love to go to the lake, but I have to work. Ethan is designing a new summer floral ensemble. I'm working on a chiffon dress with a sheer pink overlay."

"You said Ethan is out of town now."

"He'll be back Monday. I promised I would be finished...."

Domenico put his finger on her lips and smiled.

"You're crazy," Antoinette said, exasperated.

"Come on. It'll be fun."

"Alright, but I have to be back at a reasonable hour to finish my work."

She changed into her bathing suit and slipped a summer dress over it. It had white gardenias on a background of cream. She had designed it with the help of her grandmother.

"Do you have a wine opener?" Domenico called out from the kitchen.

"Yes, it's in the drawer on the left. Why?"

"I bought two bottles of Rosso for us to enjoy."

She slipped into the low-slung passenger seat. A large basket covered with blue-checkered cloth sat on the backseat. "This is nice," she said.

"What's that?" She leaned back and lifted the cloth to take a peek.

"It's our lunch." He put the top down, and they drove off.

Once they escaped the city's smog, the air smelled fresh and clean.

The wind blew through Antoinette's red hair as they sped along winding roads.

"I can't believe I found you," he said. "You're so beautiful."

"Remind me to kiss you later when you're not driving."

"I definitely will."

"How much farther is the lake?"

"It's on the other side of this mountain."

When they arrived at the lake, they walked to the shoreline. Purple flowers climbed up the trees at the water's edge. The scent of Wisteria made her feel woozy as they neared the bank.

"Where are we going?"

"It's a surprise." He led her down a trail by the side of the woods. Domenico held her hand as they walked along the narrow path.

Deep in the thick green forest, the sound of trickling water grew louder. Sunlight filtered through the leaves in silver streaks along the ground.

"Is it much farther?"

"Not much. It's only around the bend."

They came to a small cabin tucked away in the woods. He had a mischievous look in his eyes.

"Whose house is this?" she asked.

"It belongs to my family."

"Your family owns this cabin?"

"Yes. It was a summer escape for my father. When I was a boy, I spent many nights in this cabin with my brother and cousins."

Domenico picked up the front mat, where a key was hidden, and opened the door. He tried the light switch, but the electricity was off. He took a lantern from the hall shelf. A flare of light burst forth as he lit it.

"Well, what do you think? It's a little musty, but we can open the windows and air it out."

"I love it!"

The light shined through, giving enough light to shut the lantern. Domenico pulled off the sheets that covered the furniture. Dust particles hung in the sunlight's rays.

"Let's see if we have running water," he said and headed toward the kitchen. He turned on the faucet and smiled. "We have a well — the best mountain water you'll ever taste."

"Speaking of water, I heard running water as we walked on the path.

"Yes. It's a mountain stream. Let's swim," he said, grabbing a blanket and two towels.

She followed him to the shore, where he shed his pants and shirt.

Antoinette's face flushed at the sight of him in his underwear. She touched the strap of her dress nervously.

"What are you waiting for," he shouted over his shoulder.

Looking around, she hesitantly took off her sundress, revealing a one-piece yellow bathing suit.

Domenico stopped and swam to the bank to grab her hand.

"Be careful. The rocks are sharp. I scraped my foot."

They waded farther away from the shore.

"Is it safe?" she asked.

"Sure, as long as we don't get too close to the spring. The current is rougher there."

Antoinette had difficulty keeping her head above water. I can't touch the bottom."

Domenico swam to her side and lifted her onto his chest. She wrapped her legs around his waist, and they kissed. They splashed around in the water like children and stayed in until their skin puckered. As the world crumbled around them, they swam in the sea of love.

"I can see why you love it here. It's the perfect hideaway."

"My father wanted the cabin far from the road. No one ever comes here."

They emerged from the water and stood dripping on the shore. She gazed at his tall, muscular frame and giggled.

"You look like some strange mythical god from Greek mythology."

"Then you must be my Aphrodite." He pulled her to him, his hair dripping with water.

Antoinette blushed and wrapped herself in a towel.

"I'm feeling hungry," she said.

"I forgot the food and wine in the cabin. I'll be right back."

Antoinette dried her hair while Domenico limped to get the food. He returned with the food basket and sat on the blanket to examine the cut on his foot.

"Oh, no! You're hurt."

"It was that rock I stepped on. I guess the rock was sharper than I thought."

Ripping off the shoulder strap of her sundress, she gently tied it around his foot. "I hope it doesn't get infected."

He laughed. "If they have to amputate, will you still love me?"

"Don't joke like that!"

"I'll be fine. It's just a scratch. I have lots of scars."

"Oh." She sighed and noticed Domenico's shoulder. "What caused that scar?"

"I got this when I was six years old. My twin brother and I were fishing with our father. A storm came up and capsized our boat. My father could only save one of us. He pulled me to safety, but a piece of the hull ripped into my shoulder as he hoisted me up."

"What about your brother?"

Domenico lowered his eyes. "He didn't make it. My father couldn't find him."

"That's horrible."

"For the longest time, I was angry at my father for saving me, not him."

"What else could he do?"

"I know. My head says that, but my heart still hurts. Enough sad talk. Let's eat."

They sipped wine and ate fresh mozzarella on crusty bread with thin slices of Prosciutto. As the sun went down, the brilliant colors of the sunset reflected on the water. It slowly shifted and disappeared behind the western arm of the Alps.

"The light is getting thin," Antoinette said. "We should be heading back."

"I was hoping we could stay overnight."

Oh, God, she thought, *I'll never finish that dress by Monday.*

She wanted to tell Domenico to take her home, but her spirit longed to overtake her sense of decorum. She forgot about the dress and Ethan.

They entered the cabin, and he lit a small candle. The light flickered, creating shadows on the walls. He retrieved two glasses from the cupboard and opened the second bottle of wine.

"I never loved being here as much as I do right now," he said. He covered her cheeks and face with soft kisses. His warm hands caressed her shoulder.

The wax dripped down the candle, pooling around the holder.

She looked up at him. His dark brown eyes bored into hers. Their lips touched, and she fell into his arms without hesitation.

"I want to make love to you," he whispered.

She pulled away. "I'm not sure that I'm ready for that. It's not that I don't love you, but I eh… I want to wait until I'm married."

"If you're not ready, I understand. I would never pressure you."

"It is getting late, and you promised to get me home at a reasonable time."

"Yes, I did, but I don't want to let you go."

"You must," she said in a panic.

Domenico laughed. "Yes, of course."

They gathered the remains of their picnic and took the lantern with them to get back through the dark path.

Chapter 16

The sun was low in the sky. An Italian patrol car rolled past with speakers warning pedestrians to get home before curfew.

"You have thirty minutes to get off the street," a soldier yelled.

"The blackout begins tonight," Antoinette said. "We should get home."

"Let's not go home just yet," Domenico said. "I want to go to the fountain."

Walking to the square, he slid his hand through hers, their fingers tangled together.

The sun was setting, and the sky was streaked in orange light. Domenico reached into his pocket and bent on one knee.

"I love you, Antoinette," he said and opened a small satin box revealing a diamond ring.

"Oh, it's beautiful."

"It's my grandmother's wedding ring. I want you to be my wife. Will you wear it?"

"Yes," she whispered.

His proposal was a surprise only because of its timing. For the past month, vague thoughts of marriage to Domenico danced around her head, but she wasn't prepared to hear him ask at that moment. Her heart soared. She couldn't wait to tell her mother but wondered what her father would say. She hoped he would give his blessing but prepared for a fight. Domenico's family stood for everything her father was against.

"Please, Domenico. Can we have our wedding in Florence? I've always dreamed of getting married at the Duomo."

"That's fine. I'm sure my family will travel from Campania. They'll love your family if they don't discuss politics. My father is a socialist, and yours is a fascist."

"My family is Catholic," Antoinette said. "Will that be a problem?"

Domenico rubbed his chin. "My family is Protestant, but I stopped practicing religion, so I think they'll be happy to have a religious service of any kind."

"Faith is a large part of my life."

"It used to be for me too, but I started questioning God's existence when I saw man's corruption. My faith has been shaken."

"I could never turn away from the church."

"Your faith is one of the things I love most about you."

That night, she wondered what it would be like to be his wife. "Antoinette Defino," she repeated, tasting the name on her tongue. Her heart leaped with a peculiar mixture of fear and anticipation.

Her happiness swelled beneath the surface, and she thought she would burst if she didn't tell someone. She waited for lunch break the next day and sat next to Rachel.

"Domenico has asked me to marry him."

"Have you told Ethan?"

"No. Not yet."

"You should before he finds out from someone else."

"Yes, you're right. I'll tell Ethan today, but I'm scared of how he'll take the news."

"Ethan is in love with you, but he's not a prideful man. He'll put your happiness before his own feelings."

Ethan had been avoiding her since she told him she didn't love him. As he skirted into his office, she followed.

"I'm sorry I hurt you, Ethan."

"I thought you loved me. I must have missed the signs."

"I do, but not in the same way I love Domenico."

"You know I only want your happiness, Antoinette. I won't stand in the way if he makes you happy."

She couldn't shake the look of hurt from his eyes.

"I care about you so much, Ethan. I don't want you to think badly of me."

"I could never think badly of you, Antoinette. I need time to get over you."

*****

It had been two months since Antoinette broke up with Ethan. Although their working relationship remained amicable, he spent less time at the studio. It wasn't until he started dating another girl that he warmed up and offered to design her wedding gown.

After work each day, she met Domenico at the café for dinner, where they caught up on the day's events and discussed the future. She loved the energy and life of overlapping voices and the sound of the café machine.

One day, she thought she saw Ethan enter the café, but then he was gone. During dinner, she was surprised when he came to the table. Ethan's blond hair was freshly trimmed. He wore a fitted polo shirt and pressed trousers that made him look sophisticated.

"Congratulations on your engagement," he said with an amiable smile and shook Domenico's hand.

"Thank you," Domenico said. "Won't you please join us? We were about to order lunch."

"Sorry, I have an appointment. I just came by to pick up coffee."

Antoinette felt a tug at her heart. *Is it possible to love two men?"* she thought.

Chapter 17

Antoinette went home two weeks before the wedding to prepare. Already, she was sketching a wedding dress in her mind—a beautiful white satin gown with a train stretching from the church doors to the altar.

Domenico remained in Milan to finish a fashion shoot. He drove her to the station. She hated being separated from him, but she was excited to see her family. They kissed for a long time. Finally, the train whistle blew, announcing its departure.

"We'll be together soon," he whispered. "We'll never be apart again."

Steam hissed from the train as it slowly moved forward, picking up momentum until all he could see was the last caboose.

It took over an hour to get to Bologna, where she had to transfer to another train to Florence. A man sat across from her on the train, reading a newspaper. The headlines were disturbing. Italy joined Germany and Japan in the anti-Comintern pact to mutually resist Communism and Communist states. Surely Il Duce didn't go along with that, she prayed. The world was unstable, and it frightened her. Already, she missed Domenico.

The train pulled into the station, bringing her out of her daydreams. No one else had gotten off at the stop. Antoinette stepped off and paused on the platform. She then descended the stairs, looking around for her parents.

"Papa!" she shouted and hurried toward him.

"Where's Mama? Why didn't she come with you?"

"She wanted to, but Grandma is very sick. She couldn't leave her alone."

"What's wrong with her?"

"The doctors say she has a bad heart, but she seemed to lose her will to live after Grandpa died last month. All she does is sit by the window in the kitchen and look outside. She's heartbroken."

"I'm sure she's lost without him."

Once they were in the car, he sighed. "Speaking of marriage, your mother told me you're engaged. I'm disappointed your intended did not officially ask me for your hand."

"Oh, Papa. Nobody does that anymore. He will ask you for your blessing when you meet him." She kissed his cheek, and he smiled.

"I'm glad you returned from Rome so you can walk me down the aisle."

"When I heard you were to marry, I had to be here. If I am going to give my only daughter away, I need to know more about your young man. Where's he from? What is his family like?"

"His name is Domenico Defino. His family is prominent in Sorrento."

"Campania. Hmm. I know the area well." He frowned.

"What's wrong?"

"Politics. Naples is a thorn in Il Duce's side."

"I'm sorry, Papa, but Domenico isn't from Naples. He's from Sorrento, and he's the man I love."

Gaetano sighed. "Young love! Yes, I remember it well. I'm glad to see you are happy, Antoinette."

"Are you going back to Rome after the wedding, Papa?"

"I'm not sure. Things are changing in Italy. The future of fascism isn't clear."

"It's too dangerous, Papa. Domenico believes Italy has given Adolf Hitler too much power over our country."

"Il Duce would never let Germany get the upper hand. He's just playing it smart."

"Maybe he only thinks he's smart. Hitler is deceitful. He promised he would be neutral. Have you seen the headlines? Nazi Germany convinced Italy to sign a pact against communist states. Domenico predicted it would happen. He doesn't trust Hitler. He says he's manipulating Benito Mussolini."

"Nonsense. All Il Duce has to do is snap his fingers and…."

"Domenico believes it will be an excuse to go to war against Russia and that Italy is being made a vassal of Hitler. Il Duce would be sending good Italian soldiers to their deaths."

"My precious daughter. Is this the influence your future husband is having on you? You sound like a socialist."

"It's not only socialists who feel this way. The people closest to Il Duce are rumbling."

A pained expression washed over Gaetano's face. Antoinette thought she was finally getting through to him.

"Maybe I shouldn't give you my blessing on this marriage."

Antoinette looked up with panic. "Please, Papa," she cried. "I know you have bad taste in your mouth for Socialists, but I love Domenico and want to be his wife."

"Calm down, dear daughter. Why would I cause trouble at my daughter's wedding?"

*****

Josephina opened the door, and the familiar smell of tomato sauce and garlic brought Antoinette back to her youth.

"I've missed you so much, Mama." She gave her a tight hug.

"It's so nice to have you home again, Antoinette. We can use a little happiness around here."

"I'm sorry about grandpa. I'm going to miss him terribly."

"He was in a great deal of pain. At least now, he's at peace. I'm sure you must be tired after your long journey. Let's go to the kitchen, and I'll make us some tea."

"Actually, I'd prefer coffee if you don't mind."

Josephina raised her brow. "Since when do you prefer coffee to tea?"

Antoinette smiled. "Domenico loves his espresso. I guess I've grown accustomed to the taste. Where's Grandma?"

"She's in the kitchen. She'll be happy to see you."

"Antoinette! Grandma said, surprised to see her. "I didn't know you were coming for a visit."

"I told you this morning," Josephina said. "Her memory isn't too good," she whispered.

Antoinette rushed over to kiss her. "You look as beautiful as I remember, Grandma. Look!" She lifted her left hand. I'm getting married. It's Domenico's grandmother's ring."

"Then it is very special," Grandma said. A faraway expression washed over her face, and she turned to look outside at some unknown object.

Josephina put the kettle on the stove, and they sat at the table. "All she does is sit by the window.

I don't know what she's looking at."

"Then we should give her something," Antoinette said. "I'll see about planting a flower garden while I'm here. And maybe Papa can put out a bird feeder."

"That would be nice. Grandma would enjoy that."

"Speaking of Papa. I'm worried about introducing him to Domenico's family. They are staunch Socialists. You know how he feels about them. He promised he wouldn't start trouble, but...."

"Don't worry. Your father has spared no expense for your wedding. He wants it to be special. "What can I say? He is aware of the Defino's wealth and a proud man."

"He has nothing to feel ashamed of. Papa did well at the railroad. I don't want him to spend his life savings."

"Let him have his fun. He's rented a large tent for the wedding reception. We can decorate the tables with flowers and ribbons. Papa ordered a large wild boar and Florentine steak, which he intends to grill over roasted chestnuts."

"I was thinking of something simple. "Domenico says his family loves pasta."

"Yes, we'll use Grandma's recipe. They'll love it."

Chapter 18

Domenico and Antoinette were married at the Santa Maria del Fiore Cathedral, home of the Roman Catholic bishop, constructed of brick and marble in shades of green and pink with white borders.

As was traditional, Domenico wasn't allowed to see Antoinette before the ceremony. He waited at the altar with his brother, Marco, who served as best man.

The organist began playing the wedding ceremony processional of *Ave Maria,* and Antoinette moved toward the altar with fluid grace. Her white satin gown was adorned with tiny gardenias sewn into the hem. The train carried by her cousins from Montepulciano stretched out the length of six pews.

Mesmerized by her beauty, Domenico smiled as she walked toward him down the aisle. The underskirts of Antoinette's dress swished like the sound of an angel's wings as she walked down the silk runner.

Antoinette nodded to Ethan, who had designed the gown for her. Gabriella, her matron of honor, walked in front of her, followed by Antoinette's two youngest nieces, sprinkling daisies from their baskets.

Domenico's parents, Vincenzo and Maria Defino, sat in the front pew on the right side of the aisle with family and friends of the groom. Vincenzo wore a stylish gray suit, and Maria looked elegant in a blue chiffon gown. His Uncle Sonny and Aunt Geneva sat with most of his cousins behind them.

Vincenzo's twin brother, Uncle Lorenzo, wasn't there. His Uncle Franco and Aunt Camelia lived in America and couldn't make the journey.

After Gaetano shook Domenico's hand and kissed his daughter, he returned to Josephina's side in the front pew.

"What God has joined together, let no man put asunder."

After their vows, everyone teared up as they exchanged wedding rings. Their marriage was sealed with a kiss, and the organ played *La Primavera Allegro.*

The newlyweds walked down the aisle to Allegro as the newlyweds walked down the aisle. They exited the church in a shower of pink rose petals.

*****

After the ceremony, everyone went back to Gaetano's house, and he welcomed the guests. The fragrance of orange blossoms in full bloom floated through the garden. Servers walked around with glasses of prosecco and large silver trays of crostini piled high with chicken liver pâté.

Domenico had a large family. The women scampered around to help Josephina in the kitchen while the men stood in groups smoking and drinking wine. Domenico heard the rumble of male voices and greeted his cousins with a warm embrace.

"It's been too long, cousin," Tommaso shouted.

"I haven't seen you or Leo since we were children at holiday gatherings."

"Remember the mischief we got into?" Leo said.

"I do, and I remember Cousin Bruno was the one who instigated it."

"With help from Paolo."

"Cousin Paolo always found a way to get into trouble. Where is our dear cousin?"

"I'm sorry," Tommaso said. "Uncle Lorenzo refuses to associate with Black Shirts. When he heard Antoinette's father was one of them, he refused to attend."

"That's unfortunate. At least Bruno and Pasquale came."

"They defied their father, saying you were like a brother."

Boisterous laughter filled the air as another group of cousins drank.

Domenico laughed. "A rowdy bunch, aren't they? I wonder what Antoinette's conservative family is thinking." He looked across the garden at his lovely wife.

Antoinette stood near the table admiring her mother's four-layer wedding cake. Suddenly, a small hand appeared from under the table and snatched some white candy-coated almonds.

"Who's under there," she said, lifting the tablecloth. The children giggled and ran off.

Antoinette spotted Domenico talking to his cousins and went over to them.

He put his arm around her tiny waist and kissed her cheek.

"Cousins," Domenico said. "Let me introduce you to my wife."

"Bruno kissed her hand. "You are a vision of loveliness."

"Don't get any ideas of stealing my wife," Domenico said, and everyone laughed.

"I see my father," Antoinette said. "I must go to thank him for this beautiful spread." She kissed Domenico and glided across the lawn.

"You did well for yourself," Cousin Calogero said.

The dinner bell rang, and everyone made their way to the tables. Domenico and Antoinette sat at the head table with their parents on either side.

A six-piece orchestra played while the guests ate and sipped champagne. Glasses tinkled merrily as the guests clinked their forks and spoons, encouraging the bride and groom to kiss.

Domenico and Antoinette went from table to table, greeting their guests. The sweet scent of roasting pork drifted through the air as the pig rotated on a spit over an open fire.

The first course was melon drizzled with honey and pear soufflé. Along with the fruit were large plates of roasted artichokes and finocchio with plenty of pepper and garlic. It was a staple in the Mediterranean, and Gaetano ordered the bulbs, especially for Domenico's family. It had a mild anise flavor. Next came the pasta with plenty of sauce and fresh bread to sop it up. A server came around offering grated Parmesan cheese and creamy ricotta.

The main course arrived just as the guests were filled to the brim and holding their stomachs. Platters of sizzling meat were placed in the center of the table. On one side was the pork, and on the other was the Florentine Steak surrounded by roasted chestnuts. More wine was served as the platters made their way around the table. Bowls of salad offered a digestive element to the rich foods.

Waiting for dessert, the guests left the tables to dance on a large wooden platform Gaetano had specially built for the occasion. Everyone held hands, and they surrounded the happy couple. They danced around in a circle to the music, to the tune of Tarantella.

While everyone was working off their dinners, the tables were cleared for the fruit and nuts.

Cousin Pasquale pulled out the scissors and cut a large portion of Domenico's tie. His cousins then held an auction to raise money for the newlyweds.

Chatter and laughter vibrated through the garden.

*****

At the end of the evening, Domenico and Antoinette were relieved everything had gone smoothly between their families. They changed into their traveling clothes in anticipation of the drive to Montepulciano, where their honeymoon suite awaited them.

The couple made one last appearance in the garden before they left.

"I'd like to make a toast," Cousin Pino said. He raised his glass. "To the bride and groom. May they have a long and fruitful life."

Gaetano stood up. "Also, to our Benito Mussolini. May God bless him and his family."

Vincenzo stood frozen with his glass mid-air, then returned it abruptly to the table.

Gaetano's face turned red. He had promised his daughter not to make a fuss, but liquor loosened his tongue. He slowly walked toward Vincenzo.

"You did not toast Il Duce," Gaetano said with studied politeness. "Is there some reason for this disrespect of Italy?"

"It has nothing to do with Italy!" Vincenzo tried to control himself but failed. "I don't agree with Il Duce's politics."

"How can you not?" Gaetano's passion was getting the better of his sense of being a good host. "Il Duce is bringing Italy back to its past greatness. Fascism is moving the country forward. Look at all the roads, bridges, and sporting facilities he has built."

"It's a ploy to keep his loyalists in line by convincing them of Italy's progress toward the future. You can't be blind. Where do you think he's getting the money for all these great projects? What do we need with sporting facilities when so many people in the country struggle to feed their families?"

Each tried to convince the other he was wrong. The argument heated—liquor fueling the flames.

"My family has a long-standing belief in Social Democracy."

"Your ways have brought nothing but lawlessness and indiscipline in the country. Socialism causes people to become lazy," Gaetano insisted. "Look what they did to the industrial and trade unions."

"That is because the wealthy industrialists took advantage of cheap labor."

Mussolini was right to outlaw all strikes. When Il Duce took over, nothing worked in Italy. With him in power, Italy can become a great empire as it was in the days of Julius Caesar."

"Before Mussolini's fascist party took over, the people were free to speak out," Vincenzo said. "Now, if anyone dares go against him, they risk death. Like the Mafia, Il Duce operates outside the law to repress and weaken his opposition. His secret police protect the political power of his dictatorship. He has blood on his hands. How does that make Italy a great nation?"

"Even Germany admires Mussolini," Gaetano argued. "He's in Berlin as we speak, attending a dinner in his honor by the chancellor."

Vincenzo's face turned into a scowl, and he raised his index finger.

"The chancellor? Do you mean Hitler? The world's warmonger? He is declaring himself Führer now, the leader of Germany and the entire world. You can't trust him."

Gaetano's impatience rose.

"So, do you prefer Stalin? Comrade Stalin, who has crushed the churches? At least Hitler has respect for our religious heritage. Do you want to be ruled by the Slavs? "Would you rather be under the influence of the Butcher of Moscow? We must choose. Berlin or Moscow? I'll take Berlin."

"The Germans look down on the Italians as weak and disorganized!" Vincenzo sneered. "Hitler is using Mussolini to wipe out the Jews. Can't you see that? The Allies are coming for us now, as well as the Germans. Italy will be part of the wreckage Hitler is bringing about in Europe."

Antoinette stood by helplessly as the voices of the two men rose over the music. All conversations stopped.

Domenico stepped in between with a smile to separate them. "You promised you wouldn't bring up politics, Father," he whispered.

"It was Antoinette's father, Gaetano!" He's trying to push Mussolini down my throat."

"Let's go," Domenico said, hustling his father away.

Gaetano couldn't resist getting the last word. "Berlin or Moscow?" he shouted.

Vincenzo twisted his head to send a parting shot. "The will of the people should not be silenced! Fascism will die an ignominious death!"

Chapter 19

Domenico and Antoinette spent their first night as a married couple in his house.

When he unlocked the front door, it felt strange. Antoinette had been there many times, but this was different. She wouldn't be leaving at the end of the night like before. His home was now her home.

"Would you like something to eat before we retire for the evening?"

"No, but my mouth is a little dry. I need a drink of water.

Antoinette followed him into the kitchen. He ran the faucet, waiting for the water to get cold, then filled a glass.

She took a few sips and then put the glass in the sink.

"Well, I guess it's time," he said, looking at her amorously.

She nodded, and they entered the bedroom. The moon came through the windows, casting just enough light to see in the darkened room. Domenico unbuttoned his shirt and sat on the edge of the bed.

"I think I'll change in the bathroom," she said and hurried away with her trousseau. Antoinette stayed there for a long time.

"Are you all right in there?"

"Yes, I eh." The door flung open, and she stepped into the room wearing a long silk nightgown.

Tension hung in the air, laced with breathless hunger, as he pulled her close to him and kissed her tenderly.

"Your eyes sparkle like diamond dust."

Slipping the straps of her nightgown off her shoulders, it fell to the floor, exposing the curves of her body.

Antoinette moved her hands to cover herself. He pulled them away and kissed her neck.

"I'm scared," she said, looking at the floor.

Domenico lifted her chin. "There's nothing to fear. I would never hurt you."

He unpinned her hair, freeing it to cascade to her shoulders. "I'm glad that you let your hair grow out." He put his arms around her waist. "You're so beautiful," he whispered against her neck. His kisses trailed down her throat and past the curve of her breasts.

Antoinette could feel the heat building like a storm in her groins as he guided her to bed. His fingers traveled up and down her spine, making her tremble.

"Oh," she whimpered, her breath caught in her throat. Longing and the want of him pushed away her fear. Closing her eyes, she exhaled, surrendering to his touch. Domenico gently entered her, and her breath hitched as their bodies came together. Antoinette gasped at the mixture of pain and pleasure. Her teeth pressed into her bottom lip, followed by the copper taste of blood on her tongue. Feeling him deep inside her, she cried aloud. Her nails dug into his back as she felt the thunder roll through him and into her. She coiled tighter, her body tightening around him until she exploded in a release. A few moments later, he did, too, and collapsed beside her.

They lay in each other's arms, breathing heavily. Their bodies glistened with passion.

"I'll remember this night forever," she whispered breathlessly.

*****

Antoinette's eyes fluttered open the following day as the sun peeked into the window. Marveling how right it felt to be in his arms, she sighed and touched his face, waking him up. He turned to her and pulled back the covers. The air held a morning chill, but the room warmed as they kissed.

"From the first time I saw you, I knew you would be my wife someday. I love you, Mrs. Defino."

"Mrs. Domenico Defino. Yes, I love being your wife."

After breakfast, they drove to Montepulciano in the southern hillside of Tuscany, where Aunt Beatrice ran a small farm. Ponies, pigs, goats, and calves, along with chickens, rabbits, and ducks, roamed freely across the sixteen acres of grapes and other crops.

Uncle Antonio's family handed down the property through five generations. Although it was an active vineyard and farm, the property had three guest houses, some dating back to the 1700s. The honeymoon suite was Beatrice's gift to her niece. They would have five days of rustic living away from the growing political pressure in Milan.

Unlike her brother Gaetano, Beatrice was not fond of Mussolini, especially after he interrupted the sale of alcohol.

*****

During the day, they took walks in the countryside. Ancient villas, some falling into ruins, inhabited by stray sheep and wild ducks. They passed orchards of fragrant lemons with a shepherd at their heels. Bees buzzed over their heads while the dog did his job of rounding up the cattle.

They went on picnics and rode the horses in the stable. A dozen horses shuffled in their stalls and didn't seem to mind the felines when they rubbed against their legs. Antoinette always stopped to pet the cats that bedded down in the hay, unafraid of their massive companions.

When she asked her uncle about the strange roommates, he said the cats controlled the rodent population. The rats would eat the horse's food if they weren't there.

Chapter 20

Ten months later, Antoinette was on the way to the hospital. Josephina came to Milan to help because the doctor put Antoinette on bedrest for the last three months of her pregnancy.

After twenty-two hours of labor, the baby went into fetal distress, and she passed out.

When she opened her eyes, Domenico was by her bedside.

"Where's our baby? Please don't tell me it's dead."

"On the contrary." He smiled. "I'd say it's a miracle."

The nurse rolled in a cart carrying two white baskets.

"Congratulations," she said. "You have twins."

"Twins?" Antoinette looked at Domenico, who was smiling.

The nurse lifted the first baby, wrapped in a blue blanket, and placed her in Antoinette's arms.

"He's beautiful," she said, kissing the baby's head.

The nurse gave the second baby to Domenico, also wrapped in a blue blanket.

"We have two boys," he said. "What shall we name them," he said.

"One will be Domenico after you," she said. "And I'd like to name the other after my grandfather, Vittorio if that's all right with you."

"Vittorio. I like that." The baby opened his eyes. "I think he likes that name too."

Josephina was waiting at the front door when Antoinette was released from the hospital with the babies. She reached for the first infant and cooed. His mouth twisted into what she thought was a smile.

"Look, he's smiling at me."

Antoinette laughed. "It may be gas."

"No, I'm sure he knows his grandma." She cooed again. "This one has your father's dimples."

"They're twins," Antoinette said. "They both have Papa's dimples."

Domenico was grateful that Josephina agreed to stay on to help out with the feedings and diaper changes.

*****

On their fourth birthday, Antoinette took a moment to admire her sons. Although they were twins, their intellectual makeup could not have been more different. Domenico Junior was quieter and more thoughtful. Vittorio was a free spirit and didn't think before he reacted. He had a keen sense of humor, especially around the dinner table. It was hard to discipline him with a straight face.

After dinner, they sat around the radio every night to learn the events that affected Italy.

Il Duce was broadcasting his speech from a military base near Bari to relieve concern about his upcoming meeting with Germany's Chancellor in Rome.

"He is a friend of Italy," Mussolini said. "I am looking forward to meeting him."

"I want to assure you," he bellowed. "My meeting with Herr Hitler is necessary. I will not tolerate interference when Italy makes a presence in Africa. We cannot trust Britain. They try to mask their thirst for power behind civility. They want to control everything in the world. Well, they can't control Italy!"

The crowd cheered.

"We will have our second empire!"

The titanic crest of cheering and screaming grew louder. "Duce, Duce," they repeated.

"Even if we have to create it with our own blood."

Domenico shut the radio. "I think we heard enough for one evening."

Chapter 21

Happily married for seven years, Antoinette worked at home as a seamstress. It allowed her to be with her boys. Domenico took a job as a photographer for the local newspaper, *Avanti*, the official voice of the Italian Socialist Party. Politics drove Domenico. He had absorbed his father's socialist ideals in complete conflict with Milan's strong Fascist sympathies.

After work, he delivered secret papers every evening, careful to be off the streets by curfew. He wasn't sure what information was inside the sealed envelopes, but he suspected they were identification papers. Whatever the contents were, he knew the Gestapo would arrest him on the spot if caught. Domenico was clever. He reconstructed his camera case with a false bottom.

The Germans were everywhere in Milan. Domenico had to stay alert for officers checking papers. The fear didn't deter him from carrying correspondence to secret hideaways out of sight from Nazi eyes. His best friend Dante did the same.

"You should hide that envelope," Domenico warned.

"It will be hidden inside my jacket."

"If I were you, I wouldn't take a risk."

"I've been doing this longer than you. Trust me. I'll be fine."

"Meet me back here before curfew," Dante said.

They walked to the Piazza and then went in different directions.

Domenico stepped up his pace and maneuvered through the back streets to avoid a potential roadblock. It was safer to be off the main road, but his deliveries took longer.

When he arrived at the designated apartment building, he climbed the stairs to the specified address. He looked around nervously before knocking lightly on the door.

"Who is it?" a man asked.

"Pepino sent me."

The chain slid to the other side, and the door cracked open a few inches.

"I have a delivery for Stefano."

The door opened. "I'm Stefano."

As soon as Domenico pulled out the envelope, Stefano snatched it, and the door shut with a click.

The sun was setting as Domenico left the building. He headed to the Piazza to meet Dante. In the distance, he saw him walking to the corner where two Nazi soldiers were talking. One stared Dante up and down and held up his hand. *Turn back. Don't go that way.* It was too late.

They scrutinized his papers and were about to let him pass when one spotted the envelope.

Domenico couldn't hear the conversation but sensed it wasn't going well. The two Nazis pushed Dante's face against the wall. One held a rifle while the other searched him. Pulling the envelope from Dante's jacket, he opened it and glanced at the contents.

Before Domenico could react, the Nazi with the rifle fired, putting a bullet into Dante's head. He crumpled to the ground. His blood pooled on the pavement.

Domenico escaped unseen. He had to hurry home before curfew, so he ran, making it just in time. Out of breath and thirsty, he stuck his head under the faucet in the small hall bathroom, gulping the metallic-tasting water.

"Where have you been?" Antoinette asked. "Dinner was ready an hour ago."

"Sorry, I had some last-minute business to take care of."

If she knew what he was doing, it would be a risk for her. He hated lying to her, but he felt he had no choice.

Chapter 22

Domenico ran into the house. "Antoinette," he called, out of breath.

"What is it?" She came out of the kitchen wiping her hands on a dishtowel.

"Hitler has organized a youth military. Now, Il Duce has started one too. He wants children five or older to unite and prepare to be soldiers. He is calling them Sons of the Wolf."

"But Dom and Vittorio are only five years old."

"They would be trained to be part of the Fascist army. It isn't safe here for our children. I've made all the arrangements for you to return to your family. Take the boys and go back to Florence. Stay there with your mother until this all blows over."

"What about you?" she asked with a confused expression. "Aren't you coming with us?"

"No. I'm leaving for Campania. I'm going back to establish a network of freedom fighters to work against the German occupation. Yesterday, a plane dropped leaflets on the streets, urging citizens to join the fight against the Nazis. I need to stand with my village."

Her stomach lurched. "No! If you get caught—you'll be killed," she cried, throwing herself into his arms.

"What would you have me do? Ignore what I see happening. If I stay, I'll be working for the Germans. I refuse to take orders from the Third Reich."

Tears flowed from under her lashes. "Why do you have to go? Can't your cousins take care of things?"

He caressed her cheek with the back of his hand. "They need me. I can't turn my back." Domenico pulled her close. "I'll come to Florence as often as I can."

She pulled away and sobbed. "It's too dangerous."

"It will be more dangerous if Italians do nothing. I won't stand by, and...."

"The Americans are moving in from the south. Can't you leave it to them? They'll put an end to all this."

"More Nazis are infiltrating Italy every day. Il Duce can't do a thing about it. Once, he was in control, but his power was waning. Hitler's using Mussolini to advance his extermination plans for the Jews."

"Why does Hitler hate the Jews?"

"He thinks they have too much economic power and control over the media. He's convinced they are the reason for Germany's problems and using them as a scapegoat."

"Is Italy going to be drawn into a world war?"

"It's quite possible. Mussolini is fascinated with Hitler's military might. He doesn't want Italy perceived as weak."

Antoinette was devastated about separating from Domenico, but she saw its necessity. After tucking in the boys, they sat on the front porch staring at the stars. The galaxy seemed like the only thing unaffected by the horror of war.

"The crickets sing as if nothing is wrong in the world," Antoinette said, "or maybe they know, and they're talking amongst themselves about man's stupidity." She felt the dissolution of their life as they knew it and the end of her dreams.

A warm evening breeze fanned her cheek. "It's such a beautiful night. I don't want it to end."

Domenico put his arm around her and looked passionately into her eyes. "Morning will come no matter what, but we're together now. I love you more than you know."

They made love, whispering afterward about their plans when the war ended. Exhausted, Domenico fell fast asleep. Antoinette stared lovingly at him, checked on the boys, and then she, too, succumbed to exhaustion.

*****

The following day, they had their last breakfast together before parting ways. Spreading jam on her bread, Antoinette took a few nibbles, but her appetite was gone. She dressed the boys and clicked the locks on her suitcase.

Domenico hated putting distance between himself and his family, but he didn't want his sons to be wolves—just boys. He carried their bags to the car and opened the back door for his sons. Antoinette, forlorn, sat in the passenger seat. They spoke little as they rode to the central rail station. Antoinette studied her husband, stunned by his bravery. She wasn't as strong as he, although she refused to quake at the sight of a Nazi soldier. He feared nothing and would join the partisans to fight the Black Shirts and Nazis.

Italian soldiers no longer guarded the transit hub at the train station. Instead, a sea of olive uniforms worn by German soldiers moved along the platform directing men in shabby gray clothing marked with yellow stars into cattle cars with no windows.

"Where are they going, Papa?" Dom asked.

"I'm not sure, but you and your mother are taking a trip to see Grandma."

"Aren't you coming with us?"

"No, I must take care of some business. Don't worry. We'll be together soon."

"I want to go with you," Vittorio whined.

Domenico bent down and looked into his son's eyes. "I'm sorry, son, but it's too dangerous."

"We're not afraid," Dom junior added.

He tousled his hair. "You are my two brave boys. You need to take care of your mother while I'm gone."

Antoinette stepped into Domenico's arms, and they embraced. "I don't want to lose you," she whispered. Their bodies pressed against one another. "Promise you will come back to me."

Domenico kissed her gently on the lips.

"I'll come back to you as soon as this is over. I promise."

The ear-splitting screech of an incoming train drowned out their conversation.

Domenico waited until they safely boarded the train. He watched it slowly move down the tracks until his precious sons and devoted wife disappeared. The wind picked up, and his hair wafted about his face. His heart ached, but he was relieved that Antoinette and his sons were leaving Milan.

"Our love is eternal," he whispered. "Nothing will tear us asunder."

Chapter 23

Gaetano felt strongly about the fascist party and Benito Mussolini. In his eyes, Il Duce was the only man capable of restoring Italy to glory by building infrastructure and reducing unemployment.

Recalling stories about Ancient Rome and bolstered by the rhetoric, Gaetano had been swept up in the propaganda. But the Nazi occupation changed conditions in Italy. Gaetano began to see the truth and a different side to Il Duce. Already, the streets were packed with Germans and their vehicles. He knew it was only a matter of time before Nazi commandos took control.

Protests were organized throughout the city, and students demonstrated in the Piazza del Plebiscito. In retaliation, German troops burned the library.

A Kubelwagon filled with men roared past with a Nazi flag streaming behind it. Curious to find out if the rumors were true, Gaetano followed it in his car.

The S.S. vehicle stopped, and two guards stood in the back with rifles as scraggly men filed out. *Italian Jews!*

They were dirty and skinny—some too weak to jump down. Their expressions were dead.

Each prisoner was handed a shovel and directed to the edge of a field. They assembled in a row with only one foot between them. German soldiers ordered them to dig. The lieutenant clicked his heels and approached a man moving slower than the rest. With the quickness of a snake, he lashed out and clubbed him with the butt of his rifle. The man dropped to the ground and lay there motionless.

"This is an example of what will happen if you fall short," he barked. "You will be whipped and beaten until you collapse."

Another Kubelwagon arrived with younger prisoners, around twenty-two years old. Gaetano presumed they were some of the protesting students. Hooded Black Shirts armed with pistols jumped down after them. They lined up the students, shoulder to shoulder, facing forward, with their backs exposed.

"Shoot at the base of the neck," the major in charge instructed as the firing squad took their position.

One of the students was crying. "Please don't kill us," he wailed.

One of the Black Shirts gagged him, muffling his cries.

Raising their rifles, the executioners aimed and waited for the major's signal.

The soldiers opened fire, and the students fell forward and sprawled face-first in the dirt.

"This one's still alive," one said. The young man wiggled in agony on the ground.

The Fascist laughed and shot him in the face. Gaetano was stunned at the callousness of his compatriots. Filled with shame and disgust, part of him wanted to rage and shoot the Black Shirts and the Nazis. Every one of them. But that was unrealistic. He wouldn't get off more than six rounds. Still, it gave him a sense of resistance as he briefly entertained the idea.

A guard noticed Gaetano's car and walked toward him. He backed up and dropped the transmission into third gear. As he pushed his foot down on the gas, his tires spun on the dusty road. The guard ran toward him but couldn't catch up in the trail of dust. He rounded a corner and looked in his rearview mirror for the Italian guard, but he wasn't there.

Gaetano escaped. Beads of sweat rolled down his face. Seeing those men with no life left in their eyes made him question what was happening to his beloved Italy. *Why is Il Duce allowing this?*

Chapter 24

Gaetano kneeled in Saint Peter's Basilica, a place of refuge from the horrors he had witnessed.

Father Hubert approached him. "Gaetano. I'm surprised to see you here. Is everything all right with the family?"

"Yes, Father, but I fear for their safety. I heard the Germans are pushing north."

"The devil has found his way into Rome," Father Hubert said. "S.S. troops are surrounding the Vatican as we speak. None of us is safe. Especially the Jews. Mussolini has introduced anti-Jewish legislation."

"Father, is it true what they say about poison gas at the camps?"

"Yes, I'm afraid so. A priest I know in Germany witnessed a group of Jews herded into a gas chamber. They were ordered to strip. Violin music played to keep them calm. Thinking they were taking a shower, they left their belongings in a pile and willingly entered a small concrete room. When the screaming and banging sounds behind the locked door stopped, the bodies were loaded into ovens. Thousands of Jews have been burned to ashes in these ovens."

"How are men capable of such wickedness?"

The priest made the sign of the cross. "Only God knows. Perhaps there is a greater work to be done with mankind."

"I'm losing my faith, Father."

"Gaetano, my son. Your faith has never been tested until now."

"Why are Italians going along with this evil?"

"I believe a demagogue has captured the Italian people. Hitler is an anti-Christ."

"I'm thinking of going back to Florence."

"Perhaps that is a good idea. Leave before things get worse. Your family needs you."

"What about you, Father? Will you be safe?"

"It's in God's hands, my son."

"Please, Father, may I receive communion before I leave? I'd have to confess my part in the suffering of so many innocent people."

"Of course." He went to the altar and removed a chalice containing hosts.

Gaetano kneeled before him, making the sign of the cross.

"I absolve you from the deeds you are confessing. All glory and honor are yours, almighty Father, forever and ever through him, with him, in him, in the unity of the Holy Spirit."

"Amen," Gaetano said after receiving the host.

"You are a good man, Gaetano—a good man who believed in the principles of democracy only to be misled. Go in peace."

"Grazie, Father."

"Take the back roads. They might be safer."

Gaetano returned to his flat to pack his things. As he approached the building, he saw an older man sitting outside. The man smiled and blinked at him through foggy spectacles.

It wasn't until he reached the landing that it hit him. Something about the man didn't seem right. *He looks much younger than his appearance.* Gaetano went downstairs to talk with him, but the man was gone. Again, he ascended the stairs and entered the apartment. He filled a small case with only what he needed. Trying to leave quietly, he didn't bother locking the door. A gust of window from the open kitchen window slammed it shut behind him.

"Where are you going?" his neighbor Giuseppe across the hall shouted.

Startled, Gaetano put his finger to his lips. "Shush." He looked down the stairwell to make sure no one was there.

"I'm going back north to my family," he whispered.

Giuseppe looked puzzled. "Why?"

"Things are happening that must be stopped. Mussolini allowed Hitler to take over the country. They are slaughtering Jews."

He waved his flipped his hand. "That's only a rumor started by Partisans who want to expel him as minister."

"I've seen it with my own eyes. Germany is turning Italian citizens against each other and using our military to round up Jews. Don't you see what's happening?"

"I have nothing against Jews personally," Giuseppe said, "but we must keep faith in our principles. Il Duce wouldn't do such a thing. He knows what he's doing. You must trust him."

"He has betrayed us. Maybe he didn't mean it to turn out this way, but he's backed Italy into a corner. Germany is now in charge."

Gaetano looked down the hall nervously for any sign of intruding ears. "Where is our fearless leader now?" he whispered. He pretends to remain in power but hides in Milan. Il Duce is nothing but Hitler's puppet."

"You better watch what you say." Joseph's voice went low. "Certain people might call you a traitor. You could be put on trial or, even worse—hung by the Germans."

"I hold this country close to my heart, but I can't stand by and watch them murder innocent people."

Giuseppe sighed. "What are we to do, Gaetano? There is danger in every corner."

"You are right. The partisans grow stronger every day and kill Fascists. The Fascists are shooting every partisan they see. My family is in danger. That is why I must leave."

"How will you get out of Rome?" Giuseppe asked. "German tanks are on the main roads. They've set up checkpoints."

"I can't stay here. I think someone is watching my apartment."

"There's a tavern around the corner that stays open late. "Maybe you can wait a few hours. There won't be as much military presence on the roads."

"Yes, perhaps you're right." He picked up his suitcase and turned to leave.

"Wait," Giuseppe said and went back into his apartment. He came out holding a bag.

"Take this, Gaetano. You have a long journey ahead of you and may get hungry."

Gaetano took the sack. "Thank you, Joseph. You are a good man. Stay safe."

Once he was outside, he looked into the bag. Between the fruit, bread, and cheese was a gun. He tucked it into his jacket pocket and took a bite of the apple.

*****

Gaetano took a stool at the end of the bar. The tender came to him first, ignoring the other patrons.

"You look like you've had a rough night, my friend," he said. "What will it be?"

Gaetano nodded. "A bourbon, please."

The bartender pulled out two glasses and poured them both a bourbon. He drank his in one gulp and banged the empty glass on the counter. "This one is on the house," he said and returned to serving the other customers. Nursing his drink, he thought about his daughter. *Antoinette is right about Mussolini.* He only cares about his power and influence in Italy. At that moment, there was an explosion of gunfire outside.

"Partisans," the bartender said.

The heavy tavern door swung open. A half dozen rowdy men entered with rifles slung over their shoulders.

"Resistance fighters, drunk on power," the man next to Gaetano whispered. "If they start drinking, things could get bad in here."

Gaetano knew one of the men. The man with the brown cap was Alfredo, one of the men he met when he first arrived in Rome. He also recognized the man next to him. *He was the man in front of my building tonight.*

"Bartender. Pour us some bourbon. We're celebrating the arrest of Benito Mussolini."

Gaetano crossed his arms to hide the ax and elm rod symbol on his sleeve and looked down, hoping he wouldn't be recognized. He didn't move a muscle.

The resistance fighters drank their ale, hooting and cheering over their latest victory against Mussolini. One of the men stepped closer and studied Gaetano.

"I know you!" His eyes danced over Gaetano. "*Fascista!*"

"No," Gaetano said. "You are mistaken."

"Yes, now I remember. You were the chap that led the march on Rome," he said, his face close enough to Gaetano's that he could smell the Bourbon on his breath. "It's because of people like you that Italy has fallen prey to Fascists and Nazis."

"I protested for the good of Italy," Gaetano said, trying to salvage the last shreds of his dignity.

"The good! Surrendering our people to Hitler and his S.S. soldiers!"

"No. That is not what we stood for."

"Nazi! Swine!" Alfredo yelled, practically frothing from the mouth. "Mussolini is a traitor, and I condemn all who supported him." He hit Gaetano with the butt of his rifle.

Gaetano grunted and hit the ground, blood gushing from his head.

"Death to all Fascists!" Alfredo shouted.

"Stop!" the innkeeper shouted, aiming a gun he had hidden behind the bar.

Shots rang out, and the innkeeper fell.

With trembling legs, Gaetano stood up and reached for the gun his neighbor had given to him. Before he could shoot, Alfredo fired a bullet, hitting him in the neck. Gaetano coughed and fell to the floor. Dark blood dribbled from his mouth as his head rolled back.

*****

News of Gaetano's murder reached Domenico, and he was saddened to learn it was at the hands of a Partisan. He didn't want Antoinette to find out about her father from anyone but him, so he rushed back to Florence.

Chapter 25

Antoinette stood on the porch and looked at the fiery orange clouds. Rockets streaked across the sky like fingers grasping to crush the life out of Florence. She felt a heaviness in her chest, which made it hard to breathe. After making a cup of tea to calm her frazzled nerves, she crawled between the sheets of her empty bed. She had trouble sleeping. Images of the war swirled in her brain.

All through the night, the sound of explosions in Florence jarred her. Sick of the war, she missed her husband. Pulling Domenico's pillow to her chest, she folded her arms beneath it and curled onto her side. Soon she surrendered to sleep. She dreamed that her father was trapped in Rome. Antoinette wished he hadn't joined the Black Shirts. Although she respected his political ideology and patriotism, she questioned political violence and war as a means of national rejuvenation.

*****

Domenico drove to Florence to tell her that her father was dead before she heard it from someone else.

Everyone was asleep when he entered the house. He climbed the stairs and looked in on his two sons, who were fast asleep. Bending over their beds, he kissed his sleeping sons, then headed to the main bedroom.

"Antoinette," Domenico whispered.

She stirred. A faint smile spread across her lips. "I've missed you," she sighed.

"Antoinette," he said again.

She sat up and massaged the sleep from her eyes.

"Why aren't you in Sorrento?"

"I have news of your father."

"My father?"

Before Domenico reached out for her, she jumped out of bed. "What's wrong?"

"He's.... he ran into some trouble in Rome. "He's been shot."

"Is he all right?"

"He's dead."

"No!" she cried, pushing him away. "I don't believe you. Where did you hear this?"

"A friend of my cousin lives in Rome. He contacted him with the news. I'm sorry."

Antoinette narrowed her eyes.

"You must be happy! You never liked my father because he was a fascist. I suppose you think he got what he deserved."

"That's not true. I knew he was a good man."

Domenico hated seeing her grieve. He took her in his arms. She tried to pull away, but he tightened his grip. Her body went limp as she wept into his shoulder.

"They killed my father! Our own people killed my father!"

All the violence between the fascists and the rest of the country was suddenly personal to her. The foreboding that something bad would happen to her father had gnawed at her since she left Florence. Her premonition came true.

*****

Father Herbert, in Rome, identified Gaetano's body and arranged for him to be sent back to Florence.

Domenico went to the Duomo and made all the arrangements. He even had posters made to announce Gaetano's passing and personally nailed them to posts around town.

A rain shower had passed that morning, and the streets were dark and wet. Dressed in black with veils over their faces, Josephina and Antoinette made their way to the church. Domenico walked in the middle, supporting them.

Aunt Beatrice and Uncle Antonio embraced Josephina.

"Look at what they did to my husband?" she cried.

The service was open to the public, but only the staunchest fascists dared show themselves. Now that it wasn't as popular, his friends scattered like roaches in the light. This embittered Antoinette. Aunt Beatrice sank to her knees and prayed. His death was a high price for her family to pay for Gaetano's loyalty to Il Duce.

They mounted the worn marble steps to the cathedral and entered the vestibule. The lighting was dim, except for the candles. Antoinette could smell death mingled with the heavy scent of melting beeswax. The wooden coffin containing Gaetano rested in front of the altar. The cover was open for the family to kiss him. Tears filled her eyes as immeasurable grief tightened in her chest. She blinked them away.

Father Baccari waited by the confessional dressed in his black capuce over garments of white.

Josephina entered to confess her sins so she could receive the sacraments. Antoinette was next, but she took confession only for her mother's sake. Her faith had been shaken. Soon after she pulled the curtain closed, she thought she would suffocate in the small confessional.

*****

After the funeral, Domenico debated whether he should return to Campania. He realized Antoinette wasn't safe. Although she wasn't actively behind their politics, her family had political ties to Mussolini. A growing number of Partisans openly condemned Fascists.

Still, he was needed in the south. The Germans had invaded Russia and were advancing toward the Ukrainian Soviet Socialist Republic. A black cloud formed over the fashion district as the Nazis infiltrated northern Italy. He knew it wouldn't be long until they claimed all of Italy.

"Please don't go back," Antoinette cried. "I don't want to be alone."

"I'm sorry, Antoinette. I don't want to leave, but the Germans are closing in on Italy. I have to defend Campania."

"Then take me with you. The boys can stay with my mother."

"No, it wouldn't be safe. Besides, Josephina is grieving the loss of your father. She's still in shock."

"I feel so useless."

"No. You're strong, Antoinette, as is your mother. The two of you will be safe here in Florence. Vittorio and Domenico need you here."

"This will be over soon, I promise. Campania will not give up without a fight."

Domenico kissed his wife goodbye once more.

Chapter 26

A knock on the door woke Antoinette in the middle of the night. Hastily, she grabbed her robe and turned on the porch light before opening the door.

"Ethan, Rachel. What are you doing here?"

"Please, turn out the light. We don't want anyone to see us."

Antoinette flipped off the switch. "Come inside. Hurry."

"I'm sorry, Antoinette. We didn't know where else to go. The Germans are surrounding Milan. They're rounding up all the Jews."

"I don't understand. Why are they doing this?"

"Because we're Jews. Hitler wants to wipe us off the face of the Earth. He's arresting everyone and shipping them to God knows where."

"That's awful," Antoinette said. "He can't do that! Il Duce wouldn't let that happen."

"Mussolini is no longer in power. Germany invaded Italy without firing a shot."

"What about the Italian Army? Surely, they'll stop the Nazis."

"Mussolini and Hitler formed an alliance. More like a surrender. Now, the Gestapo runs everything. They are determined to exterminate every Jew and take the property. They raided the synagogues and took anything of value they could find, including a list of the names and addresses of all the Jews in Milan."

Rachel's eyes were glassy with tears. "It's all gone—everything we worked for. But worse than that, they took Mama and Papa."

Ethan stroked her arm. "Don't worry. We'll find them when the war is over."

"No," she cried. "It'll be too late. The Rabbi saw them loaded onto the train. They were sent to one of those so-called work camps. They're really death camps."

"Oh, I'm so sorry," Antoinette said.

"I was hoping to get to Switzerland," Ethan said, "but the Nazis are like ivy on a Cypress tree. Their tendrils and branches spread everywhere. They have patrols on all the major roads. We'd have to go through the woods. Even if we could get around them, Rachel is pregnant. I don't know how far we'd get."

"Pregnant?"

"Yes, she was raped by a German officer. He had been watching her for weeks and followed her to the textile factory."

"I shouldn't have been working so late," Rachel said. "I knew the dangers of being alone. As I was about to lock up, he came out from the shadows and...."

Tears welled in Antoinette's eyes, and she embraced Rachel. "I'm so sorry."

"When he found out Rachel was having a baby, he wanted to eliminate any trace. It was no longer safe to stay in Milan. We had to leave."

"How did you get to Florence?"

"We stowed away in a cattle truck heading south. There's a priest here in Florence who is smuggling people out. He arranged for us to hide in a cattle truck."

Josephina heard them talking and came out of her bedroom. "Ethan, you did the right thing. You can stay here with us."

"That's truly kind, but we don't want to put you and your family in danger. If you help us, you'll be risking your life. The Germans will see it as treason, punishable by death."

"I will not turn my back on you and Rachel," Antoinette said.

"The Gestapo will kill you, your mother, and your sons if we're caught here!"

"Then we won't get caught," Antoinette said.

"We have a wine cellar in the basement, with living quarters," Josephina said. It doesn't have windows, but it has everything you need."

"All right," Ethan said, "but it's only temporary until we can find a way over the Alps."

Ethan and Rachel followed them to the basement. "It's a little dusty, but you'll be safe here. She pulled the covers off two mattresses.

"Help me move this cupboard in front of the wine cellar, Josephina. It can serve as an emergency hiding place."

"Thank you, Josephina," Rachel said. "We'll forever be grateful for your kindness."

"There's a small wash closet. You can wash up in there." She pulled some towels from the linen cupboard and handed them to Ethan.

"Are you hungry?" Antoinette asked. "We have some leftover dinner on the stove."

"We're fine," Ethan said.

Rachel nudged him. "I'm starving," she whispered.

"I'll bring you food." Antoinette reached over and tried to rip the yellow star from his coat, but it was sewn on tight. "Give me your coats," she said. "You won't be needing these any longer. I'll burn them."

Antoinette climbed the stairs to the main floor. Her body stiffened with sudden fear. Maybe they were right. She didn't want to put her mother and sons in danger. What if the S.S. Jew hunters found them? Perhaps there is another place to hide them, she thought and decided she'd visit Father Baccari. Maybe he knows a way to get them to Switzerland. Antoinette knew that wasn't practical with Rachel in her condition and that they would get caught. *No! I will not let my friends die.*

Chapter 27

Antoinette made Ethan and Rachel as comfortable as possible in the basement. They would stay there during the day when the Nazis were more likely to make their rounds.

Knowing how hard it was for them to be confined, Antoinette closed the curtains every evening and invited them upstairs to have dinner. They crowded around the dining table to eat.

"You're pretty," little Vittorio said.

"Thank you," Rachel replied, folding her napkin on her lap.

"Why do you live in the basement?" Dom asked. "Is it because you're Jewish?"

She exchanged a glance with Antoinette across the table and concentrated on taking a helping of potatoes. "It's just temporary until we can go back home."

"Why do they hate Jews?" Vittorio asked.

Ethan pressed his fingers onto the tablecloth, unsure of what Antoinette had told her sons about the war.

"It's all right," she said. "The boys know what's going on. Domenico told them."

Ethan looked into Vittorio's eyes. "Have you ever had a classmate who hurt other kids?"

"Yes, my teacher said they were bullies. She said they didn't like themselves and had to lash out at others."

"Well, sometimes adults act like bullies. But don't worry. There are more good people on the earth than bad."

This seemed to satisfy Vittorio, and he resumed eating his dinner.

"What's going on in Milan?" Antoinette asked.

"I won't lie. It's not like you remember," Ethan said. "There were changes after you left. The church bells stopped ringing, and Jews were afraid to attend synagogue. We had to pray in secret. Once the curfews went into effect, the theaters closed. Markets had limited amounts of produce and meat. If you weren't in line early, the shelves were empty, or there was only a small selection. I wish I could say that was the worst, but…." He glanced at the children and stopped talking.

"It can't stay this way forever," Rachel said. "Can it?" Her eyes pleaded for reassurance.

Ethan patted her arm. "We just have to wait it out."

Rachel was optimistic the war would end soon. Antoinette didn't want to alarm her about the fact that things were indeed getting worse. Ethan asked Josephina if she had a radio so he could hear news of the war, but Antoinette lied and said it was broken.

One night at the dinner table, there was a loud knock. Ethan and Rachel fled to the basement. Josephina quickly cleared the extra dishes, and Antoinette rose from the table to answer the door. The pounding sounded again. She moved to the front entrance and took a deep breath before opening the door.

Their Ukrainian neighbor stood outside. He stared into her eyes and twirled his thick drooping mustache.

"Good evening, Vasiluk. Can I help you?"

"Buonasera. I came to see your mother." He walked past her into the dining room, where Josephina sat eating.

"Hello, Vasiluk," she said, putting down her fork. "What can we do for you?"

"My wife and I have been concerned about you and your daughter living here alone with two small children. She suggested I come to see if you needed anything."

"That's kind of you. Thank you, but we have the basics we need."

"Your dinner smells wonderful." He adjusted his spectacles and scanned the table. Antoinette noticed a food stain on the empty place Ethan had been sitting and moved the cake over to hide it.

"Is that an apple cake?" he asked.

"Yes, I baked it today," Josephina said.

"A celebration?"

"Yes," Antoinette said. "It's my mother's birthday."

"Would you like to take some home for you and your wife," Josephina said.

He smiled. "That's very kind of you. It's hard to find a cake in the stores."

Josephina cut two pieces of cake and wrapped them in a napkin.

"Grazie," Vasiluk said. "My wife will be delighted."

Antoinette walked him to the door. After he left, Antoinette was able to breathe easier.

"Mother, do you think he was spying?"

"The Nazis have eyes everywhere. It's hard to know whom to trust. We must be cautious in the future."

Chapter 28

At first, life went on pretty much as normal. Then they were issued food rations.

Antoinette headed for the church in the center of town. She passed a long line of people snaking down the street, waiting to buy groceries. They didn't need to rely on the monthly issue of food rations. Her father's garden supplied ample food. They even had chickens and one duck which they planned to eat on Christmas day. She only had to go to the crowded, frenetic market to buy baking ingredients. She preferred to bake her own bread when she could get flour.

As Ethan had said, huge swastikas were scrawled and pasted on storefront windows.

Despite his warning, the appearance of the German soldiers was a shock. German troops paraded in the square, singing "Deutschland, Uber Alles" with unfamiliar words. Loudspeakers spewed propaganda about alleged atrocities committed by Jews.

Antoinette held her head high, walking with purpose as she moved past a dark cluster of S.S. soldiers standing on the corner. Her Florentine looks made it possible to avoid the pointed questions of street patrols. She crossed the town square and went inside *Santa Maria del Fiore Cathedral.* Antoinette spent more time helping Father Baccari. He had recently replaced Father Benito, who had disappeared.

Father Baccari was an older priest. His white hair was cut short, and he had difficulty moving due to arthritis. He came to the cloth late in life.

Antoinette slid into a pew and clasped the small, silver crucifix hanging from her neck. She stopped to make the sign of the cross in front of the wooden crucifix. A statue of the Madonna clutching her heart was to the left. She was looking up toward the heavens, and the candlelight flickered on her face. The weight on Madonna's heart seemed as heavy as Christ's body suspended from the nails in his hands.

As the priest prepared the Saturday confessional, a young German came into the church with two small children trailing behind him. He dipped his hand into the holy water, crossed himself, and instructed the children to kneel at a pew. The man slipped into the confessional.

"Bless me, father, for I have sinned," Antoinette heard him say.

"Go on," the priest said.

"Are you Father Baccari?"

"Yes. Do I know you?"

"I was told you hide Jewish children."

"Where did you hear that?"

The priest stepped out of the confessional box and saw the children.

"Who are you?"

"My name is Hans. "I promised to get these two children to a safe place. I was told you could help."

"I don't know who would tell you that. I'm a simple priest trying to lead my poor parish through this terrible war."

"Please," Hans said. "I don't have much time. I'm trying to save these children. They're so young and innocent."

"Where are their parents?"

"Deported to Auschwitz. They begged me to look after their children."

"How do I know you're not a Nazi spy?"

"I assure you that I'm not. Not all Germans agree with what Hitler is doing. Some of us are decent human beings. We do what we can."

Father Baccari looked into the frightened eyes of a boy of six and a girl of four.

"What do you want me to do?" he asked.

"I was hoping you could get them to Switzerland."

"Perhaps, but that will take time."

"I want my mama," the girl cried.

Her brother put his arm around her shoulder. "Don't cry. We'll see her soon."

Father Baccari rubbed his salt-and-pepper beard. "I suppose I could find someone willing to take them."

"Thank you, Father," Hans said and turned to the children. "You're in good hands now. Be brave."

He was almost to the exit when two Nazi soldiers appeared, cutting like a wide shadow across the doorway.

He pushed past them, bolting outside.

"Quick, hide," Antoinette whispered to the children. "Under the pews."

She ran outside with Father Baccari.

Hans sprinted toward the bell tower. A bullet kicked up dirt at his heels as he entered the side door.

"He's climbing to the top," Father Baccari whispered to Antoinette. "I pray it doesn't ring, or he'll be deaf."

Spotting the young German on the roof, one of the Nazis raised his rifle.

Hans ducked behind a gargoyle as a bullet whizzed through the air, piercing the stained-glass window of the vestibule behind him. The glass panels shattered, spraying crystalline fragments through the air and tingling as they fell on the stone roof. He staggered back as another bullet struck him in the chest. He clutched the edge of the arch until his fingers gave out. Gazing one last time at the sky, Hans plummeted to the ground.

The Nazis loaded his body into the bed of their truck and drove away. Once they were gone, the priest gathered the children hiding under the velvet-cushioned pews.

"What's your name?" he asked the boy.

"My name is Samuel, and my sister is Marion."

"Those are lovely names," Antoinette said.

The priest lost his smile and turned to Antoinette.

"I'm sorry to put you in this position, but I may need your help with these children."

"What can I do, Father?"

"I'm involved in setting up a network of safe houses where Jews can escape the Germans. We must resist them and help the Jewish people. I need your help with these children until I can find a way to smuggle them over the Swiss border. I'll understand if you refuse."

"I'll keep the children until you can find safe passage across the Alps."

"It will be a significant risk to you and your family. Since your husband is involved with the Partisans, the Germans may see you as a person of interest."

"Don't worry, Father. I know what I'm doing."

"All right, but make sure no one sees them enter your house."

Father Baccari let them leave with Antoinette. She was one of the few people he could trust.

Ethan and Rachel were surprised to see the children.

"This is Samuel and Marion," Antoinette said. "They will be staying with us for a brief time. I promised to take care of them until Father Baccari finds a group to lead them safely over the Alps."

"Hello," Rachel said, excited to see the children. "Would you like me to brush your hair?" she said to Marion.

The little girl nodded.

"I hope you realize the danger," Ethan said.

"These children were bound for the German camps. What else could I do?"

"Hiding them is admirable," he said. "Getting them out of Italy will be difficult."

*****

The next day, the Gestapo came back to the church. Antoinette was there praying in one of the pews. She at once stopped and went to Father Baccari's side.

"I hear rumors, Father, the Nazi said."

"Rumors?"

"Yes, perhaps you are aiding Jewish children to escape Italy."

"Why do you concern yourself with the children," Antoinette interrupted. "Don't you have enough slave labor with their parents?"

The Nazi raised his brows and fixed his eyes on Antoinette. He spoke English. "Do you know who I am?"

"Yes, I do. Your rudeness is insulting, sir."

He raised his pistol as if to strike her with the butt.

Father Baccari stepped between them. "She didn't mean that. She's just trying to protect me."

The Nazi lowered his luger. "You're lucky I don't bash your head. Now, get out of here before I change my mind."

In a flurry of anger, Antoinette strode out of the church and into the sunlight. As her temper cooled, she rebuked herself for inviting attention.

Chapter 29

Father Baccari had someone waiting to take a small group of people over the mountains. He informed Antoinette that they'd be leaving the day after Christmas.

"Before sunrise, someone will knock twice, then three times. She won't stay to talk. Just have the children ready to go."

Christmas was only two days away. Josephina promised Ethan and Rachel they would have a place at the table. *If things were different,* she thought. *I might have adopted the children myself.*

"Isn't that too risky?" Ethan said. "I don't want to see you in trouble."

Antoinette weighed the consequences.

"Don't worry. I don't think they'll bother anyone. Even the Nazis take time off for Christmas. The children have gone through an ordeal. They miss their parents and live in constant fear. They deserve a little happiness."

Knowing it was also Hanukkah, Antoinette decided to combine the holidays. She wanted a couple of dreidels, but the Jewish toy was hard to find. Instead, she tried to make the small tops from some wood she found in her father's workspace. She had a Jewish friend who taught her how to play the game during grade school. Antoinette etched a Hebrew letter on each side. Together, the letters formed the meaning, "a great miracle happened there." Dom and Vittorio helped by painting them.

Josephina reminded her of a doll tucked away in the attic. She could give that to Marion. While up there, she found an Egyptian board game her father had given to her. Gaetano was fascinated at the time, watching the two children move the round discs across the board. They learned the game quickly.

The family left it on a train, so he brought it home for Antoinette.

Domenico wanted a toy airplane, but she couldn't find one since most of the toy shops were owned by Jews and closed. She explained the problem to her sons and said she'd teach them how to make their own planes with paper and a wooden clothespin. They loved the idea.

For Ethan, Antoinette wrapped a bottle of vodka her father had stored in the back of the kitchen cabinets. She found the perfect dress for Rachel in her closet.

Josephina spent the afternoon cooking a fresh pot of tomato sauce. Homemade pasta noodles hung around the kitchen to dry. She layered the noodles with plenty of sauce and ricotta cheese she made from heating milk and skimming off the curd. A duck roasted in the oven, filling the house with its succulent scent. Before the meal, she brought a few bottles of wine from the cellar.

"Best we enjoy this before the Germans confiscate it all," she said.

They passed the bread and the last of the butter Josephina had made when milk was still available. After pasta and meat, everyone groaned, their bellies bursting. Still, they waited anxiously for dessert. Josephina outdid herself with a plate of assorted Biscotti. Antoinette preferred to end her meal with a cup of tea, but the smell of expresso was so delicious that it gave her pause. Josephina had hidden it away for a special occasion.

Ethan sat back and smiled as he puffed one of Gaetano's old cigars. Josephina couldn't bear to get rid of them when her husband died, even though she didn't know anyone who smoked. Antoinette put a Bing Crosby record on the Victrola as the women danced around the room, being silly.

The children stayed up playing with their toys while the adults played cards. For a few hours, they put the war out of their minds.

*****

The following cold and snowy day, there was a knock on the door. Antoinette had prepared the children for their journey with layers of sweaters and a pouch filled with food.

"Are we going on a train?" the little girl asked.

"No. We have to walk in the snow," Samuel said.

"Are we going to get wet?"

"I'll make sure you are dressed warm," Antoinette said. "It won't take long. You'll be nice and dry once you get over the mountains."

Rachel wanted Ethan to go with them, but he refused to go unless she came too.

She gave him a weak smile. "I don't want to give birth to my baby on a snowy mountain."

"Then we stay together," he said.

Before Antoinette could hug the children goodbye, the woman whisked them outside and hurried them away. If things were different, she might have adopted the children herself.

It saddened her, but now that she was helping Father Baccari, there would be other children to save.

Chapter 30

Now that the Germans had fully occupied the area, the danger increased. Daily raids created new terror for the people of Florence. The Gestapo muscled their way into homes unannounced. Going upstairs was no longer safe, so Ethan and his sister had to stay in the basement. They slept until the evening and then came out to eat in the small kitchen. Their days were opposite the outside world, so there was less chance that anyone would know they were there.

The Nazis continually harassed Father Baccari, convinced that he and his parishioners were behind the Jewish people fleeing to Switzerland.

Father Baccari prepared the Holy Eucharist at the altar for Sunday mass. Even as the door of the church opened, he sensed danger. Four men came toward him, and he recognized one as Franz Hadler.

"We have some questions for you, Father."

Father Baccari tried to rise to his feet. Hadler pressed his fingers into Baccari's shoulder and tightened his grip on the priest's collarbone.

"A man was here a few days ago. He had two children with him."

"I didn't see any children."

"If you're honest, this will be painless, and we'll leave you in peace. If not, well...." He smiled and backhanded the priest, splitting his lip. "I hate to inflict pain on a man of the cloth—but I will."

"He did not have children...."

"You will tell me what I want to know."

After a smack to his knees with a truncheon, Father Baccari's legs gave out. The priest grimaced at the pain.

"I believe these children were Jewish. It is a treasonable offense to hide Jews."

"I know nothing," Baccari said and made the sign of the cross.

"Pray, pray for your mortal soul," the lieutenant said. He raised his pistol and shot him between the eyes.

Father Baccari tumbled down the altar stairs, his white robes saturated with blood.

*****

Father Baccari's replacement was younger. Father Capella was a tall man who wasn't intimidated easily. He arrived from Rome to soothe the parishioners, fearful of returning to the church for Sunday mass. His vestments flowed with ease and confidence as he performed the sacred duties of the parish.

Like Father Baccari, he had the propensity to aid refugees but wasn't as careless as his predecessor. He was well aware that the Germans were watching, waiting to implement their strict form of law and order.

Alone in the church, he fell to his knees in front of the altar and prayed. He knew it was only a matter of time before the Nazis would be back to interrogate him. Below the abbey, six orphans waited for Sister Maria of the Sacred Heart to collect them. Once they were gone, he took a deep breath and retired to his bed chambers.

He was about to fall asleep when there was a pounding on the heavy oak door. Father Capella pulled on his robe and opened the portal. Outside were three military officers, two in gray uniforms and one in black. His name badge said, Franz Halder. The other two were of lesser rank.

"I see we have a new priest," Halder said. "It surprises me that you're so young. What is your name?"

"I am Father Luca Capella, and I'm old enough to lead my flock," he said piously. "What can I do for you?"

"I want to make you aware of the fate that befell your prior colleague and give you fair warning. We are watching who comes to your church."

Father Capella's pulse surged as he stood to his full height. "All are welcome in the house of God."

"There was a nun here today."

Father Capella swallowed and took a deep breath. "She was sent to assist me with paperwork Father Baccari left unfinished."

"I see," Halder said. He ran his fingers across his jaw. "I'll be watching, Father. If I find any evidence that you have lied to me, there will be no warning next time," he said and turned to leave.

Chapter 31

Antoinette looked down the road at two military vehicles followed by a German lorry billowing black diesel smoke. The brakes squealed to a stop outside her house, and a top official stepped out and paused to straighten his black uniform coat. A soldier with a rifle jumped from the second vehicle and clicked the heels of his calf-high boots. “Heil Hitler.”

“Heil Hitler,” the lieutenant returned the salute and turned his gaze to the house. His face was severe. He slapped his baton in his hand and stepped toward the stairs.

“Are you Antoinette Defino?”

“Yes, Commandant,” she said and swallowed the lump in her throat.

“I am Lieutenant Franz Halder.” He gave Antoinette a cold, sharp stare.

“How can I help you?”

“I’m looking for your husband. Is he here?” he asked, eyeing her closely.

"No, my husband is in Sorrento, visiting his family."

The officer smiled. "Is that so?" he said and pulled a cigarette from his pack. He looked at the house, the unlit cigarette dangling from his lips. "Would you mind if I came inside to look around?"

"Of course not," she said, trying not to tremble.

He walked past the living room and into the kitchen. Hearing a noise above, he looked up.

"Do you live alone?"

"No. I live with my mother. She isn't feeling well today and has remained in bed. I beg you not to disturb her."

"Josephina, right?"

"Yes, how do you know my mother's...."

"And where are your boys?"

"My boys?"

"Yes, your sons, Domenico jr. and Vittorio."

"They're in school." She tasted acid in the back of her throat.

He nodded and looked up at a trap door in the ceiling. "Is that the attic?"

"Yes," she said, "but we don't use it."

"How do you get up there?"

"The stairs pull down."

"You do know that harboring fugitives is a criminal offense."

"Fugitives?"

"Your husband is part of the resistance. We arrested him last week. Instead of the firing squad, he escaped. Franz lit his cigarette and inhaled.

Her rapid heartbeat throbbed in her fingertips.

"Domenico?" Her puzzlement registered in her eyes.

"Have you heard from your husband?" he asked, heading toward the kitchen.

"No, I haven't heard from him in weeks."

Franz Halder gazed at her coldly with ice-blue eyes. He stepped closer. "Do you hide Jews?"

His expressionless face made her shiver.

"I'm afraid that you're lying to me." He raked his fingers through his cropped blond hair as his eyes focused on the basement door.

"No, sir, I assure you, there are no Jews here."

Antoinette's breath hitched.

As his hand reached for the knob, there was a commotion outside. His aide entered, stiffened his heels, and whispered something in Franz's ear.

Hadler frowned and said something to him in German.

Hadler turned to Antoinette. "It seems I have a pressing issue that requires my attention." He looked back at the basement door.

Antoinette followed him outside. She reached for the railing to steady herself.

Franz ground his cigarette out beneath his heel and entered the vehicle. She waited for his entourage to pull away from the curb. When the lorry disappeared around the corner, she ran to check on Ethan and Rachel, still hiding in the wine cellar.

"They know," Ethan said. "I'm sure they'll be back. It's no longer safe for us here, Antoinette. We have to leave your house."

"Don't be foolish. The Gestapo is everywhere and checking papers. You wouldn't get far."

"That's why I need to ask another favor."

"What is it?"

"I have a friend who lives near Ponte Vecchio. I've already been in touch with him. He forges Identifications. The papers are ready, but I dare not pick them up myself."

"Do you want me to get them?"

"Yes, please, but you must be careful not to attract attention. Pretend you're shopping. Take the boys. Go to this address." Ethan scribbled the location on a piece of paper and handed it to Antoinette. "Ask for General Wolff."

"Wolff? Isn't he a commander of the S.S. in northern Italy?"

"Yes, that's why I didn't sign his name. Be discreet when you ask to see him. Once you get the papers, we will leave, and you will be safe."

"All right, I'll go first thing in the morning. My mother will be upstairs if someone is looking for me or I don't come back."

That evening after checking on her mother, she tucked the boys into bed and turned off the lights. As a half-moon appeared between the clouds, the not-so-distant sputtering of mortar fire interrupted the silence and menaced the house.

Her sleep was troubled. Even as she plunged deep into slumber, her mind would shudder and wake.

Through a crack in the curtains, blasts south of the city backlit the hills against the night sky. *Is my Domenico still alive?* Antoinette missed him so much. It seemed like just yesterday when they stood at the station. She could still smell his aftershave. *Come back to me, my love.*

Chapter 32

As Domenico approached Naples, he passed abandoned cars and broken wagons lining the roadside. A few pedestrians came into view from time to time, but they moved in a haze. They seemed confused as if they didn't know where they were going or what to do. He thought about his wife and sons. He missed them more than he could imagine. He contemplated returning to Florence, but his family needed him.

Since he was in Naples, he stopped in Castel Nuovo to visit his uncle Sonny. He was alarmed to see how many Nazis were around the Palazzo del Telefoni. Demonstrating were students gathered near the university. Suddenly, there were screams and shouting as soldiers began beating the crowd. Nazi generals ordered the Italian soldiers to open fire. The air reeked of cordite from rifle fires. Blood pooled on the street. People ran in all directions, but they didn't get far. They were rounded up and placed in a van.

Domenico pulled out his camera and instinctively took pictures.

*****

As he was coming up the street, he noticed two German vehicles stopped in front of the shop. A German soldier wearing an ugly gray uniform jumped out and entered the shop.

Domenico sneaked around the building through the alley to the back door. Inside, he saw his uncle with his hands up. The soldier hit his uncle in the head with the butt of his gun and demanded Sonny open the cash drawer. He filled a bag with money, pulled food from the displays, and shoved it into the same sack.

Domenico crawled along the aisles until he was behind him, then wrestled the soldier to the ground. Uncle Sonny reached under the counter for his pistol and shot the Nazi in the chest.

"Quick, Uncle. Get out of here before the others come. I'll divert them and meet you back home.

Sonny left through the back door, and Domenico dashed through the front door. The soldiers spotted him and chased him through the streets.

Domenico had hoped to escape to Via Santa Brigida, but he was captured. He was taken to prison and locked in a cell. The prisoner in the next cell pushed his face close to a crack in the wall. "Who are you?"

His voice was familiar. "My name is Domenico Defino.

"Domenico?" For a moment, there was silence.

Before he could answer, an Italian soldier showed up. "Come with me," he said and grabbed him by the arm.

"Where are you taking me?" Domenico asked.

"Lieutenant Franz Hadler of the Third Reich has a few questions for you."

"He's a German. Why would I have to answer his questions?"

"I'm sorry," the Italian soldier whispered. "We are under German law now." He led him to a room with three Nazis. Domenico could tell he was a high-ranking German. Two other Nazis of lower S.S. rank stood by his side in gray fatigue uniforms.

Franz smiled. "Your family are troublemakers. Do you know what happens to troublemakers?"

"The only troublemakers here are German swine who think they can take over our country."

"We already have one of your cousins locked up. Paolo, I believe."

"Tell me. What treasonous activities are you and the Defino family planning?"

"I just arrived in Campania. I have nothing to say."

Franz lashed out like a snake and struck him with his baton. "That's for your insolence," he said.

White light flashed before Domenico's eyes, and he slumped to the floor, coughing blood.

"What should we do with you?" Franz said. "We could make you an example and have you shot in the square." He scratched his chin. "But no, that might make you a martyr. Better to send you to a work camp for the rest of your days. We'll decide if you live or die when you get there."

Two men dragged him out to the courtyard and threw him in the back of a van. As the vehicle weaved along the road, Domenico remembered the penknife he had hidden in his boot. After many attempts, there was a click, and the back doors swung open. He jumped out of the speeding van and ran into the woods. When the Nazis stopped to figure out the commotion, Domenico was gone.

*****

Aunt Geneva prepared a cold compress for Sonny's head as he explained what had happened to his three sons.

"Do you think Domenico got away?" Calogero asked.

"We can only pray that he slipped through the German patrols," Sonny said.

"What if he was caught?" Accursio asked. "The Italian police arrested Cousin Paolo for inciting a demonstration of students at his college last week. No one has heard from him since."

"I already called Uncle Lorenzo," Tomasco said.

"Good. We had better send word to my brother in Sorrento," Sonny said. "I'm sure he'll want to know."

"Maria hasn't been well," Geneva said. "This is the last thing they need."

"It's unavoidable. We can't just stand by and watch our sons be plucked off the streets of Italy."

"Someone has to go back to the shop and secure the store," Sonny said.

"Don't worry, Pop," Accursio said. "We will take care of it."

*****

Paolo couldn't remember how long he had been imprisoned. When he first arrived, Italian police questioned him about his family. He refused to tell them his name, even when they broke his arm and left him in the cell without medical attention. Somehow, they found his family name Defino, but it didn't mean anything at the time.

Now, he was pulled out and led to a small office. The man standing inside was a German officer.

"Sit down," he yelled, pushing Paolo into a chair. "I'm going to ask you some questions. If you tell me what I want to hear, you will not have any trouble."

"Why should I cooperate?" Paolo said. "I'm already in trouble."

The Nazi looked down at him and smiled.

Paolo's mouth went dry.

"I am Lieutenant Halder. I am first in command of the Gestapo in Naples."

Two fascist soldiers moved aside as Hadler brought back his steel-toed boot and kicked his shin.

Paolo yelped in pain.

Chapter 33

Uncle Lorenzo showed up with his four sons, Bruno, Leo, Pino, and Pasquale. An hour later, Domenico's father, Vincenzo, arrived with his brother Marco.

Soon, the whole family was sitting around the table discussing how they would take back the region and expel the Germans.

"The American allies are advancing in southern Italy," Accursio said. "We can assemble a group of resistance fighters to cooperate with them to propel the liberation of Campania."

"Yes, but don't forget the once dedicated fascists who turned against the regime," Leo said. "They no longer follow Mussolini."

"I have a friend who quit the police department. He said no one is happy about taking orders from the Germans."

There was a knock on the door. Tomasco went to answer.

"Cousin!" he shouted when he saw Domenico. "We were just leaving to search for you."

"I'm so relieved to see you made it here alive," Sonny said. "We worried you might have been shot or arrested."

"I was, but I was able to take apart the hardware to open the door and jumped out of the speeding van. I ran into the woods when the Nazis stopped to figure out the commotion."

"How is your head, Uncle Sonny?"

"I'll live, but I don't know what would have happened to me if you didn't show up at that moment."

"One more thing," Domenico said. They have Paolo."

"My Paolo," Uncle Lorenzo said. "Are you sure?"

"Yes, the Nazi who interrogated me said so himself."

"I must return to Sorrento," Domenico said."

"No, you can't come home," Vincenzo said. "That's the first place they'll come looking for you."

"But mother… she's ill."

"Don't worry. Marco's wife, Teresa, is taking care of her until we get back."

"You need to stay here and fight," Leo said. "We can organize a group to rid Naples of the Germans. Together, we are a small army."

"First, we need to free my brother Paolo," Bruno said.

"How?" Domenico asked. "We have no weapons."

Bruno smiled. "We have lots of weapons."

The cousins followed Bruno outside to his truck. He pulled the cover off a large wooden crate in the back.

"What's in there?" Domenico asked.

"Me and Pasquale raided a local artillery battery and acquired a couple of MP-40s. Then one night during a German hunt, we stole rifles and ammunition from a Nazi jeep. Oh, and a couple of Mills Bombs."

"Mills Bombs?"

"Yes, grenades. We'll toss one in their vehicles. The explosion will send them charging out of the gates."

"I thought the plan was to sneak in quietly," Leo said.

"They won't know what hit 'em. We'll go through the gates and bust inside the prison as they run in the other direction."

"I have five sticks of dynamite," Marco said.

"Bring them. We can use it once we're inside."

*****

A delegation of uniformed Germans stood in front of the prison, talking. Their vehicles were unattended.

The group stood ready at the gate while Bruno and Pasquale crept along the walls of the prison compound.

Bruno threw a stick of dynamite into one of their jeeps, and Pasquale tossed a live grenade in the other.

The first blast alerted the Nazis, who ran to their vehicles.

A second explosion killed several of them as the concussion sent metal flying.

Automatic weapons clattered at Bruno as he ran.

Distracted, the Germans overlooked Domenico and his cousins, who rounded the corner and rushed into the prison.

The string of naked bulbs didn't provide much light in the narrow prison passageway. Coming to a fork, Domenico stopped.

"This way," he said, leading them down a long tunnel to the prisoners. Weapons drawn, Domenico, Marco, Leo, and Tommaso followed.

"Kill every fascist you see," Tommaso said.

Italian guards stood at the entrance to the cellblock of the imprisoned demonstrators.

Tommaso pulled the pin on a grenade and tossed it into the corridor toward the guards. They yelled and ran. The explosion blew them down the passageway and blew the corridor gate open.

"This is it," Domenico said, "but we need the keys to open the cell door."

"Leave it to me," Marco said. "You men stand back." He wedged a stick of dynamite in an opening beside the lock. "Cover yourselves," he yelled to the men inside. Marco lit the fuse and ran back down the hall with the others. The blast was deafening in the confined space.

Once the debris settled, they moved toward the cell. The cell door hung by a single hinge. Domenico kicked it open with his boot. The prisoners inside were crouched along the wall to avoid damage from the explosion.

Paolo, wolfish and lean, stared into his cousin's eyes.

"Domenico!" he shouted, shaking and white-faced.

"I knew my cousins would not leave me to rot in this cell." Overcome with emotions, he embraced Domenico, kissing his cheeks.

"How are we going to get out of here?" Leo said.

"There's a secret exit," Marco said. "It's on the lower level. That's where they torture people."

"Do you remember how to get there?"

"Yes. We have to go back. There's another corridor."

"That must be where we came to the fork," Domenico said.

Staying close to the wall, they made their way to the other tunnel. It ran downhill deeper into the prison. A metallic stench permeated the air.

"We're close," Marco said. "I smell old blood."

They came to a concrete room with long tables and rows of torture implements. An ancient rack for stretching humans sat ominously in one corner.

"What the hell do they do with that?" Pino asked, pointing to a chair with a vice on the arms.

Domenico stepped closer to look at the vice. He startled and jumped back.

"Those are fingernails. They must have squeezed them off some poor soul."

"That's nothing," Marco said. "You should see the tongue remover."

"Let's get out of here," Leo said. "Where's the exit?"

"I could have sworn there was a door here," Marco said. "They must have sealed it."

"Wait!" Domenico said. "Did you hear that? Someone is out there?"

"Stand back and take cover!"

"That's Bruno," Paolo yelled.

They crouched under a metal table as the side of the wall exploded, sending concrete in all directions.

Chapter 34

Naples was the first city to rise against the Nazis as the Allies leapfrogged from Sicily to the mainland. The insurgence of Italians grew stronger.

The Delfino cousins organized the volunteers to resist the encroaching Germans.

"It won't be easy," Domenico said. "Men will die, but we can hold the city."

"It's important we stick together," Peppino added. "There is strength in our numbers."

"We have a group offshore at the Sicilian Channel," Pasquale said. "They are ready to burn the oil reserves to keep it out of German hands."

"Let's hope it doesn't come to that," Domenico said. "Pray the Americans will get here first."

*****

There came news of a major battle. The Allies had landed at Bagnoli, four miles from Naples. Tommaso knew the area well, and they made their way to the beachhead.

A parade of American ships dotted the coastline. Having spent the night patrolling the streets, they'd set up small campfires on the beach. Domenico and six cousins cautiously approached a group of American soldiers. They raised their weapons.

"Don't shoot!" Bruno called out. "We're Partisans. We've come to aid the removal of German forces in Campania."

Keeping his rifle aimed at them, the Lieutenant in charge ordered them to surrender their weapons and put their hands up.

Paolo held back, unwilling to be left defenseless.

"We need to trust them," Domenico said.

One by one, they laid their arms at the feet of the Americans and put their hands up.

After two hours of intense questioning, the Americans finally believed and welcomed Domenico and his cousins. Lines of communication were formalized for future joint efforts.

*****

Domenico and his cousins became spies for the Allied troops. They supplied the Allies with information about German plans. Domenico stayed closer to the university in Naples, where a group of resistance fighters was.

Outraged Neapolitans united, and a civilian uprising ensued. Over fifty protestors were rounded up and arrested. They included eight sailors and fourteen Italian police officers who had offered armed resistance in the center of the city. The Nazis ordered the citizens to witness the executions scheduled for the following day.

The Germans demanded that all Italian citizens surrender their weapons within twenty-four hours. To suppress the population and create a military security zone, a German general ordered the evacuation of anyone living within three hundred meters of the waterfront. Males over eighteen and under thirty years old were deported to work camps. They sent soldiers into Naples to round up and execute resisters.

Domenico and his cousins organized a group of rioters to oppose the Nazi roundups.

The Neapolitan uprising prevented the Germans from defending against the Allied offensive and saved Naples from destruction.

Knowing the Allied forces were approaching, former Italian soldiers came out of hiding and joined the resistance. The insurgents sprang into action when the Germans tried to destroy the bridge to isolate the city.

The train station there was overrun by Germans soldiers retreating to the north. Domenico and a group of forty men set up a roadblock. Armed with rifles and machine guns, they pushed the German soldiers back. Enzo Stimolo, an Italian lieutenant, led a group of resistance fighters against German reinforcements sent from a nearby camp. His men then captured a weapons depot and plundered an armory.

After the resistance soldiers had rested, taken care of the wounded, and replenished their ammo and weapons, volunteers were requested to seek out the Nazis below ground. It was rumored that some had barricaded themselves in one of the two principal catacombs beneath Naples.

Entering the back of a church shortly after dawn, the cousins entered the catacombs and snaked through the dark tunnels.

"What's that smell?" Marco said, covering his nose with his sleeve.

The stench grew stronger as they pushed forward. They came to a chamber where dozens of German soldiers lay on the ground. Flies swarmed the bodies, streaming in and out of their open mouths. Domenico picked up a capsule lying next to one of the corpses.

"Cyanide," Leo said. "Looks like they've been dead for days. They killed themselves rather than surrender. They believe us to be as cruel as them. The idiots. Serves them right."

Chapter 35

In the distance, Domenico saw the silhouettes of low-flying bombers. Rockets lit the sky like daytime in brief flashes.

"They're getting close," Domenico said to Alessandro.

"He's right," Marco said. "I can feel the blast waves under my feet."

Air raid sirens moaned and wailed, followed by antiaircraft guns and bombs raining down on the train station. Domenico hit the ground close to the building and instinctively curled into a ball. Glass from the ticket window exploded and showered his back. He buried his head in his hands and covered his ears against the loud explosions as they grew nearer.

Domenico stayed low until the bomb blasts were farther away, and everything quieted. He smelled smoke all around him. The pain in his shoulder was searing. He raised his head and felt the back of his shirt wet with blood. Dizzy and disoriented, he forced himself up, but his knees buckled.

Marco was lying a few feet away, close to the tracks. Domenico crawled toward his brother, whose chest heaved as his lungs struggled to get oxygen. Marco's breathing was shallow, but he was still alive.

Domenico looked around for his cousin Pasquale but saw no sign of him. Then he turned to look for Bruno. He lay motionless on the tracks below. Domenico ripped off Bruno's bloody shirt exposing a large hole in his cousin's chest. Domenico fainted. He woke up in a hospital with a nurse plucking shards of glass out of his back. He moaned as the nurse packed alcohol swabs into his open wounds.

"I'm sorry," the nurse said. "I know it's painful, but you'll be fine. The glass didn't hit any vital organs."

"Is my brother, Marco, still alive?"

"He's in the next bed. He came out of surgery two hours ago."

"Will he be all right?"

"Yes, the effects of the anesthetic will wear off soon, and he'll be in a lot of pain."

*****

After one week, Domenico was able to leave the hospital. He went to his uncle Sonny's house to check on his cousins. There was only one casualty.

"Everyone made it home," Sonny said.

"Even Pasquale?"

"Yes, but the whole family is in mourning."

"I'm sorry about Cousin Bruno," Domenico said. "I don't think he made it."

"No. Uncle Lorenzo is distraught but proud of his son. We're all proud of how you boys stuck together to fight for Italy."

"Is there news of the war?"

"The Grand Council voted to return Victor Emmanuel's full constitutional powers. Mussolini was removed from his position and arrested as he exited the royal residence."

"I hope he pays dearly for what he's done to our country."

"What of the Germans?" Domenico asked.

"The Allies liberated Naples and drove them north. The Germans are north of Florence now. They have built fortifications across Italy, ten miles deep.

Panic washed over Domenico's face.

"Florence? Why? There's nothing there for them except art and historic buildings."

"Exactly. The Nazis are hiding in plain sight. They know the Allies and the Italians won't wage a battle there. It would destroy the city."

"They plan to detonate the Renaissance bridges across the river Arno to slow the Allied advance."

"That's where my wife and sons are," Domenico said. "I have to go back."

"You can take my car, but I'm not sure how far you'll get. You'll have to go through Rome. The Germans have checkpoints on all the main roads."

"I have a paper with the letterhead of the Vatican," Domenico said. "I'll write a letter from the Pope to the mayor of Florence and pretend to be a messenger."

"If the Nazis question your papers, they'll execute you."

"That's a chance I'm willing to take."

"Then I suggest you leave now and drive through the night. It'll be safer on the roads."

Chapter 36

Antoinette and her sons crossed over Ponte Vecchio to the shopping district south of the Arno river. German soldiers eye-balled them as they sped past in military vehicles. The hairs on the back of her neck raised. They were halfway down the street when the air-raid sirens wailed. Buildings shuddered from the impact of a bomb on the bridge. Screaming people stampeded the roads to avoid bombs, debris, and death. Antoinette pulled her sons close to her side to shield them from the hurtling chunks of debris and tried to keep up with the surging crowd, but holding Dom and Vittorio's hands slowed her down. A deafening roar overpowered her as they reached the square. German bombers flying overhead were targeting the bridges. Knocked off her feet by the concussion of an explosion, she hit her head on the pavement. Darkness enveloped her.

Vittorio opened his eyes slowly. He screamed as blood dripped from his forehead into his eyes.

"Mama!" He scrambled to his feet but fell to his knees. His head throbbed. Again, he stood up. "Mama!"

Choking on dust, he looked as the crowds pushed past him. He struggled through a sea of ripped bodies, shouting for his mother. She was nowhere in sight.

As the crowds kept pushing past him, he ran back.

"Don't go back that way," a man yelled, reaching for his arm.

"I have to find my mama and brother."

"It's too dangerous."

"Let me go!" Vittorio squirmed free and pushed against the mob.

In the distance, he saw bodies on the pavement. Reaching the smallest one, he looked down at Dom's brown eyes, which had rolled back into his bloody face. Vittorio pulled Dom up, only to realize the back of his head was missing.

"Mama!" Vittorio screamed. Letting his brother's body fall, he held his stomach and vomited. Sobbing, he slumped to the ground next to his brother.

"Come, my son," a priest murmured. "You can't do anything for him now."

"Have—have you seen my—mother?" Vittorio gasped, searching among the dead and dying bodies.

"We must get to the safety of *Palazzo Pitti*. Maybe she's there." The priest led Vittorio down the street, blood trickling from the boy's head wound.

When they arrived at the palace, Vittorio ran inside, searching for his mother.

"Mama!"

A young nun pulled him to her bosom as he cried. "We'll find her, don't worry. She put a bandage on his wound and rocked him until he fell asleep.

People huddled together in the church, listening to the atonal music of air raid sirens.

"We're all going to die," a lady cried, clutching at her husband.

The bombing continued for nearly an hour. When it finally stopped, the priest gathered able-bodied men to help the wounded. Volunteers helped load the wounded into carts for transport to the hospital. Many injured were missing arms and legs, their stubs bound with tourniquets to control the bleeding.

Vittorio was one of the last to be taken to the hospital. Falling in and out of consciousness, he had no way of knowing his mother was in the same wagon.

Chapter 37

Remnants of the dusky gray light vanished over the horizon. Domenico drove for two hours, hugging the coast until he reached the outskirts of Rome. Traveling around the city, he wove his way around the north side, passing deserted barricades of sandbags along the way until he reached the main road out of Rome. As his uncle had warned, he saw a heavily fortified roadblock in the distance.

A Wehrmacht patrol in calf-high black leather boots and armbands displaying a large black swastika staffed the checkpoint, stopping any cars trying to leave Rome. The men were sitting around a fire and drinking wine they had stolen from Tuscany. They were ordered to shoot retreating Italian soldiers who refused to fight.

The bodies of Italian soldiers trying to retreat lay in a heap by the side of the road. They'd all been executed. Shot in the face.

Amid raucous laughter, one guard dragged himself away and stood in the road. He had a Walther pistol sheathed in his holster on his black leather belt.

"Halt!"

Domenico stopped the car.

"Papers!" the guard demanded.

Domenico handed him his identification and the forged letter of passage. "I'm returning to Florence. I must deliver a message from Pope Puis."

The guard spat in the dirt and stared at the papers impatiently, looking back at his companions, drinking from a bottle.

"Hey," he shouted. "Leave some for me." He waved Domenico on and returned to the drinking party.

As Domenico continued past the checkpoint, he saw the bodies of more Italian soldiers face down in the dirt beside the road. He rolled up the windows to reduce the smell of the dead men's rotting flesh. Domenico drove north toward Florence as fast as he could, ignoring the beautiful countryside he'd once enjoyed. The roads were good until he reached the outskirts of Florence. Bomb craters made driving treacherous. Smoke billowed above Ponte Vecchio, and fire ravaged the buildings. He abandoned his car and ran through the narrow streets toward the burning buildings.

The roads were vacant as he approached the town center of town. Smoke escaped from gaping holes in the roofs of the shops. Domenico surveyed the damage.

A building across from him groaned and crumbled with a crash. Piles of personal belongings lay among the shards of glass from the windows—clothing, shoes, purses, and furniture. Seeing a high-heeled shoe of a woman, he stopped. There was no sign of the woman it belonged to.

It resembled a pair that Antoinette had worn. "Oh, dear God!" he cried, wondering if it might be his wife.

"Did everyone die?" he asked a man sifting through the rubble.

"No, some made it to the church. They took the wounded to the hospital."

Gasping for air, Domenico forced air into his lungs and ran. His legs trembled and burned, but he didn't slow down until he reached the church. Antoinette wasn't there. Without stopping to catch his breath, he vaulted to the hospital. His lungs felt as if they might burst.

"Can I help you, sir?" the head nurse asked.

He drew in a lungful of air. "I'm looking for my wife and children," he said, his chest heaving.

"Name?" she asked without looking up.

"Antoinette Defino."

She slowly flipped through a listing. The pages were an inch thick.

Impatient Domenico ran past the reception area and pushed through the double doors leading to the patient rooms.

"Sir, you can't go in there," she shouted.

The nurse was right behind him with a security guard.

"It's all right, Sally," a kindly nurse said.

"Please, can you help me?" he asked. "I need to find my family. They might have been wounded in the bombing."

"Feel free to look around, but please don't disturb the patients. They've been through a horrible experience."

Domenico went from room to room, hunting for his family. He went back to the nurse.

"I've searched everywhere," he said, "but...."

"They may be in the morgue," she said, feeling sympathy for Domenico. "You should check there. I'll take you." She led him down the stairs to the lowest level of the hospital.

"I have to get back to my patients," the nurse said. "I'll be back in ten minutes. Take your time."

Domenico was alone with the dead. He moved from gurney to gurney, lifting the sheet that covered each body. Breathing in the putrid air of death, he searched for Antoinette and his sons. Domenico came to a tiny corpse and froze. The tip of the child's shoe poked out from under the sheet. Every nerve ending in Domenico's body pulsed. He lifted the sheet, revealing his son. The boy's hair, matted with dried blood, stuck to one side—his white tee shirt stained with dark purple blotches. Fighting the compulsion to vomit, he pulled Dom up, hugged his broken body, and rocked him in his arms.

"I failed you, my son. I should've been here to protect you. Forgive me."

"He's at peace," a voice said.

Domenico looked up to see the nurse had come back.

"Have you found your wife?"

"She isn't here." He pointed to a door. "What's in there?"

"Body parts—arms, legs, torsos. You don't want to go in there."

A lump rose in his throat. "No!" he cried and sank to the floor and sobbed, the finality of it smothering him.

The nurse gave him a few moments to collect himself before they returned to the hospital's main floor.

As he turned to leave, a child's voice called out, "Papa!"

It came from a small boy lying in a bed. Domenico came closer. Although Vittorio's face was swollen, he knew him at once. The bandages made it hard to see his face.

Domenico grabbed his son. "Vittorio!"

The floor nurse rushed over.

"This is my son. Where is his mother?"

"Mother? He was alone when they brought him in. I have a list of confirmed dead. What is her name?"

"Antoinette Defino."

She looked at her chart. "I don't see her name among the survivors."

"Check again."

The nurse shook her head. "A lot of the people didn't survive the bombing."

Domenico kissed his son gently on his head.

"Is he going to be alright?"

"Yes, he has a slight concussion, but the lacerations are healing. He should be fine in a few days. He needs rest."

"I have to leave you for a little while," Domenico said. "I must search for your mama."

Vittorio tried to hold onto his father's arm but was too weak.

"Don't worry, son. I'll come back tomorrow. Sleep. Soon you will be better, and I'll take you home."

Domenico walked six blocks to their house.

American soldiers drove along the pot-holed streets in their tanks. The Allie troops had broken through the Gothic Line, driving the Nazis farther north and reclaiming Florence.

People on the sidewalk waved, throwing flowers and kisses as they went by. Domenico was happy to see them but sorry they didn't come sooner.

Chapter 38

The sky had turned dark by the time Domenico reached the house. He ducked under the porch canopy when the rain came down in sheets. The front door hung by one hinge. T*he Nazis have been here,* he thought, *but why?* He entered slowly, checking each room. Everything was in its proper place.

When he descended the stairs to the basement, he found bloodstains on the floor. A half-eaten dinner sat on the table. Someone's meal had been interrupted. Broken dishes were strewn about—evidence of a struggle. The cupboard that had guarded the wine cellar had been riddled with bullets until it was no more than splintered wood surrounding a gaping hole. Domenico treaded upstairs, his stomach churning. Dry and acrid air filled his lungs.

He closed the basement door. Passing the hall mirror, he glimpsed his reflection. A tired old man looked back at him. He appeared older by at least ten years. His face had weathered, and stress lines encircled his eyes. War and strife had taken a toll.

Antoinette's scent lingered in the air like a loving embrace. Walking from room to room, he touched things that belonged to her as if they held her life force. He could feel her presence in every detail of the décor.

His fingers danced over the perfume bottles on the bedroom dressing table. Exhausted, he crawled between the sheets to hug Antoinette's pillow. A kaleidoscope of terrible images he had seen spun in his mind. The darkness gradually dissolved into a milky gray sky. Finally, limiting his memories to Antoinette, he found refuge in sleep.

Abruptly awakened by the light of day, he opened his eyes. For a moment, he thought perhaps he was only having a nightmare. He rolled over to reach for her, but all he felt was the cold, empty space where she should have been.

*****

Domenico went back to the hospital. Vittorio was much better and eating on his own.

"Papa," he cried. "Are you here to take me home?"

"The doctor says you must stay a few more days, but it won't be much longer."

"Where is my brother? Where's Mama?"

Domenico looked into his son's anxious face.

"Vittorio," he said and sat close to him on the hospital bed. "They won't be coming home."

"Are they dead?" he asked, eyes brimming with tears.

"Yes, son. I'm sorry."

Domenico tried to explain the best he could.

When he left Vittorio, Domenico arranged to have Dom's body transferred from the hospital morgue to the funeral parlor and then went to see the priest. It felt strange walking into the church where he and Antoinette were married—the same church where both of his sons were baptized. There was a new priest. Domenico explained what had happened to his family.

"I'm sorry about your wife. Father Baccari was fond of Antoinette. He spoke highly of her."

"Thank you. I don't have Antoinette's body, but I'm sure she's at peace with her father, Gaetano, and her mother, Josephina."

"Would you like the service to be here in the church?"

"No. Only me and my son will attend."

"Might you lay him out at home? Of course, it would have to be a closed coffin."

"That won't do. My son, Vittorio, has been through too much. I think it best not to traumatize him. I suppose it's better to deliver his coffin to the cemetery."

"If you like, I will come there and perform a small service. We can pray over Dom's coffin before he's buried, and I can say a few words for her too."

Domenico had never been religious, but he knew that Antoinette would have wanted the church to help accompany Dom to the next world.

"Si, grazie, Father. I'll make the arrangements."

Tombstones were unavailable due to the war, so Domenico had to mark the grave with a wooden cross.

He had Antoinette's name carved above their sons. He also had Josephina's name etched into Gaetano's gravestone.

Rage and guilt encircled him like the hungry vultures that flew above the cemetery as he watched the stone cutter work.

The war was over, but Domenico couldn't find peace. Vittorio seemed despondent. Memories were everywhere, making their loss inconsolable. There was only one solution—to leave the country. He wanted Vittorio to have a future and thought America would be the place for him to make a new life. His uncle had left for America before the war. He was living in Manhattan and would sponsor him.

"We need to pack, Vittorio. We're going on a long journey."

"Where are we going, Papa?"

"America."

"I don't want to leave Mama."

"I'm sorry, son. There's nothing left for us here."

Chapter 39

At the central station, Domenico bought two tickets to Naples. They boarded a train filled with vacant-eyed American soldiers. They looked battle-weary and scarred. Domenico assumed they harbored horrific memories of what they had seen. The train lurched forward, pinning everyone to their seat for a moment as it gained momentum.

When they arrived at the Naples station, Domenico hired a driver to take them to the port, where the S.S. *Columbia* prepared for the long and grueling journey across the ocean. The only space available in the crowded ship was in the hull. Domenico added their names to the manifest of passengers traveling to New York. Instead of using Defino, he shortened his name to Fino, ending any trail to his destination.

The smells in steerage were overpowering, and they tried to stay outside on the deck as much as possible. Luckily, there were other children, and Vittorio could play and run around freely.

Domenico preferred to stay alone and stare out at sea, wondering what life in America might hold for him and his son.

A storm hovered over the sea, sending waves that moved the ship up and down. They couldn't see anything past the curtain of rain ahead of them. Everyone ran for cover below deck, but Domenico smiled into the rain, letting the water kiss his face.

Finally, it subsided, and the Statue of Liberty was visible on the distant horizon.

"Look, Papa. There's a lady in the water."

Domenico smiled. "That's the Lady Liberty. She's there to welcome us." Even though he'd heard about the statue in the harbor, his heart pounded faster. Believed to be inspired by the Roman goddess Libertas, she symbolized freedom.

"How did she get here, Papa?"

"I don't know. Maybe the lady swam across the ocean."

"Oh, Papa," Vittorio said. "She didn't do that."

Domenico laughed and tussled his hair. "I suppose she came here the same way we did, on a ship."

The sunrise reflected on her in the harbor as they approached Ellis Island.

The ship docked, and they disembarked under the watchful eyes of port police and immigration staff. They stood in a lengthy line with the other passengers hoping to be approved for entry into the United States. Some were denied for medical reasons, and Domenico worried. Vittorio had just gotten over a cold and still had a slight cough. Luckily, they made it through.

*****

The air was sweet and clear in the early morning as they walked toward Uncle Franco's apartment on Hester Street in Manhattan. Italian men congregated outside of shops, smoking cigars and watching people pass. *It's like they moved a part of Italy to America,* Domenico thought.

Clam sellers displayed their wares on a cart at the corner of Mulberry and Canal Street. The scent of freshly baked bread floated from a bakery and tickled Vittorio's nose.

"I'm hungry, Papa. Can we buy some bread?"

"No, son. I'm sorry. I only have lira. We'll have to wait until we get to Uncle Franco's house. Then we will eat."

They passed the butcher and the chicken vendor and soon came to Hester Street. They knocked on the door. A woman in a calico dress answered. Aunt Camelia looked older than Domenico remembered.

"Oh," she cried. "They're here, Franco! Come out and greet our nephew."

Leaning on a cane, Franco came from the bedroom, his back bent with age.

"Domenico," he shouted. "Welcome. I thought you weren't coming until tomorrow."

"The ship arrived early. I hope that's all right."

"Of course it is," Aunt Camelia said, looking down. "And this must be little Vittorio."

"Your cousin Antonio should be home soon, but he prefers to be called Anthony."

"That sounds very American," Domenico said, relieved no one mentioned Vittorio's twin brother.

"Uncle Franco. What's with the cane?"

"I had a stroke a few months ago. It's affected my right side. I'm getting my strength back slowly, but it takes time."

"Have you eaten?" Aunt Camelia asked.

"No. Not since this morning."

"Well, come in and eat!! I have mozzarella, tomatoes, and eggplant on the table. When Anthony gets home from work, we'll have dinner."

"What's he doing?"

"He's working on the subway system in Manhattan. It's expanding now that the war is over."

"That sounds dangerous."

Camelia flipped her hand. "Most jobs they give to Italians are dangerous. No one else wants to work in the sewers, subways, tunnels, or bridges. Anyway, he works up an appetite. He'll be starving.

Vittorio's eyes lingered on the fresh loaf of bread in the middle of the table.

"Would you like some?" Aunt Camelia asked.

He nodded.

She sliced a thick piece, smeared it with gobs of butter, and handed it to him.

Vittorio shoved it into his mouth, devouring it in seconds. Everyone laughed.

Aunt Camelia sliced another piece. "Here you go, sweetheart, but save room for the pasta." She turned to Domenico. "Let me show you to your room."

He followed her down the hall to a small room with two single beds.

"I hope you don't mind. The room is small, but the beds are comfortable. The bathroom is across from the hall. You can wash up if you like."

Anthony came home with the grime of the city on his face and hands. He was ten years younger than Domenico.

"Cousin Domenico!" Anthony reached out and hugged him. "Sorry. I must stink. Let me go shower, and then we'll talk."

The whole family sat around the table. Everyone talked at once. Vittorio thought about how different things were in America as he spooned Polenta into his mouth.

Uncle Franco sat down, picked up a small ball lying on the table, and squeezed his fingers around it a few times.

Vittorio watched with interest.

Franco smiled. "The doctor says I can regain the strength in my hands if I do this exercise."

"Domenico," Anthony interrupted. "We heard you were a spy for the Allies in Italy."

"Not a spy—a freedom fighter. I aided the Allies when I could."

"The Germans could have killed you," Anthony said.

Domenico glanced over at his son, who didn't seem to pay attention to the conversation.

"No, I was quite safe."

"You risked your life," Aunt Camelia said. "You're a hero."

Domenico shook his head. "I never looked to be a hero, and I don't know anyone else who did."

"Maybe a few young men looked for chances to be brave, but there were no heroes where I was. People cared about their country or families. They were trying to survive. Those who volunteered were often people who hadn't calculated the risks. You can find them among the dead."

"There are a lot of children your age living on the block, Vittorio, Aunt Camelia said, changing the subject. "Sometimes, the fire department opens the fire hydrants on the street so kids can play."

Vittorio's eyes opened wide. "Really?"

"Yes, you will love living in New York."

When dinner ended, Uncle Franco and Domenico went to smoke cigars in the living room. Cousin Anthony and Vittorio stayed in the kitchen to help with the dishes.

"Vittorio," Anthony said as he dried the last pot. "Would you like to go to the park?"

"The park? Yes, Cousin Anthony. Could we?"

"Go ask your father if it's all right."

Vittorio ran into the living room. "Papa. Cousin Anthony wants to take me to the park. Can I go?"

Domenico turned to face his uncle. "Is it safe?"

Franco laughed. "We're in America. Of course, it's safe. Besides, Anthony won't let anything happen to him except a tummy ache. If I know my son, he'll fill him with ice cream and treats."

"All right, but Vittorio, make sure you listen to your cousin."

Vittorio and Anthony left the house for the park.

"I'm sorry about your other son," Franco said. "He was too young to lose his life like that."

Domenico broke down. "You talk about heroes, but I am not. It's my fault Antoinette and our son are dead. I wasn't there when they needed me. I failed my family."

"There was nothing you could have done." His uncle fixed his eyes on him. "It's not your fault. It would be best if you put it behind you. You still have a son. Have faith."

That night, shadows crawled across the ceiling from the headlights of the passing cars. Yearning for the warmth of Antoinette next to him, Domenico closed his eyes and conjured her face at them. Her memory clung like spider silk. It was all he had to comfort him. He fell asleep to the hypnotic tick of the radiator.

The drone of the radio in the kitchen woke him in the morning. The news interrupted the pleasant melodies. The static backdrop of the voices seemed far away. He already missed Italy. It would take a little time for Domenico to get accustomed to America. The country he knew so well was now far away.

Chapter 40

In and out of delirium, Antoinette underwent three surgeries to repair her broken body, but they couldn't fix her brain. She stayed in a coma for seven months. Her eyes twitched, and distress lined her face, but no one could reach her. In her dreams, she heard two boys crying out for her. Mama, Mama, Mama. The words drummed in her head like rain as she remembered the explosions. A wave of sickness filled her stomach, knowing she couldn't protect her children.

Antoinette heard the highs and lows of distant voices. People around her were speaking, but at first, she couldn't understand what was being said.

"She's awake," a female voice said. "Get the doctor."

There was a flurry of activity around her and then a white light. It was shining in her eyes. She tried to shut them, but someone was holding them open. She moaned.

"You're going to be fine," the doctor said. "You've been unconscious for almost a year. We didn't know if you would ever wake up. Do you know your name?"

Antoinette tried to speak, but the words blurred together.

"An-toin-ette-Def-ino. Where am I? How long have I been asleep?"

"Shh," the doctor said. "Rest now. We can talk later. He turned to the nurse. "Get this woman something to eat. Perhaps some soup."

Although she knew her name, her past had been brushed away like a tear. Her past was a shadow—as if an artist drew the faintest lines of the landscape—an incomplete portrait.

The hospital staff considered her a miracle when she awoke. They located her residence in records at City Hall and sent someone to the apartment, but there were new residents. There wasn't much they could do for Antoinette, so they transferred her to a long-term care section of the hospital.

Whenever she closed her eyes, she saw images that made no sense. The illusions were engraved on the retina of her memory. At the edge of her thoughts, they slipped away. Plagued with nightmares, she feared everything and everybody.

*****

Antoinette had been awake for three months when a strange man came into the hospital looking for her. He walked up to the reception nurse. "I'm looking for a woman treated in this facility. Her name is Antoinette Defino."

"Yes, we have a patient by that name. Are you her husband? "

"No, I'm a friend."

"I'm sorry. Only family members are allowed to visit."

"I will not leave until I see her!"

"No, no. It's against the rules."

"What rules! Our country was at war."

"Step aside, or I'll push my way in."

She picked up the phone and whispered into the receiver. When she hung up, she huffed. "Take a seat in the waiting area. The doctor will be here shortly."

"Thank you," he said and sat in the waiting area.

Soon, a man in a long white coat came to talk to him.

"Hello, I'm Doctor Anderson. I understand you have been inquiring about one of my patients."

"Yes, Antoinette Defino. She is a close friend, and we lost touch during the war. Can I please see her?"

"Antoinette is unable to recall anything from her past. She has retrograde amnesia, a common aspect of head trauma."

"Maybe I can help."

"I don't think she'll recognize you, and I don't want to upset her."

"I know more about her life than anyone."

"Hmm. Perhaps it's worth a try. I'll have the receptionist take you to her."

The woman was flustered but did as she was told and took Ethan to a special unit for patients who needed long-term care.

Ethan entered the room, where everything was white, from the walls to the sheets. A crucifix hung above the iron bed. He moved slowly toward the bed.

"Antoinette," he whispered.

His voice came to her, soft and familiar. It rose from somewhere deep in her mind.

"Wake up." He touched her brow.

The light intruded as she opened her eyes and tried to focus. For a moment, something flashed across her face, and Ethan smiled. He thought she remembered him.

"Who are you?" She asked. "Do I know you?"

"It's me, Ethan. Don't you remember?"

"Have we met before?"

"Antoinette! It's me. She noticed the faint, shaded circles under his eyes and stiffened. "I'm so glad to have found you." He reached for her hand, but she pulled away.

She shook her head. "I don't know you! Go away."

"You hid my sister and me from the Nazis in your basement. If only I hadn't sent you to pick up new identity papers." He reached out to hug her.

He rubbed his chin. "I'm sorry. I feel terrible since I'm the reason you were in town."

Antoinette covered her ears with her hands. "Don't tell me anymore. I don't want to hear."

"Nurse," she called hoarsely.

The nurse came to her bedside.

"I don't know this man."

"Ethan is your friend."

"No! Send him away."

"Please, Antoinette. The doctor told me about your memory loss." Ethan reached out to embrace her.

She thrust him away. "Leave me alone."

"I'm sorry, sir. You'll have to leave."

Ethan drew away from the bed. "I'm sorry…." He took one last pleading look back, but Antoinette closed her eyes.

The nurse guided him toward the door.

"Don't give up," she whispered.

Chapter 41

After leaving the hospital, Ethan returned to the house where Antoinette lived.

"Buongiorno, Sadie. I hope you remember me."

"Ethan, right? You are the gentleman who was looking for the Definos."

"Yes, I have found Antoinette Defino. She was at the hospital like you said."

"Splendid. I hope she is recovering."

"She has lost her memory, and I'm trying to help her. The last time I was here, you said you had photo albums. Do you still have them?"

"Yes. I put the photos in the attic. It seemed like such a shame to throw them in the trash."

"Can I have them? They may help her get better."

"Yes, of course. I'll get them for you."

Ethan thanked her and returned to the hospital.

"Please, don't push me away," Ethan said before she could throw him out. "I have something to help you remember."

"What is it?"

He opened the book of memories and sat on the edge of her bed.

Antoinette flipped through the photographs of smiling faces. She felt she was spying on someone else's life. The worst part was the expectation. The hope for everything to come back.

At the back of the book was a pressed gardenia. The faint scent still lingered. Antoinette closed her eyes and pressed her fingers on the lids.

"I can't," she cried, thinking it would be a kinder road to forget.

The nurse hurried into the room. "Are you having one of your migraines?"

"Yes. Please make it stop."

"I'll get a cold compress for your head." She closed the curtains, blocking out the daylight.

"That's enough for today," the nurse told Ethan.

"I'll come back tomorrow," he said and kissed Antoinette's cheek. She didn't pull away.

*****

During the night, a warm image of Ethan came forth in her dreams. They were walking along the shore under the moonlight. She could feel his love for her and remembered kissing him.

Antoinette began looking forward to Ethan's visits.

By the glint in her eyes when he walked into her room, he thought she was happy to see him.

"I had a dream last night," she said. "I remembered that we were more than friends."

"Yes, I had thought we would be married back then, but things didn't turn out the way I had hoped."

"Is it because I married Domenico?"

"Yes, but we always remained close, even after you left Milan. When the Germans began rounding up Jews, Rachel and I escaped. You and your mother were the only family we had left, and you were kind enough to take us in, but the Gestapo suspected we were there and came snooping around. It wasn't safe for us to stay. I sent you to the town to pick up new identities so we could leave. While you were gone, the Gestapo returned to your house and found Rachel and me hiding in the wine cellar. They came in the dark. Josephina stood up to them, but she was no match for the Gestapo. They dragged us away."

"Who's Josephina?"

"Your mother.

"My mother?" She closed her eyes and held her head. "Why can't I remember her?"

"Maybe in time," Ethan said reassuringly.

"Where is she now, my mother?"

"I'm sorry," he said. "I don't know."

Ethan knew what had happened to her mother, but he couldn't tell her. His mind went back to that dreadful day.

He recalled how the Nazis barged into the house.

"Wir Uchen Juden," they had screamed, demanding to know where the Jews were hidden.

Josephina had bravely stood up to them. "Jews? There are no Jews here! Get out of my house."

The officer shoved her out of his way. "Spread out," he instructed his men.

Ethan remembered hearing the commotion and knew they were in danger. Leaving their half-eaten dinner, he and Rachel hid in the wine cellar behind the cupboard. They sat in the dark, listening to the upstairs floorboards creak. The heavy thud of boots descended the stairs to the basement. He held his sister with her face pressed against his chest. Suddenly, an explosion of bullets pierced the cupboard, exposing the crawl space. One hit him in the arm, and blood poured onto the ground.

The S.S. soldiers dragged Ethan and Rachel outside to a waiting van. Ethan felt helpless. He caught one last glimpse of Josephina lying in a pool of blood in the doorway. The Gestapo had beaten her with clubs. She was still alive, but a Nazi soldier towered over her with his rifle. Before the door closed, Ethan heard a single shot ring out, and his heart sank. The van backfired, and the gears ground as it drove off.

"What happened to you when the Germans found you in my basement?" Antoinette asked, returning him to the present.

"We were taken to a field next to the train station. We were separated from your mother."

"Rachel and I joined more than five hundred other Jews," he continued. "They loaded us onto a train and sent us to Auschwitz." He held out his arm to show her his tattoo, number 200164.

Ethan had given Antoinette an enormous amount of information. She rubbed her temples and moaned in pain.

The nurse rushed into the room. "I'm sorry, but you need to leave now, Ethan."

*****

The next time Ethan visited Antoinette, she was less anxious. His presence no longer bothered her.

"How did you find me?" she asked.

"When the Allies liberated the camps, I made my way to Milan. I don't know what I expected—maybe everything would be as before the war. I searched for my family, but nothing was the same. My house had been bombed. The roof looked like it would collapse any minute. But I took a chance and rummaged inside in case I found something of value. All I found were a few trinkets of sentiment. The yard was the only sign of life. Although the lawn was overgrown, the plants and bushes vibrantly reached for the sun. After that, I didn't know where to go, so I came to find you. There were new tenants in your house. They told me you were alive but didn't know where your husband was."

"Husband?"

"Yes, you are married. I asked the tenants about your husband, but they didn't know. Domenico left everything behind, the furniture, the paintings, the china, and even his photo albums."

Domenico. His name echoed in her head until it felt like a rock lodged deep inside her.

Ethan wasn't sure if she was ready, but he didn't want to hold anything back. You also had twin sons, Vittorio and Dom."

"Sons?"

Ethan opened the photo album and handed her a picture.

"They must be the boys I've been dreaming about." She studied the life in pictures—a life that was no longer hers.

"They were with you during the bombing. Do you remember anything?"

"I remember an explosion at the old bridge, but everything went black."

"The Germans bombed the streets to delay any advances from the Allies. They spared the city center."

"Did they blow up the bridge?"

"The Ponte Vecchio was hit, but it wasn't destroyed. Alas, the other bridges sustained heavy damage.

"If I have sons and a husband, where are they now?"

"The boys died during the bombing. I guess that's why Domenico left Florence."

Pulsing pain shot to every nerve ending, and her head throbbed.

"Why can't I remember?" she cried.

Ethan put his arms around her. "Don't worry. I'll help you to remember."

Chapter 42

Domenico awoke and looked across the room. Vittorio's bed was empty. Aunt Camelia had taken him to register him for fifth grade at the public school down the street. Vittorio thrived in the new environment and made many friends in the neighborhood during the summer. However, Domenico still felt out of place in America. He went to the kitchen and poured himself a cup of coffee. A subway train heading to Coney Island passed, causing the glasses in the cabinet to rattle.

Anthony was eating a large plate of fried eggs and bacon. "What are you doing today?" he asked with his mouth full of food.

"I'm not sure. I've walked almost every inch of Manhattan from the South side to the North."

"What you need, dear cousin—is a job!" Anthony said. "You're a photographer. Why don't you go down to the Fashion District? They're always looking for new talent."

"Perhaps you're right."

"Once you're working, you'll blend right in." Anthony drew a rough map of the Fashion District.

Domenico thought about taking the subway but was still nervous about going underground. Besides, he wanted to get a feel for the city. As he walked uptown along Broadway, the demographics of the population changed. He observed the commuters. American men dressed in suits with crisp white shirts and ties hurried along with suitcases in their hands.

As he continued to 7th Avenue, Domenico came to a massive button on top and a large needle leaning against the structure. Alongside the giant button was a sculpture of a garment worker sitting behind a sewing machine. He studied the map Anthony drew for him.

Domenico knew he was in the right place--fifteen blocks of textile factories and garment stores spanning from 35th to 40th Street and stretching down 7th to 9th Avenue. On the corner was a man passing out flyers for Fashion Week.

"Excuse me," he said. "*Per favore*. Can you tell me where the Norell Fashion House is?"

"A few blocks that way." The guy pointed.

"*Grazie*," Domenico said. As he turned to go, the guy mumbled. "Just what we need. More WOPs."

He had heard about Italian discrimination. He wondered how they could tell.

Domenico looked down at his drab brown pants and matching vest.

Feeling self-conscious, he ripped off his Coppola cap and stuck it in his coat pocket. *I can't possibly apply for a job wearing this.*

He stopped in the first men's clothing store he came across.

"Can I help you, sir?"

"Yes, I'm job hunting, and...."

"Say no more. You have come to the right place. We have a new arrival of stylish suits. I'm sure we can find something to your liking."

The sales clerk pulled out a streamlined suit of smooth polished fabric. "This is the newest fashion, straight off the runways of Milan."

"I know Milan well."

"Yes, I thought you looked Italian. I'm from Avellino."

"Really? I'm from Sorrento."

"That was a lovely area before war ravaged the hillside."

"Yes, it's a shame the country put their trust in the wrong leaders. It will rise again, I'm sure."

Domenico looked at the price tag. "I'm sorry. I don't even have enough money to buy a shirt."

"I see," he said with sympathy. "I may be able to find something in your budget."

Domenico followed him down the aisle.

"I've been in your shoes, so I know how it is. No one would give me a break when I first arrived in America."

At the back of the store, he stopped at a clothing rack. "These suits are last year's style. I can sell one to you at half the cost."

Domenico looked through the rack and found two that he liked, gray and navy.

"You can try them on in the dressing room. Buy one today. I'll throw in a shirt, free of charge."

Thank you," Domenico said. "You are a kind man."

He tried on the suits and settled on the blue. Feeling more confident, he left the store and continued on his way.

Even in Italy, Domenico had heard of the famous designer Norman Norell Levinson. He dressed many clients of wealth, including film stars, socialites, and politicians. Arriving at the Norell Fashion House, he paused before entering the first building.

Although he was good at photography, the loss of Antoinette had shaken his confidence. She had always been his favorite subject.

He walked up to the receptionist's desk in the front lobby. "I'm here to apply for the photographer job."

She looked him up and down, then handed him a clipboard. "Fill this out and have a seat," she said, pointing to the chairs along the side of the room.

Domenico took a seat along with four other men filling out applications. One at a time, they were called into an office.

The third applicant went inside for the interview. Domenico waited patiently for his turn, but the receptionist returned to announce that the position was filled. She thanked everyone for coming.

The other two men mumbled and left, but Domenico stayed behind.

"Please," he said. "I need this job. If only I could speak with the recruiter. I'm sure he would be impressed with my credentials."

"I'm sorry. Mr. Norell is not seeing anyone else."

With his head hung low, Domenico turned to leave.

"But I do know where they need a photographer," she said. "It's in the Theater District."

"The Theater District?"

"Yes, Broadway photographers are important. They work only for the show's marketing team."

"What does a Broadway photographer do?"

"They capture the magic, beauty, and wonder of a brand-new show every night.

"It sounds interesting. Where do I apply?"

"Go to 44th Street and look for the Hudson Theater. Ask for Mr. Harris. Tell him Gina sent you."

Chapter 43

When Ethan arrived at the hospital, the nurse blocked him from entering the room.

"Is she all right?" he panicked.

"Calm down, sir. Antoinette is fine. The doctor is here to examine her. You can't go in yet."

"But I have questions to ask him."

"I'm sorry. Once the exam is over, you can ask the doctor questions."

Ethan waited for the doctor and caught his attention when he was leaving.

"Hello, Doctor Emmett. Do you remember me?"

"Indeed, I do. You're the chap who insisted you could help Antoinette. How is that going?"

"She still doesn't know who I am," Ethan said, "but at least she isn't trying to get me thrown out anymore. I think she's starting to get more comfortable with me. Tell me, doctor, will she get better."

"Physically, she's in good health."

"Will she ever get her memory back, doctor?"

Dr. Emmett shook his head. "Her brain sustained major trauma. It might never heal. There's no point in reaching back for something that is gone."

Seeing the disappointment on Ethan's face, the doctor added, "That's not to say it can't happen. I've seen patients wake up one day and remember everything before their accident. The problem with that is they sometimes forget recent memories. She might not remember the time spent with you."

"That's a chance I'll have to take."

"I'm releasing her from the hospital tomorrow. Does she have anyone who can take care of her? If not, she'll have to go to a convalescent home."

"I'd like to take her home with me," Ethan said. "I can take care of her. I'm sure she would prefer that to the home. I have a lovely old house overlooking the Arno river."

"I have no objections," the doctor said. "It's up to her."

Ethan entered the room.

"The doctor wants to send me to another facility," she said.

"Yes, I heard. I told the doctor you could come home with me."

Antoinette said, seeming flustered.

"You don't have to decide today," Ethan added. "Think about it." He kissed the top of her head and got up to leave.

"The nurse told me there's a garden on the hospital grounds. I want to sit outside and feel the sun on my face."

"Are you strong enough to walk?"

"Yes. I have to get out of this bed."

Ethan helped her slippers the hospital had provided. He held onto her arm as she took small steps. Once they were outside, her breathing was labored.

"Let's sit on this bench," he said.

"No, I want to sit next to the birdbath. I love birds."

Ethan laid the blanket he took from the room across her lap. She closed her eyes and lifted her face to the sun.

"I believe the color is coming back to your cheeks," Ethan said.

She smiled. "Tell me about your house."

"It's quite small but comfortable. I have a good view of the river from the back, and there are plenty of birds."

"I haven't seen a bird yet," she said after twenty minutes. I wish I had some seeds."

"Maybe the nurse can give me a little bread from the lunch tray," he said.

Light shined in her eyes. "That would be wonderful."

"Will you be all right here alone?"

"Yes, I'll be fine."

"I'll be right back."

As the day grew long, the sun sank behind the hospital.

"I should get you back to your room," he said, supporting her arm.

Once inside, he helped her into the bed.

"You look exhausted, Antoinette. I'll be leaving now."

"No, don't leave me," she cried. "I'm afraid."

"I'll be back in the morning."

"Yes, please. Come back for me. I want to leave this place."

"Don't worry. I love you and will take care of you."

Chapter 44

The next day, Ethan came back for Antoinette.

"I brought you something to wear. The old lady next door lost her daughter. She was happy to put her clothes to good use."

Antoinette put on the dress. It was much too big for her small frame.

"We'll buy you some new clothes once you're settled," he promised.

She slipped on the shoes, which fit perfectly.

"I'll call for a chair," the nurse said.

"I can walk on my own. It's my memory that's impaired, not my legs."

"Sorry, it's a new hospital policy."

The hospital attendant wheeled her out to Ethan's car. He helped her into the passenger seat, and they drove to a small house on the other side of town.

She stared up at the windows, hesitant to go inside, but then climbed the porch stairs to the door. They entered a narrow hallway. She could smell the musky scent of generations who had lived there before.

"Is there anything you'd like?" he asked.

"A cup of tea would be nice."

"I'll make it. You can freshen up in the bathroom down the hall."

"Yes, thank you." She closed the door, leaned against the sink, and fogged the mirror with her breath. Using her finger, she wrote A. Defino. It lingered for a moment, then disappeared. She heated the glass with her breath again, rubbed it away with her sleeve, and went to the kitchen. Ethan was setting the table, and she looked out the window, overlooking the river.

"Birds fly by every morning. That's the best thing about this house."

"I thought you said the Germans confiscated your wealth."

"Yes, I lost everything—my factory, the family jewelry, and all the cash I had in the bank."

"She looked at him with a puzzled expression.

"My sister Rachel was a shrewd one. Instead of depositing the entire daily cash intake, she stuffed half in a metal box and buried it in the yard. When I returned to Milan, I searched the yard. Although the lawn was overgrown, the plants and bushes reached for the sun. I found the spot and dug. There it was, just as she said."

The kettle whistled, and he poured the boiling water into a cup. "How do you take your tea?"

"No sugar. It's such a small detail, but *that* I remember."

Staring at the stark white wooden cabinets, she blew on the tea and took a sip.

"Once you're stronger, we'll redecorate," Ethan said. "I'll paint the walls whatever color you want. Maybe a peachy shade will brighten the room."

"That would be nice." Antoinette sat on the red vinyl chair and ran her fingers across the ridges of the silver edging on the table.

"This table was left here by the previous owners. I've been meaning to replace it."

"No, don't. I like it. It's very modern."

"That reminds me. If you ever need money for something...." He opened the icebox. "I keep it here."

"That's a funny place to put money."

"Better than a safe. No one would expect to find money among the frozen foods."

After her tea, Antoinette's eyelids drooped with exhaustion.

"It's getting late," Ethan said. "I set up the guest room for you."

*****

Silver slivers of light from a full moon poured through the open blinds. Antoinette lay in bed, tired but unable to sleep. She raised herself to one elbow and slid out of bed. Careful not to awaken Ethan, she tiptoed past his bedroom and went to the kitchen. The linoleum floor was cold beneath her bare feet. She rifled through a cabinet, expecting to find glasses, but it held dishes. Her eyes darted around the room. She thought it was her kitchen, but it didn't look familiar. She opened the drawers, emptying the contents onto the counters—batteries, tape, glue, a screwdriver, and an array of keys. Ethan appeared in the doorway.

"What are you doing?"

"I'm looking for… I'm looking for… something."

"It's after two. I heard you all the way upstairs."

"I feel like I misplaced something and have to find it."

"I'll help you search in the morning."

She slid everything back into the drawer and closed it. When she turned to Ethan, tears welled in her eyes. He pulled her close, and she pressed her face against his chest. They held each other for several moments, unmoving, unspeaking.

"Let's go back to bed. You'll feel better in the morning."

"No! I don't want to be alone. Please don't leave me. I'm scared."

"If you like, you can sleep in my room. I'll sleep in the chair."

"I hate to put you out of your bed."

"Nonsense. I'll be fine. The important thing is to make sure you feel safe."

"What if I don't know you when I wake up?"

"Don't worry. I will never let you forget me."

Antoinette swallowed hard, but her panic lodged in her chest, making breathing difficult. "I'm sorry for being so much trouble."

"You're no trouble at all. You are the light in my life. I promise things will get better," he said.

Chapter 45

Ethan had searched for a job requiring his design skills, but all he could find was a job doing laundry. It didn't pay much, but he had no choice.

Antoinette refused to leave the house and disliked being alone. She watched the clock all day, waiting for Ethan to return home. Sometimes, he found her sitting in the dark when he returned from work.

Seeing the pictures of her sons spread on the table, he knew she was crying but came to ignore these episodes because they made him feel helpless.

In her dreams, she saw a man, but he wasn't Ethan. He called out to her, and she floated toward his vision. She felt an overwhelming love for this brown-eyed stranger. He slid his hand through her hair and rested it against her neck, drawing her close. When he kissed her, she could smell his cologne and heard his joyous laughter echo through her mind. When she woke, his image faded like smoke. Before she could acknowledge the memory, it faded away. Antoinette bit her tongue to keep from calling out to him.

Feeling someone shaking her shoulder, she awoke with a start. Antoinette felt out of place for a moment and wanted to cling to the dream.

Ethan lovingly caressed her cheek. She blinked away the last remnants of sleep. Haunted by another's kiss, Antoinette longed to return to her dream. Guilt washed over her as if she had betrayed Ethan. Still, she wished she could remember the details of her dream.

Before leaving for work, he rummaged through the desk drawer in the hall and returned to the kitchen table with charcoal, pencils, and a sketchpad.

"Do you remember how to draw?"

"I don't know." She picked up the pencil and touched the page. Her hand flowed with an unknown force. The image bloomed, becoming sharper and more defined until it took the shape of a dress. Despite the absence of her memories, her brain served her well. Her talent was still there.

"That's wonderful," Ethan said, checking his watch. "Will you be alright if I leave for a couple of hours?"

"Yes,' she said. "I think so."

She heard the front door shutting behind him. The sound made her stomach drop. Once he was gone, Antoinette reached for a piece of charcoal and a pad. She tried to conjure the face of the strange man she had seen in her dream. Closing her eyes, she pictured the curve of his mouth and the shade of his hair. Her fingers twitched for a moment, then she brought the pencil to the page and began drawing. The lines of a face emerged, cheekbones and a brow. The shape of a man materialized before her. Black curls, brown eyes, and a strong jaw. The image was pleasant, and the resemblance to someone she knew tugged at her memory. *Domenico!* She tucked it in the back of the book and returned to the dresses. After sketching for an hour, she became restless. Looking through the bag of clothes in the bedroom closet, she found a yellow sundress. It was two sizes too big. She had seen a sewing machine in the spare room, so she went to work. Smiling with pride, she admired her reflection in the mirror.

The clock read 2:00 pm. Antoinette wanted to make a special dinner for Ethan. She couldn't remember specific details of her past, but she knew how to make fresh gnocchi. A flash of memory made her grandmother's face appear in her mind, and she smiled, but it sank like a rock in a river and was gone. Antoinette opened the icebox and removed the money jar. She took only enough to buy dinner and set out into the late Florence afternoon.

She bought sausages from the butcher, then headed for the bakery to buy bread. After paying the baker, she saw a boy with his mother. She felt an old familiar ache in her chest. Her eyes prickled and burned. Tears blurred her vision as she ran from the store, but once she was outside, she became confused. She knew she was in the shopping district but couldn't orient herself.

Urgently gravitating toward a familiar street, she continued until she stood in front of a house and stopped. The purpose slipped like a thought out of reach. She closed her eyes and imagined this was her house, her life. Her heart raced. It looked like the house in one of the photos. Maybe Domenico was inside. Antoinette felt off-center as her world slid from its axis. She reached to knock on the door, then realized it wasn't her home anymore. She collapsed in the doorway.

A woman held a cold compress to her forehead when she awoke.

Antoinette jumped up. "Who are you?"

"I'm Sadie. I live here."

"How did I get here?"

"I found you outside my door. My neighbor helped me get you inside."

Antoinette gazed around the room. "Did I used to live here?"

"Yes, during the war with your husband. I bought this house from Domenico."

"I'm so confused."

"Don't worry, dear. I called Ethan. He's on his way. He told me the whole story about your memory loss."

"How do you know, Ethan?"

"Ethan came by to inquire about Domenico's whereabouts. I didn't have any information, but I promised to call if he ever returned. I'm the one who gave him the photo album."

The doorbell rang, and Sadie went to answer it. Ethan came into the living room and rushed to the sofa. His brow was tight with worry.

"Thank goodness, you're all right," he said, kissing her forehead with concern. "You weren't there when I came home from work. You gave me quite a scare. I thought I'd lost you." He looked into her eyes, which were frightened and troubled. "You're safe now."

Her body relaxed, almost with a sigh. "I'm sorry. I don't know what happened to me. One minute I was shopping, and the next, I woke up on this kind lady's sofa. She knows Domenico."

"I'll let you know if I hear from him," Sadie said as Ethan guided Antoinette to his car.

He helped her into the passenger side and turned to thank Sadie.

"Thank you for your compassion. Antoinette will be fine once she has some rest."

"Maybe it isn't a good idea for her to look at those photos," she whispered.

Ethan nodded.

Chapter 46

Antoinette's dreams shifted to another time and place. She had the same recurring dream of being in a basement consoling a woman with sad blue eyes.

"Don't be sad, Rachel," she said, turning a Victrola on. It came to life, and she placed the needle on the record.

Happy music made the women smile and dance while Ethan looked on with a smile. She tried to reach out and grab the memory when she woke, to hold on, but it slipped away. Except for this time, she remembered the girl's name.

She found Ethan sitting at the kitchen table, eating breakfast.

"Tell me about Rachel," she said and sat across from him.

"Rachel? Do you remember her?"

"She was in my dream."

He released a heavy sigh. "Sadly, my sister Rachel didn't make it out of the death camps. When we arrived at Auschwitz, she was seven months pregnant.

They put her in a barracks with mothers, young children, and older ladies. We only caught a glimpse of each other across the courtyard in the mornings. I wanted to put my arms around her and hear her voice again.

"One night, while I was lying on the hay mattress, I heard the voice of an angel singing. At first, I thought maybe I was dead, but no—it was Rachel. At first, I was afraid they would kill her, but they didn't mind because her song was so sweet. The S.S. enjoyed it and even made her entertain top officials when they visited the camp.

"From then on, her song soothed everyone in the barracks, and we forgot about our pain for a few moments as we drifted off to sleep. When her voice filled the night air, I felt safe, but they sent me to Theresienstadt to build more ovens for the work camps. I didn't want to leave my sister. I pleaded to be left behind, but one of the guards threw me in a van.

"What happened to her baby?"

"I've been told that after Rachel gave birth, a few women helped to hide the baby. Knowing that the Nazis would take it away, they pretended she was still pregnant by padding her dress. My sister had three days with the infant until another prisoner informed a German commander. She had had her baby taken away and thought it unfair that Rachel should be with her baby. Rachel and the baby were sent to the same gas chamber."

Antoinette shuddered. "That's horrible."

“I wept many tears because I couldn’t save her from her fate.”

“It wasn’t your fault.”

He shook his head sadly. “I try to forget. I must keep my mind on the present.”

Chapter 47

Antoinette had misplaced the photos of her past life. They were the last thread of her old life. Without the aid of the pictures, her visions made little sense.

Ethan had hidden the pictures in the back of the closet, thinking it best. But she wasn't ready to let go of the past. If her husband and children were alive, Antoinette needed to know. For months, she kept searching, then accepted they were gone.

"Maybe Domenico went back to his family," she remarked one night at dinner. "You said he's from Campania. He could have gone back there."

"Campania is a large area. There are five provinces: Caserta, Benevento, Napoli, Avellino, and Salerno. I wouldn't know where to start."

"Perhaps he took a ship across the ocean. Many people relocated to America."

"Even if that's true, we would have no idea which ship he took. If you like, we can check manifests, but that will be difficult from Florence."

Tears filled her eyes, and she wept.

"If it eases your mind, we can take a trip to Naples," Ethan said. "There's a major port there."

She looked up at him with hopeful eyes.

"I'll make the arrangements."

"Thank you, Ethan. I'm sorry to be a problem, but I must know."

*****

Ethan and Antoinette traveled to Naples by train and checked into a boarding house two blocks from the port.

The following day, they went to the immigration office and asked if they could see the manifests. The woman behind the counter laughed. "Do you know how many ships have left here since the war ended?"

"I realize there are many," Antoinette said, "but I need to find someone."

The woman led them into a back room with shelves of heavy volumes. She pulled the first one down and put it on the table.

"It would be quicker if each of you took one," the woman said, grabbing another register ledger and laying it on the table. "When you finish, put them back on the shelf. Let me know if I can help." "I have to get back to work," she said, walking toward the door to leave.

Once she was gone, Ethan and Antoinette quietly scanned each page. They had each skimmed through eight books by the end of the day. They were about to pull down two more when the woman came back.

"The office is closing for the evening. I'm sorry, but you have to leave now."

"Can we return tomorrow?" Ethan asked.

"Yes, that will be all right, but I won't be here." She smiled. "I apologize if I seem crass, but many people come here looking for their loved ones. My name is Jane. Tomorrow is my day off. I'll leave a note for Linda."

"Thank you," Antoinette said.

They returned the following day. Linda was accommodating and helped them look through the manuals during her lunch break. Antoinette confided in her, and they became friends by the end of the day.

Domenico Defino was nowhere to be found. Even with Linda's help, it was no use. Ethan had to return to Florence for work.

"Don't worry," Linda said. "I'll go through one book every day and call you if I find him."

"I'm sorry, Antoinette. I know you're disappointed. We can come back again next month."

"Shh." She put her finger on his lips. "I can't put you through this any longer. My past wants to remain behind me. I have to accept it."

She willed herself to stop thinking of Domenico and emptied her head, making space for Ethan.

Chapter 48

Antoinette awoke to the sound of a branch rubbing against the window and sat up. The bed was empty.

"Ethan!" she called. "Are you here?"

For a fraction of a second, she thought maybe she was alone again. She put on a robe and rushed to the kitchen. The window was open, and a flock of birds flew by. She opened the cabinet, finding the tea where she expected it. Familiarity settled in, and her anxiety eased.

Well into her second cup, Ethan entered the kitchen with a bakery box wrapped in red and white string.

"I thought I'd be back before you woke, but the line was around the corner."

"What's in the box?"

"Cornetti! The best in Italy."

"I love Cornetti!"

"Yes, I remember. Your mother made them before...."

"Yes, I helped her mix the dough." A smile crossed her lips as a childhood memory flashed before her eyes. "My mother? Where is she?"

He had told her about the Nazis who dragged her mother out of the house and beat her. It was one of the hardest things he'd ever had to do. Now, he was faced with the same task again.

"I'm sorry, Antoinette. She's gone."

"Oh, yes. I remember you told me that." She bit into a Cornetti. "You're right. These are quite good."

"It makes me happy to see you smile."

"You make me happy." Antoinette wasn't sure she was in love with Ethan, but even if she wasn't, she did love him. It was enough. "Maybe it's time we get married."

Ethan looked stunned. "The pastry is *that* good?"

"It's been months since we went to Naples, and we haven't heard anything about Domenico. I'm afraid he must have perished during the war."

"I love you, Antoinette. "If you want to get married, we will, but is it too soon?"

"No. The life I had is gone. I'm ready to start a new life with you. I spoke to the priest, but he said without Domenico's body to bury, I'm still married in the eyes of the Church."

"Then we'll go to the courthouse as soon as you like."

"No, I'd like us to marry at the synagogue."

He brushed back a stray lock of her hair. "Really? You would have to convert."

"Yes, that's what I want to do."

She made a quick sketch on her writing pad.

"This is what I want my wedding gown to look like," she said, pleased with her ability.

Ethan leaned across the table to kiss her and tasted the powdered sugar on her lips.

Focusing on their wedding, the strange man in her dreams slipped farther and farther away as time passed.

Chapter 49

Sunlight streamed weakly through the curtains. Domenico jumped out of bed and dressed quickly, his mind still sluggish with sleep. He didn't want to be late for work. His new job as a Broadway photographer was challenging and rewarding. Every morning, he left the apartment and walked to the subway on the corner to take the train to Manhattan. Blending in with the other commuters, the hum of the train lulled him into complacency. After all the bad things in Italy, it was a change for the good.

"Where are you going so early?" his cousin asked when he entered the kitchen.

"To work, of course. Why aren't you dressed?"

Anthony laughed. "It's Saturday. There's no work today."

"I guess I lost track of the days."

"You've been working so hard lately. You need a day to relax. Why don't you go to the park? A handful of men your age sit around talking about the old country. They'll make you feel right at home."

"Maybe I'll take Vittorio," Domenico said. "Where is my son?"

"My mother took him to buy new shoes. He's growing so fast."

"Your family has been so kind. I don't know how we will ever repay you."

"You don't need to. That's what family is for. We stick together."

Domenico changed into casual clothes and left and walked down the street. Garbage bags along the sidewalk. *The rats will feast tonight,* Domenico thought.

As Domenico passed the corner deli, he smelled the aroma of the coffee. Inside he purchased a coffee and cheese Danish to take to the park. The puffy pastry was gone when he arrived, so he sat on a bench and sipped his coffee.

Children played under the watchful eye of their mothers, and others wheeled babies in their strollers. Others sat on benches talking while their children ran around the playground.

Three men sat at a concrete table, smoking cigars and playing cards. They spoke Italian in a Sicilian dialect.

Domenico understood enough to approach them.

"Buongiorno," he said.

The men stopped playing to look at him.

"Buongiorno, indeed," said a scruffy man wearing a cap similar to a newsboy. It was the typical hat worn in Sicily.

"My name is Domenico Fino. I've just arrived here in New York."

"What part of Italy are you from?"

"The Campania area."

"I'm from Catania. Not too far from the mainland."

"It amazes me how many Italians left Italy," Domenico said.

"We all have our reasons for leaving," the scruffy man said.

"Many of us went back after the war, but it's not so bad here. My name is Luca," he said and offered his hand.

Domenico shook it. He had his own reasons. It was easier to be alone in a city full of people. Still, he couldn't come to terms with leaving Italy.

"I have a sister who lives in Campania," the third man said. He was holding the cards. "Do you play Scopa? We're short one man."

*****

Listening to the lonely sound of the train heading to Coney Island or Manhattan, Domenico tossed and turned at night. Domenico could always tell which direction it was traveling by the different sounds that bounced off the buildings. When it was going toward Manhattan, it always seemed faster.

Domenico thought about his brother. When Marco called to tell him their father had passed away, he wanted to go back for the funeral, but he couldn't get off work and didn't have enough money for a plane ticket.

Vincenzo was buried with his wife, Maria, who had died of cancer after the war. Now that his parents were gone, Marco took over the olive business. He begged Domenico to come back to Sorrento and help with the farm.

Marco had married a Sicilian girl. They had six children, and another was on the way. Domenico promised to visit soon, but time slipped by quickly as he and his son settled into the rhythm of American life.

With a new circle of friends, New York seemed natural to him after a while.

Domenico made peace with losing Antoinette, his one true love. At times, he yearned for a warm body beside him, but he didn't want another wife and never remarried.

Chapter 50

One day, a man came into the shop where Ethan was working. He looked familiar, but many customers who reminded him of someone else came through. The man handed him his laundry ticket, and Ethan cranked the wheel to rotate cleaned and pressed clothes on hangers. He rang up the purchase and waited for the patron to sort through his billfold.

"Ethan?" The man looked at him intently. "Is it you?"

Ethan looked up into his eyes, and his mouth dropped open.

"Jakub Kaminski! I thought you were...."

The Polish man had worked for him at his studio. Now, he looked older.

Jakub smiled, revealing a chipped tooth on the top row of his teeth. "I saw the writing on the wall and moved my family to a small town at the Swiss border. We stayed with my sister, who had married a French diplomate. It was safer, but still, we faced risks. We were lucky. Our family had remained in Poland and were sandwiched between Hitler and Stalin. Most of them perished."

"It's good to see you are safe," Ethan said.

"Good to see you too. You were a wealthy fashion designer the last time I saw you. Why are you working in the laundry?"

"When the Nazis arrived in Milan, they confiscated Jewish-owned businesses. I lost everything."

"They were crooks! It's a shame that you lost your studio. I have always admired your work. Your talents are wasted."

"It's not so bad. I escaped with my life and married the girl I always loved."

"Unfortunately, I lost my wife last year. She had cancer."

"I'm sorry to hear that. What have you been doing since the war?"

"I have a small dress factory at the edge of town. I learned so much working for you. I want to repay the favor."

"How so?"

"I need skilled dressmakers. Perhaps you would like to work for me. You'll be compensated properly for your talents. I'm sure I can pay you more than you earn here."

"I'd like that. Thank you for the opportunity."

"Of course." Jakub laughed. "What are friends for?"

"I will talk to my employer. They are counting on me to be here this week, but I will give him notice that I will not be working as of next week."

Jakub nodded and wrote his address on a piece of paper.

"Come and see me next Monday. I'll be waiting."

Ethan put the paper in his pocket. "I'll be there."

*****

The following Monday, Jakub met Ethan at the door and gave him a tour of the facilities. As they walked through the main factory, ideas for improvements sprang to Ethan's mind.

"Jakub, moving the machines to the back would be best. It would give you…."

"Ethan, you're a good man and a diligent worker. I'm sorry for your losses, but this is my business. You now work for me, and I must treat you like any other worker."

"I understand, Jakub. I'm grateful for the work, and I promise not to overstep."

Ethan had fallen a long way from having his own design studio. Working for someone else was limiting. He ached to do his designs without having to answer to someone else.

Chapter 51

Six months after they wrapped their fingers around the wedding chalice and drank the ceremonial wine, Antoinette settled into her life with Ethan. The sun streamed through the window.

She took a sip of her tea, feeling the warmth and flavor bloom in her mouth. She sat on the terrazzo to watch the Arno river pass by. It captured a scene that many artists had reproduced on canvas. Flashes of memories still haunted her, but they slowed down as she adjusted to a life beyond her past. She loved Ethan.

Antoinette examined her image in the mirror when she awoke that morning. It had been six weeks since her last period. Her breasts were swollen, the nipples larger than normal. She felt a nervous sickness that rattled her body, and a familiar sensation stirred within her. Even though she couldn't remember being pregnant with her sons, she knew a baby was inside her. *Ethan will be so pleased.* She put her hand on her stomach, feeling for movement, and hoped it would be a girl. Jewish custom believed showing happiness before the second trimester could be unlucky. Antoinette didn't believe in curses and omens, but now that she had converted to Judaism, she followed Ethan's beliefs. Eager to design the baby's nursery, she opened her sketchpad and drew a crib draped in sheer voile Gasa fabric.

For the rest of the day, she sketched baby dresses. So enthralled with her designs, she didn't hear Ethan come into the house. He stood behind her and gasped, his eyes fixed on her sketch pad.

"Ethan, you're home. I didn't hear you come in."

"What's all this?"

"I was planning to tell you, but I wanted to wait another month. We're going to have a baby."

"A baby?"

Oh, please be happy, Ethan. I am."

He looked at her with earnest affection. "I love you, Antoinette. Of course, I'm happy, but... I worry about you. Can you handle it?"

"Yes! It's just what I need. I don't want to look back all the time. This baby is a blessing."

Ethan's worry disappeared as she entered her second trimester. Her mind cleared, and the color in her cheeks returned. There was a joy in her eyes he hadn't seen before. The pregnancy seemed like a healing salve. Ethan was convinced they were having a boy. They decorated the nursery together, laughing as they painted the walls blue.

Chapter 52

The fashion world was slowly returning to its glory days. Shopping had become a recreational activity in the United States and London, not the discouraging chore it had been during the war.

Jakub had a few contracts, but it wasn't enough to keep the factory going. After only six months, he approached Ethan.

"The department store buyers aren't purchasing from small houses like mine."

"Women are tired of utility clothes produced during the war rationing," Ethan said. "They yearn for something different."

"Okay, so what do you suggest, my friend?"

"I have designs for a younger clientele. With new material, you can create glamor without charging prices people can't pay."

Jakub scratched his head. "Good. Come up with three garments, and let's see how they sell."

"I'll get to work on it right away. You won't be disappointed."

That night at dinner, Antoinette was excited when he told her about the design work. She enjoyed watching him sketch. The charcoal glided over the page until an image appeared. He was a master at his craft.

"Please, Ethan. Let me help. I may not remember people in my past, but I remember fashion."

He massaged his right temple. "I don't see why not. You always had an eye for design."

Antoinette helped by pointing out how he could improve the designs. Drawing on her sketchpad gave her a new focus. She found comfort in Ethan's world. It was a place where she could focus her talents and block out her bad dreams.

They worked on innovative designs until they were perfect. Each could guess the other's thoughts. Their bond strengthened as they silently worked through the night. Together, they sketched a soft, feminine collection of dresses with a floral theme for spring. Antoinette called it a revival of living and regrowth.

Antoinette spent the next day on the back porch sketching a new line for Ethan's collection. Jakub welcomed Ethan's ambitions, encouraging him. He sent him to Milan for the International Apparel and Clothing Convention. Ethan traveled to the fashion district with a dozen handmade dresses to negotiate contracts with department stores and boutiques and called on old contacts.

Enthusiastic buyers loved the clean lines of Ethan's clothes. His look was designed to appeal to America's newly cosmopolitan atmosphere.

Although the shops in Paris were slow to commit, orders poured in from London.

Within several months, Ethan set about reviving Jakub's business model. Before long, they were shipping to New York.

"At this rate, we're going to be as big as the great Gucci," Jakub said with a glint.

Italians, sick of conflict and eager for new prosperity, fell in love with his unique designs and quickly shed their old bourgeoisie styles.

Ethan's ready-to-wear designs brought Florence to the cutting edge of fashion as many young women shunned their mother's seamstresses.

When Jakub had trouble catching his breath, Ethan took over most of the business dealings and worked longer hours.

Chapter 53

Adelina was a lovely blue-eyed girl, as bright as a summer day. Antoinette breathed in the baby's essence, which filled her with a sense of peace she hadn't known for so long. The nursery had a bassinet, but Antoinette found it hard to leave the child alone.

"She's fine," Ethan assured her.

After six months, Adelina outgrew the bassinet and was in a crib.

Ethan and Antoinette peeked into her room, watching her hold onto the bars of her crib to hoist herself up. She'd inch her way around, falling every few steps. Pulling herself up again with determination in her bright blue eyes, she'd try again.

*****

Antoinette sometimes dreamed she was falling, but only for a moment. She learned to step between her memories, short visions of an image or a voice. Time seemed to skip ahead. Dreams of Domenico had slipped from her grasp. She no longer dreamed of her past. Her head was filled with new memories, and the old ones faded. Her daily activities took center stage for the next five years.

Adelina was scheduled to start kindergarten as summer ended.

Antoinette's intense love for Adelina triggered anxiety attacks. She was obsessed with keeping her safe. Ethan said she was behaving irrationally, but a part of her thought such vigilance was her obligation as a mother.

"I don't want her to leave," she said. "She's too young to be separated from her home."

"Adelina needs to be around children her age," Ethan said.

"I know you're right, but what if something bad happens?"

He put her arm around her shoulder. "Don't worry. She'll be fine."

*****

Antoinette walked her daughter to the elementary school four blocks away. The students lined up inside the gated courtyard. She kissed Adelina and let her join the other kids but stayed outside the gate until the school bell rang. Once her daughter disappeared into the safety of the school, she took a deep breath and walked home.

After brewing tea, Antoinette sat at the table and curled her fingers around the warm cup. She opened her drawstring pouch, reaching for the worn-down pencils. Bits of charcoal spilled onto the table. She swept them up with her fingers darkening the stains on her skin. Usually, her pencil glided over the page. Concentration eluded her as she continuously checked the clock on the kitchen wall. Time seemed to be standing still.

The day dragged on until it was time to get Adelina. She walked back to the school thirty minutes early and stood by the gate, waiting eagerly for her daughter to appear. When Adelina came outside, she spotted her mother and ran to her.

"How was your day?"

Adelina's eyes widened. "There was a bomb drill. The sirens were so loud. We had to get under our desks."

Antoinette tensed. "Oh, that must have been scary."

"No, it was only pretending."

That night, Antoinette dreamed she was in the middle of town, frantically searching for something, but she didn't know what. Fireballs rained down around her, and she ran as fast as possible, seeking shelter. Drenched with sweat, she awoke with a start.

"Adelina!" she cried, jumping out of bed and rushing to her room. She opened the door and gazed at her daughter, sleeping peacefully.

She broke down. "I thought I lost her."

Ethan pulled her close. "You will not lose her. You must stay strong, for our daughter's sake."

"You're right. I'll try harder."

*****

Every day, after taking Adelina to school, she went home and stared at the clock until it was time to pick her up. When she reached the school, an elegant woman with a Betty Grable hairdo was waiting by the gate wearing a mid-length tweed coat with a red scarf. She looked familiar. Antoinette had seen her before at the market.

Adelina came out of the school holding hands with a girl her age.

"Mommy, Mommy," she cried. "I made a new friend. Her name is Lucy. She said I could play with her. She has a dollhouse with lots of furniture. Can I?"

"Lucy's mother smiled. "Hi," she said. "I'm Vera. I think we're neighbors."

"Neighbors? Oh, yes. You live down the street from us," Antoinette said. "I've seen you before, but my memory is not good."

"My husband and I moved here recently from Sicily, Vera said. "After the war, the Mafia took hold. My husband, Giovanni, and I thought it best to move."

"It's nice to meet you, Vera. I'm Antoinette, and my daughter is Adelina."

She laughed. "I know. Adelina is all my daughter has talked about for weeks. They sit next to each other in class. It seems they have become very close."

The two women talked as they walked home, and their daughters laughed and whispered to each other. When they approached their street, Antoinette felt enthusiastic about the possibility of a new friend—for her and her daughter.

Reaching Vera's house, the girls ran up the stairs of the stoop.

"Would you like to come inside for a coffee, Antoinette? I made a limoncello cake yesterday. It's my mother's recipe."

"Please," both girls cried, jumping up and down.

"That would be lovely," Antoinette said.

Chapter 54

Ethan cleared his plate and went to his office, leaving Antoinette and Adelina to watch a show on the new television they bought with his pay raise. Every night after dinner, he scrolled through countless photos. He had contacted an organization in New York to reconnect families displaced by the war. Using his connections in the newspaper, Ethan circulated pictures of survivors. He also collaborated with the Red Cross in Germany.

There were numerous accounts of displaced family members. One family in Florence took a young girl off the streets and gave her a home. They believed her parents and older sister had perished in the camps, but the sister had escaped and made her way to America. She saw her photo and contacted the agency. After filing the proper papers and paying for her ticket, the sisters were united in Brooklyn.

People were happy to find loved ones they had presumed dead.

Ethan was glad to have a hand in healing the scars of broken hearts, but he pushed himself. It began to take a toll on him. After working all day at the textile studio, he stayed up late into the night searching for the missing. He became thinner over the next few months. His skin sagged from his bones, and he slid downhill fast. Antoinette begged him to cut back on his work. Still, he insisted on going to the shop and continued his research with displaced Holocaust survivors at night.

Ethan was especially intent on finding Marion and Samuel, the two children who briefly stayed with them during the war.

One day, the organization posted a letter from a Boston man looking for his children. He submitted an old snapshot of their faces. His wife had perished, but he survived and left the country.

Right away, Ethan saw the resemblance to the children who briefly stayed in Antoinette's basement.

He didn't want to get the fathers hopes up until he could locate the children. He called one of his contacts in Campione d' Italia.

"Hello, Sid. This is Ethan."

"Ethan, my friend. How are you doing?"

"A little tired, but I keep going. I have a favor to ask of you."

"What is it? I'll do my best to help."

"I'm trying to locate two Jewish children who escaped to Switzerland during the war. I believe they arrived safely in Bissone before the Swiss stopped taking refugees. Their father is alive, and he's looking for them."

"I know someone in that village. I'll do what I can, but it won't be easy. Many Jewish immigrants spread out to neighboring villages. Some were expelled. Do you have a photo of these children?"

"Yes, it's a little grainy, but I can send it to you."

"As soon as it arrives, I'll send their photos to various newspapers in Switzerland. Maybe someone will recognize them."

"Thank you, Sid. I knew I could count on you."

The doorbell rang. Antoinette was about to get up, but her husband was already at the door. A few minutes later, she looked up at him, standing in the doorway with an open letter.

"What is it?" she asked.

"It's a telegram. Jakub has died. Heart failure."

"Oh, that's terrible."

"The family lawyer has summoned me to appear at the reading of his will."

"You? What do you suppose that's all about?"

"I don't know. Maybe the family has questions about the business."

*****

Ethan sat in the lawyer's office, still grieving for his friend. There was no one else present.

The British lawyer was very formal. "I'll need you to sign this paper, Mr. Rubenstein."

Ethan wondered if there were debts left behind. It made him uneasy.

"What is it for?"

"It's to acknowledge you are the executor."

"I'm not sure why I was appointed executor," Ethan said.

"This will not take long. It's all here. I've already reached out to the Kaminski family, but they could not attend the reading."

The lawyer adjusted his spectacles and cleared his throat.

"I hereby leave my business assets and properties to Ethan Rubenstein."

Ethan sat back in disbelief.

"I don't understand."

"Mr. Kaminski had two bank accounts and a stock brokerage account which he left to his sons, but he wanted you to have the business. The information is on this sheet and my filing with the local surrogate's office. I estimate it is worth £250,000, but it may be more. He also left a letter. It's addressed to you. Maybe that will help to explain."

Ethan carefully opened the envelope.

He also left a letter," the lawyer said. "It's addressed to you. Maybe that will help explain things." Ethan carefully opened the envelope.

"My dearest friend Ethan,

I'm sure you are quite confused at this moment. First of all, I am ashamed of myself for withholding this information. You should know that the textile shop rightfully belongs to you. Before the Germans confiscated Jewish-owned businesses in Milan, your sister Rachel transferred the shop to my name. The business remained in my protection to ensure the primary owner was not Jewish and subject to confiscation. I had always planned to return it to you, but after you disappeared, I assumed the Nazis relocated you to one of the death camps. I sold the business and left Milan. It was just a coincidence that we both ended up in Florence. I had gone there because it was a logical location for fashion. Then, I took the money from your shop's sale and bought another. I should have told you the first day I saw you in the laundry shop. Please forgive me. I wish you and your family many years of happiness and prosperity. Telling you the truth will allow me to rest in peace.

Regards, Jakub"

Ethan released a long breath. *Why didn't Rachel tell me?*

Chapter 55

A vision of Domenico briefly skimmed her consciousness. She thought the brown-eyed stranger was gone. Antoinette tried to conjure the sound of his voice. Since Jakub had died, her flashbacks returned. She didn't want to worry Ethan, but memories lurked in every corner.

Antoinette wasn't comfortable letting Adelina wander too far. Ethan pleaded with her to loosen her grip, so she let Adelina walk to her friend Lucy four houses down.

Settling in with a cup of tea, she picked up her sketch pad. A scrap of paper fell to the floor. It was the image of a handsome stranger. She had drawn this man a hundred times, memorized the angle of his jaw and the shadow of his hairline. Tracing over the now familiar lines of his face, she had.

She tucked it in the back of her pad and turned to a fresh sheet. Pushing out of her mind, she tried to concentrate on Ethan's new winter collection. Soon, her eyes drooped, and she fell asleep. Domenico came back to her in her dreams. She reached out to touch him, but there was nothing but mist. The sound of the front door closing jolted her awake.

"Where are your brothers?" she asked Adelina in a panic.

"Brothers?"

"Aren't they with you?"

"I don't have any brothers."

Panic came over Antoinette. "Oh!"

"Are you all right, Mommy?"

"Yes, honey. I fell asleep in the chair. I guess I was having a nightmare. Please don't mention this to your father. I don't want him to worry."

"All right, Mommy."

They entered the kitchen, and Antoinette poured a glass of milk and took a cookie from the jar.

"Can I have two cookies?"

"Your father should be home soon. I don't want you to spoil your appetite for dinner."

Ethan was late. Adelina rushed into his arms, and he twirled her around.

"How're my girls?" he said and kissed Antoinette's cheek.

"We're fine, but I'm afraid dinner is now cold."

"I'm sure it's delicious. I'll go wash up, and we can eat."

Antoinette smiled and prepared the table setting.

"It was a busy day," Ethan said as he sat at the table. "I assembled a small sales force dedicated to the new line. The changes will make the company more profitable and attractive to new customers."

Antoinette forced herself to eat, self-conscious over every movement she made, afraid Ethan would know.

"Is something wrong?" he asked.

She put her fork down and looked into his eyes. "I need to work," Antoinette said. "I want to set up a boutique where our clothes can be sold."

"If it makes you happy, I'll help you find a space."

Nestled in the center of the town among buildings smudged with soot from nearby factories, Ethan found a store for rent. Concrete rubble from the bombardments had been swept aside. He signed a one-year lease, and the boutique opened. Ethan had the front of the building remodeled. Despite pockmarks from the heavy bombing of the war, the space was in a good location.

Antoinette now worked at the boutique. A little apprehensive, she also felt excited. After five years as a housewife, she felt good to be in the world again. Focusing on the future instead of the past was good and kept her flashbacks under control. Once again, her fashion background emerged. Clothing sales took off quicker than they had expected. Profits were good. Ethan calculated the boutique would make enough money to buy the building even before their lease was up.

*****

Antoinette felt the years rush past. She and Ethan happily worked together and watched Adelina grow up loving fashion, too. She collected buttons in a box she kept under her bed. After school, Adelina came to the shop and sat at a desk in the front office to do her homework. Inevitably, she wandered into the sewing room to watch the seamstresses create garments. She was especially fascinated by the vibrant colors and textures of the embellishments.

Chapter 56

Ethan continued to work long hours at the shop and stayed up late in his office at night. He looked exhausted, but Antoinette couldn't convince him to cut back. She let him sleep and stepped onto the porch with a cup of tea. There was a chill in the air, so she went upstairs to get a sweater. Ethan was rushing around, trying to get dressed for work.

"I overslept," he said. "You should've woken me."

"You needed the rest," she said and kissed his cheek. "I'm making breakfast. What would you like?"

"I'm not very hungry."

"At least have a piece of toast and a cup of tea with me."

"I'll try." He appeared to be in pain as he walked to the bathroom.

"Are you all right, Ethan?"

"Yes, just a little stiff. It's these old bones. They don't move the way they used to."

At breakfast, he spoke little and was not his usual self.

"You've barely touched your breakfast. Aren't you feeling well?"

"I don't have an appetite."

"Something's wrong. I know it."

"Not to worry, dear. It's just indigestion. I must have eaten something bad yesterday."

She had a feeling that he wasn't telling her everything.

Soon after Ethan left for work, she walked Adelina to school. Light snow fell and grew heavier by the time they reached the building. Antoinette pulled her jacket tighter against the cold and admired some of the Christmas decorations in town. The smell of freshly baked bread lured her into the bakery. She had a snap memory of her father. She smiled, remembering his face on a Saturday morning and the aroma of fresh rolls and pastries.

Lately, her visions were of childhood. Antoinette cherished the comfort of her parents' faces and small events from her youth. But she still had no recollection of her marriage or her children.

"Give it time," her doctor said, encouraging her not to lose faith.

Antoinette bought two loaves of bread for the upcoming holiday, but the temptation was too great. She broke off small pieces of one on the way home.

By the time she arrived at her house, half the loaf was gone. The phone rang as she opened the front door. She rushed into the kitchen and picked up the receiver.

"Hello?"

"Hello. I'm Kelly from Doctor Klein's office. I need to speak with Ethan Rubenstein."

"He's not home at the moment. I'm his wife. Can I give him a message?"

"Yes. Please tell Ethan that his test results are back."

"Test results?"

"Yes, he was in the office last week with severe stomach pains. We took some blood and sent it out for analysis."

"What's wrong with him?"

"I set up an appointment for Ethan on Monday at ten am. The doctor will go over the results then."

"Oh, all right. We'll be there."

Waiting for Ethan to come home for lunch, Antoinette paced, checking the clock every few minutes. Getting impatient, she grabbed her coat and rushed to the studio.

Chapter 57

Antoinette passed rows of women operating sewing machines in the factory. Needles clattered as they bobbed up and down in rhythmic chaos.

Ethan was in his office. She could see him through the large window that overlooked the production line.

Surprised to see her, he tried to hide the medication the doctor had given him to relieve the pain.

"Antoinette! What brings you here?"

"The doctor's office called. They said you were in for stomach problems. Why didn't you tell me? I'm your wife. Why didn't you talk to me?"

"Of course, you're right. I should have mentioned it to you. I didn't want to worry you until I had a proper diagnosis."

"The office made an appointment for you on Monday. I'm coming with you. We'll face this together."

*****

Antoinette put Adelina to bed and joined Ethan in the living room that night. He had a faraway look in his eyes.

"What are you thinking about?"

"Sometimes, my mind goes back to Auschwitz."

"You never talked about it," she said, sitting on the chair across from him. "I'm always afraid to ask, but I wonder about it."

"I didn't want to burden you with my dark thoughts. You have enough of your own to deal with."

"I'm your wife. You can talk to me."

"Horrific things happened there. Perhaps you shouldn't know."

"Please. Let me help you carry the burden. What happened when the Nazis took you away."

Ethan sighed. "They herded us into cattle cars with barely any room to move and only one bucket to relieve all of us. The smell was atrocious."

Antoinette shuddered.

"After days filled with tears and screams, the train stopped, and the doors opened. For a moment, I thanked God because the air was stifling inside, but it got worse. Soldiers with fierce dogs ordered us out. They directed some of us toward a large building, primarily women with children and sickly old men."

"Why did they separate everyone?"

"We didn't know, but they were deciding who would live and who would die. Some were herded into a building. They gave the rest of us shovels and made us dig trenches.

Smoke rose from the chimneys, and human ash rained down on us like snow. They stripped people naked, killed them with Zyklon gas, and then burned their bodies in ovens. The sickening odor permeated the air and into our clothing. It smelled like burned chicken feathers. At first, shock caused disbelief, but this happened every day. We soon resigned ourselves to it—perhaps because we could do nothing to stop it.

"The food rations were barely enough to keep us alive. We grew weaker every day, starving to death. Our skin sagged over our bones, and our stomachs ached with hunger. We were desperate. When the guards weren't looking, I swallowed handfuls of small stones to keep my stomach full. I can still feel it in my belly."

"You never mentioned any of this before. How did you survive?"

"When the Allies neared the camp, the Germans fled. We ran to the kitchens and filled our bowls with soup from giant pots. Some prisoners dug through bins of garbage for scraps of vegetables—anything edible.

When Soviet soldiers arrived, our condition horrified them. They gave us bread, then other food. Still, some died of starvation or disease because the food and medical attention came too late."

Antoinette put her arms around Ethan and said nothing. She hugged him as tears ran down her face."

Chapter 58

On Monday morning, Antoinette brought Adelina to Vera's house to walk to school with Lucy. Then walked with Ethan to the doctor's office around the corner and sat in the waiting room. The nurse called his name, and he disappeared into the examination room.

Finally, the nurse came out and led her to the doctor's private office. Ethan sat in the chair across from the doctor, who looked worried.

"What's wrong?" Antoinette cried.

"Well, we found some problems," the doctor said.

"Oh, no! What problems?"

"He has blood in his stool, and the x-rays show an unknown mass."

"No, it can't be. How did this happen?"

"People in the camps often come away from it with physical problems that show themselves over time. Starvation and psychological stress are traumatic for the body. They may have contributed to the development of the growth."

"There must be treatments," Antoinette pleaded.

"There are some experimental drugs we could try, but…."

"Could they cure him?"

"Possibly, but I won't know the extent until I operate. I want to admit Ethan into the hospital."

A flicker of unease passed across her face. "Operate? You mean, cut him open?"

"It's the only sure way that we know how to assess the damage. We might be able to cut out the tumors."

"Tomorrow is the start of Hanukkah," Antoinette argued. "Can't it wait eight days?"

"This is urgent, Mrs. Rubenstein. We must know what we're dealing with before we can treat him."

"No, I won't allow it."

Ethan patted her hand. "Now, now, dear. The doctor knows best."

"I want to admit Ethan to the hospital today."

Antoinette felt the room closing in on her. "I can't lose my husband!" She fought to breathe, but everything turned black.

*****

Antoinette sat in the hospital lobby the next day, wringing her hands. *God, please let my husband be all right. Please!*

The doctor came through the double doors wearing a blue surgeon uniform with a sweat-drenched cap on his head.

"Doctor," she cried, jumping to her feet. "Is Ethan all right?"

"Let's have a seat," he said, taking her arm and guiding her to a chair.

"Please, tell me. What's wrong with my husband?"

"Ethan has stage four cancer. I'm afraid it has metastasized to other organs."

"What does that mean?"

"It means the tumors have invaded several of his internal organs."

"Can you remove them?"

"No, I'm afraid there are too many to remove, and the tumors may have started where I can't detect them yet."

"What about the treatments?"

"I don't recommend them. It would put Ethan through more pain, and the likelihood of him surviving is not good."

"What are you going to do to fix him?"

"I'm sorry. The disease is too advanced. I'm afraid it's terminal.

"What are you saying?" Antoinette looked at him in disbelief.

"There's nothing I can do. He probably has six months to live, if that. It's in the hands of God."

Antoinette burst into tears. "No!"

Chapter 59

A month passed, and Ethan regained some of his strength. Antoinette was hopeful. After dinner, she filled a teapot with water and lit the stove. When the teapot whistled, she poured the boiling water into a sturdy earthenware cup and took it to the terrazzo, where Ethan sat with his pipe. The sound of the rain had a soothing effect, and she settled into a chair across from him. He had a strange expression.

"Ethan, are you alright?"

His lips moved, but no sound came out. He had a strange expression.

Antoinette jumped up. "What's wrong?"

He tried to tell her, but his words didn't make sense. Something was seriously wrong. She ran next door for help.

Vera and her husband, Giuseppe, rushed over to check on Ethan.

"I think he's having a stroke," Giuseppe said. "I'll call for an ambulance."

"A stroke?" Antoinette shook her head. "No, it can't be."

"We won't know until he's seen by a doctor. You go with him and leave Adelina with us. She won't be allowed in the hospital because she's too young."

"I'll help you pack a bag," Vera said, rubbing her shoulder. "It's going to be all right. Don't worry."

At the hospital, the doctor examined Ethan. He used a flashlight to look into his eyes and gave him instructions that Ethan did not seem to understand.

"Your husband has had a stroke," the doctor said with empathy. "I'll have to admit him."

Once Ethan was settled in his room, the nurse nodded.

"You can go in now, Mrs. Rubinstein."

"Can I stay with him tonight?"

"Yes, there's a chair next to his bed, but I'll have the nurse bring you a cot if you prefer."

"Thank you. I probably won't sleep."

Antoinette quietly entered. Ethan seemed to be asleep. She settled on the chair beside the bed and prayed for God to save him. The nurse tried to get her to leave and get something to eat, but Antoinette wouldn't budge.

"I need to be here when he wakes up."

Holding his hand, she fell asleep.

*****

The following day, Ethan opened his eyes. Feeling hopeful, she stared into them, but they looked dull and lifeless. The spark had left them, replaced by a faraway expression. She realized he was physically awake, but his spirit had flown.

"Nurse!" she called out. "We need the doctor."

Antoinette tucked the bed sheet around him and smoothed his hair. "Don't leave me," she cried. "You're my strength."

The doctor came in and examined Ethan. He shook his head. "He's gone."

"But he opened his eyes! He looked at me!"

"Sometimes, before death occurs, the body reacts involuntarily," he explained. "If it's any consolation, he's no longer in pain."

Antoinette was inconsolable as tears flowed down her cheeks.

"Would you like me to call someone to take you home?" the nurse asked.

"No. I appreciate your concern, but I can get there alone. I don't want to talk to anyone right now."

Exhaustion enveloped Antoinette as she walked home. She stared at her image in the bathroom mirror. Feeling her legs buckle, she gripped the cool porcelain sink and took deep breaths. After washing her face, she left to pick up Adelina at Vera's house. *How do you tell a ten-year-old girl that her father is dead?*

Seeing her mother, Adelina let out a cry and ran into her arms.

"Where's Papa?" she asked. "Is he better? Is he coming home soon?"

Antoinette kneeled to face her daughter.

"I'm sorry, Honey. Papa won't be coming home."

Tears filled her eyes. "Where did he go?"

"Would you like some privacy?" Vera asked.

"No, please stay," Antoniette said and turned back to Adelina. "Remember when I told you about heaven?"

She nodded. "It's where all good people go when they die, right?"

"Yes. God has called your Papa to heaven. He didn't want to leave you but had to go."

Adelina's face scrunched as she tried to process what Antoinette was saying. She then threw herself into her mother's arms and cried. They held each other close.

"You still have me," Lucy said, putting her arm around Adelina's shoulder. "We're like sisters."

Antoinette was grateful Adelina had Lucy to lean on.

"Please," Vera said. "I know you have preparations to make. Giuseppe and I want to help."

"I appreciate that. I don't know what to do first."

"You probably want to go home, but I think you and Adelina should stay here for a little while. Stay for dinner. In fact, why don't you spend the night."

"Thank you. We'll stay for dinner, but I'd like to go home. I need to be closer to Ethan and comfortable in our bed."

Antoinette picked at her dinner. "I'm sorry. I don't have much of an appetite. I'm so tired. I want to go home now."

"Giuseppe will walk with you and Adelina home."

"Thank you, Vera," Antoinette said and hugged her. "What would we ever do without you?"

"I'll always be here for you. Get some rest. I'll come by in the morning and help you with the funeral arrangements."

Giuseppe waited to leave until Antoinette and Adelina were inside, and the light was on.

"Mama. I'm scared. Can I sleep with you tonight?"

"Of course. We can snuggle together."

She tucked Adelina into the bed and slipped under the covers beside her. Adelina fell asleep securely in her mother's arms. Antoinette stared at the ceiling and spoke to Ethan in heaven.

No one will ever hurt you again, my Darling. You are free.

Chapter 60

Following Jewish scripture, Ethan was buried within twenty-four hours of his death. Antoinette thought about sending his body to be interred at the Rubenstein Family mausoleum in Milan, but she wanted to keep him near.

Mourners overflowed the cemetery for Ethan's funeral. Friends she didn't know he had showed up to pay their respects to the man who worked tirelessly to reunite Holocaust victims. People loved him for his kindness and the work he did helping others.

Adelina sat next to her friend at the temple. Lucy tenderly put her arm around her, offering comfort.

After the service, Adelina and Lucy went to the cemetery with Giuseppe. Vera stood beside Antoinette to receive condolences from the mourners.

Vera took her hand. "Antoinette, it's time to go. They're waiting for us."

"I didn't get to say goodbye," she wept. "I didn't get to tell Ethan how much I loved him." She bowed her head on Ethan's coffin and cried.

"Ethan knew how much you loved him."

Nodding, she took a long slow breath. Antoinette put her veil down over her eyes before joining the procession to the cemetery with Vera beside her.

Antoinette gazed up at the canopy of trees. She had always thought May was the most beautiful month in Florence, but not this year. Red poppies and purple wisteria painted the cemetery walls with vivid colors, but she took no joy from them.

Rabbi Samuel Margulies prayed over the gravesite. Ethan had loved him for his Zionist views. He picked up two shovelfuls of dirt and threw them on the plain pine casket, the first with the shovel upside down to signify reluctance. The second time, right side up, to show acceptance.

Antoinette had a hard time accepting his death and fell to her knees. The soil smelled rich with organic matter. She gripped the loosened earth in her clenched hand and kissed it before letting the dirt fall onto the coffin. The trees above rustled, and Ethan's voice spoke to her. "Don't cry! Be strong."

Vera and Giuseppe supported her back to the house. She arrived to find friends and neighbors bearing gifts of food to pay their respects. It helped a little, but losing Ethan shook her security, leaving her alone to bring up their daughter.

"It's just you and me now," Antoinette sobbed.

"Don't cry, Mama. I'll take care of you." Adelina brushed away her mother's tears with her tiny hand.

Antoinette smiled at her daughter's courage. She had to pull herself together to be a mother to Adelina.

"We must be strong now. "Papa would want that."
"Shouldn't we be covering the mirrors, Mama?"
"How do you know about that?"
"We learned about it at school. It's called Shiva."
"I suppose we should. It's a Hebrew tradition.

Chapter 61

Antionette wanted to hide from the world and insulate herself at home. She refused to return to work and left the house to go to the market or the cemetery.

"Oh, Ethan. How could you leave me?" She clenched her fists and squeezed them tight to stop her hands from shaking. "If only I had some of your strength. Some of your courage."

She placed a stone on his tombstone to mark her visit to the grave. The pain was too fresh and sharp, and she couldn't fathom the future. She hadn't realized how much Ethan had filled the space in her life. His clothes still hung in the closet. Antoinette couldn't bear to part with anything that had belonged to him. She felt closer to him, surrounded by his shirts and jackets.

One by one, she went through the cartons on the shelves. In the back of the closet, she found a box. It was locked, but she remembered a strange key in the night table drawer. The key was still where she had seen it. She placed it in the slot, and it fit. Antoinette opened it and stared at the book of photos. They were the pictures of her past life with Domenico—the ones she thought were lost.

She held the photo close to her heart with both hands and rocked.

"Mama?" Adelina called. She entered the room to find her mother sitting in the closet.

"What are you doing?"

Antoinette stared up at her unblinking. It scared Adelina, and she ran to get Vera, who came at once.

"Antoinette, dear, what are you doing?"

She looked up slowly from the pictures she had found.

"What's that?" Vera asked.

"My past," she said, clutching the photo of Domenico. "I thought I had misplaced these pictures, but Ethan must have hidden them in the closet.

Vera looked at a photo of the smiling faces of Domenico and Antoinette on their wedding day.

"Did you ever find out what happened to him?"

"No. Domenico must have died in the war. Ethan said he was a Partisan. He also said I had twin sons. I dream about them all the time. Maybe they're in heaven with their father."

"What about his family?"

"I'm not sure. When Ethan and I went to Campania, I tried to inquire about the family name, but no one recognized it."

Antoinette stood up, shaking off the trance.

"We should give these clothes away or sell them," Vera said.

"I can't bear to part with them." Antoinette reached into one of the boxes and pulled out one of Ethan's sweaters. She buried her face in the garment.

"They still smell like Ethan. I feel closer to him."

"I understand, but they are doing you no good here."

Antoinette held the sweater to her chest and wept.

"If I don't have something tangible of him, I fear he'll disappear from my memories like Domenico."

"These things are not Ethan," Vero reminded her. "We can sell them and raise money for the organization he was working with to find Jewish survivors of the war."

"Yes, you're right. Ethan would have wanted that. It's better if I remember him for the things he loved."

Tears pricked her eyes as she and Vera neatly folded the clothes and tenderly packed Ethan's belongings in boxes.

*****

Antoinette had to find the strength to keep the studio alive. She turned the corner on her grief, merging with a fresh new idea. Children's clothing! It was Adelina who inspired the change.

Committed to serving a new generation, she developed a line of children's clothing for a new clientele. Adelina and Lucy were her models.

The girls giggled, enjoying the pageantry of fashion shows. They loved anything with sparkles and rhinestones. Full of life, the duo kept Antoinette from falling apart on more than one occasion.

When *My Fair Lady* opened in London, Vera bought four tickets. Adelina was excited. She had developed a love for musicals and plays and enjoyed the dramatic colors and embellishments that made the costumes sparkle.

They checked into a hotel close to The Theatre Royal, Drury Lane.

London was the center of the Swinging Sixties, a youth-driven cultural revolution flourishing in art, music, and fashion. It was all Adelina talked about when they returned to Italy.

Chapter 62

Having just finished their elementary years at school, they were looking forward to spending the next three years together in scuola secondaria.

The girls were heartbroken when Lucy's parents announced they were moving back to Sicily.

The moving van had arrived to carry their belongings across the Messina Straits from Calabria to Sicily. It was packed and ready to go.

"Where's Lucy and Adelina?" Giuseppe asked. "It's time to leave, and I can't find them."

"Did you look in the house?" Vera asked.

"Yes, they're not in there."

"Maybe they're in Adelina's room," Antoinette said. "I'll go and check."

Antoinette came out, shaking her head. "They're not there either."

"Lucy!" Vera shouted.

"You don't think they walked into town, do you?" Giuseppe asked.

"They could have gone to the park, but Lucy always tells me when she goes. I'm getting worried."

"Let's split up and search. Giuseppe, you walk to town. Vera, you go to the park."

Each went off, calling for the girls. Antoinette searched the back of the house. As she was heading toward the front, she heard voices and stopped. Antoinette peered through the lattice beneath the back porch.

"Adelina, Lucy! Come out this instant."

"I'm sorry, Mama," Adelina said. "Lucy doesn't want to move. Can't she stay here with us?"

"Don't be silly. Lucy has to go with her parents."

"But we'll miss each other."

"We can visit during the holidays."

Lucy and Adelina wriggled out of the small opening. Dirt smudged their faces and clothes. Antoinette brushed them off and led them to the front yard.

Giuseppe and Vera were back. Panic on their faces.

"Here they are," Antoinette said.

Vera ran up to Lucy. "I'm mad at you, young lady. You had us worried sick."

"Don't be mad at Lucy," Adelina said. "It was my idea to hide. I'm sorry. Please don't punish Lucy."

The scowl on Vera's face softened. "I understand how hard this is for the two of you. It's hard for everyone. We'll come back to visit, and maybe you can come to Sicily when school is out for the summer."

The impatient van driver honked his horn.

Adelina and Lucy clung to each other and promised to keep in touch forever.

Antoinette said a tearful goodbye to her only friend, Vera. After Ethan died, the loss had been devastating. But now, this new loss. A profound sadness took hold of her. She wondered how it would affect Adelina.

After Lucy left, Adelina lost interest in modeling. To cheer her up, Antoinette enrolled her in a children's theater.

Chapter 63

Eight years had passed since Ethan died of cancer. The years fell away like leaves in the autumn wind. Still, memories of her life with him were vivid, unlike the distant people she couldn't identify in her dreams.

Adelina had a passion for acting. She took classes and participated in local plays at the Teatro Puccini. She was especially intrigued by American actors. Posters hung on her bedroom walls of famous people on Broadway.

She had grown up to be a lovely young lady. Antoinette wished Ethan could have seen her.

Her acting left little time to help her mother in the boutique. Antoinette struggled to keep things going by herself.

"I can't manage the studio and the boutique alone," Antoinette said. "You must cover some of the shop hours, or I may close the studio."

"Oh, that would be horrible! I'm sure Papa wouldn't like that a bit. If we close the studio, we'll lose all our contacts in Milan."

"I'm getting older, and...."

"I'm sorry, Mama. I will help out more, I promise."

While Adelina was completing her studies at the university, she worked as a cashier in the boutique.

*****

Antoinette lay in bed, listening for Adelina to return home from rehearsals. They usually lasted until ten p.m. every evening.

When she finally came in, Antoinette closed her eyes.

The bedroom door burst open, and she bolted upright.

"Mama!" Adelina was out of breath from running up the stairs.

"What's wrong?"

"Nothing! My class is going to New York to see a Broadway play called *Fiddler on the Roof*. Please, Mama. I must go."

"New York? That's an expensive trip."

"I've been saving my money from working at the Boutique. I think I have enough. Please, Mama. It's only for two weeks. Once I return, I'll take over the studio, and we can hire more seamstresses. I want to start a line of theater costumes."

"Costumes?"

"Yes, the theater purchases their costumes in Paris. I'm sure they'd prefer to buy locally. Broadway is the place where I can get inspiration."

"Do you think we can make enough money?"

"I'm positive. Please, Mama, give me a chance."

Adelina had a clever mind like her Aunt Rachel. Antoinette had no doubt she would succeed.

*****

From the moment Adelina exited the plane, she could feel the vibrations of the city.

"Stay together, class," her theater arts professor said, herding the wide-eyed group onto the bus.

Stuck in rush hour traffic, no one minded as the bus lumbered down Times Square. They leaned out the windows to stare at the marquees and crowds of people rushing to unknown places.

The bus stopped in front of the hotel, and the class stepped onto the street. The ground rumbled from the trains beneath them.

They checked into the Algonquin Hotel, only a three-minute walk from the Belasco Theatre, where the class was invited to sit in at rehearsals for a musical the next day.

Standing in the lobby, Adelina noticed a cat with a mass of orange fur sleeping on one of the sofas. She went over and petted him. He was very affectionate.

"Hello," she said and scratched him behind his ears. The cat opened its mouth, and a male voice meowed. Stunned, Adelina looked up to see a handsome young man appeared with sandy-blonde hair that fell in loose curls around his face.

Adelina laughed. "You gave me a fright. For a moment, I thought he was a talking cat."

"Oh, he talks all right. His name is Leo. He lives here. Leo lets everyone know when he wants food or to go out."

"I love cats. I'd take him home if I didn't live so far away."

"Did you notice the tip jar on the reception desk counter? I put a note on it. **Feed The Cat.**"

Adelina laughed. "You're funny."

"I've been told," he said with a smile. "Are you part of the group from Italy?"

"Yes, this is my first trip to America."

"I'm Nicholas," he said. "I'm dropping off the passes for your class to get in the theater tomorrow."

"Are you an actor?" she asked, wide-eyed.

"Nah. I'm in charge of lighting."

"Maybe I'll see you again," Adelina said.

"I sure hope so,: Nicholas said with a smile that lit up his face.

The teacher gathered the students to give out room assignments. When Adelina turned back to the front desk. Nicholas was gone.

Chapter 64

The following day, after a bus tour, the class walked to the theater.

Adelina was looking forward to seeing Nicholas again. She hurried into the theater. It took a moment for her eyes to focus once they left the sunshine outside. He was busy talking with one of the technicians near the stage.

Their eyes met, and she felt a jolt of energy. Her legs turned to jelly.

He flashed a brilliant smile. "Hello again. How are you enjoying our fair city? I bet it's quite different here. You know, all the hustle and bustle."

"Hi," Adelina said. "It's a little different from Florence. Things seem to move a lot faster in New York."

"Florence! I've always wanted to visit there."

"Why don't you?"

He scratched his head. "Well, I'm working, that's why. Our photographer, Domenico, is from Sorrento but lived in Florence for a while and talks a lot about it. He's teaching me about cameras so I can take over for him."

"Is he going back to Italy?"

"No, he's just retiring. I'm sure you have a lot in common. I'll introduce you. He's coming in later to take photos for the billboards outside." Nicholas looked around nervously. "I had better get back to work."

She kept an eye on him as he adjusted the lighting on stage. He disappeared behind the stage, and she focused on the rehearsals. As she tucked her books under her arm to leave, she heard his voice.

"Adelina, wait," he called, approaching with an older man.

"This is Domenico, the man I told you about from Florence. He's taking photos today for the billboards outside."

Domenico was unable to speak for a second. He studied her, his brow lifting behind his glasses.

"I'm sorry for staring." He extended his hand. "It's just that you remind me of someone I once knew in Florence."

Adelina laughed. "They say everyone's related in Florence if you go back far enough."

"It's your eyes. They are a unique shade of amber."

"Yes, I have my mother's eyes. She is...."

Suddenly, Adelina's teacher called the group together.

"Oh, I must go now. It was nice meeting you."

When Domenico left, Nicholas turned to her. Mesmerized by her Italian charm and beauty, he didn't want to lose her.

"I hope to see you again before you go home. I'd like to show you around Manhattan."

"I would love that, but I had better check with my teacher first. I'm not sure he would let me go off from the rest of the class."

"I'll come by the hotel later. They're hosting a reception dinner for your group. They know me well. I'm sure they won't mind if I crash the party." He laughed.

*****

Nicholas made everyone laugh with his funny New York humor. Everyone felt comfortable around him, including the professor. He soon became part of the group and spent as much time as he could with Adelina.

After dinner, she had permission to take a short walk with Nicholas. They walked for blocks, talking and laughing. The sun had gone down, but it wasn't cold.

"So, what do you think about New York so far?" he asked.

"Every block offers a different culture. It's all so much to take in in one short week."

"New York is the kind of place that takes years to know. There's always another path to discover that hasn't been explored. The city has secrets, some tucked away in small alleys."

"And you... do you have secrets?"

"Some, but basically, I'm a clean-cut American boy."

"Were you born in Manhattan?"

"Yes, my mother is Jewish, and my father is Italian. I grew up in the Jewish tradition."

"Have you ever been to Italy?"

"No, but it's on my list of places to visit. I want to explore the village where my father was born."

"Which village is that?

"It's called Castellamare di Stabia. It's not far from Naples."

"Did you always want to work in lighting?"

"No. It was supposed to be a part-time job, a way to pay for university classes. Actually, I'm a dancer. I was the only boy in dance class. The other kids in school made fun of me, but I didn't care."

"How did you learn about lighting?"

"My father taught me. It isn't my dream job, but I like it. I'm hoping to be in the right place at the right time. I need to be in the center of it all. Maybe a producer will need someone as an extra. Who knows? It's that trifecta of theater, dance, and opportunity." He began dancing down the sidewalk to a tune he hummed.

"You're pretty good!"

Adelina was enthralled by Nicholas and his grasp of musicals past and present.

Chapter 65

Nicholas came to the hotel the next day after work to pick up Adelina.

"Have you been to Central Park yet?" he asked.

"No, but it's on the schedule for a class tour."

"It's not far… just about ten blocks. I can come by tomorrow. We can take a tour around Central Park in a horse-drawn carriage."

Adelina blushed, her eyes bright. "That would be lovely."

They walked along Sixth Avenue toward one of the many entrances to Central Park until they reached Columbus Circle. It was still early enough to see the sunset as they approached one of the buggies.

The old man who owned the horse was feeding him an apple. Adelina looked into his big brown eyes and petted his mane.

My name is Giuseppe, and this is Barney. Would you like to take a ride?"

"Yes, Nicholas said and helped Adelina into the carriage.

Giuseppe was from Sicily and told them stories about his village as they rode along the winding paths of Central Park, enjoying views of the city between the trees.

The sun was setting as the horse clip-clopped along, and it was starting to get dark by the time they returned.

"That was wonderful. Thank you for sharing that with me. I'd best get back before my professor begins to worry."

As they walked back to the hotel, he held her hand, and she wondered if he might kiss her goodnight before he left her. Feeling awkward, she shifted from one foot to the other when they returned to the hotel lobby. He stared into her eyes, searching for a sign that she liked him before his lips touched hers. His kiss was sweet and gentle. It was a perfect end to the day, and she practically floated to her room with the promise of seeing him again.

*****

While the rest of her class gathered on the roof to watch fireworks, Adelina waited in the hotel lobby for Nicholas. The soft purr of Leo emanated from the couch, and she took the opportunity to pet him. Usually, she couldn't get near the cat because the customers were drawn to him as soon as they entered the hotel.

Nicholas rushed in with restless energy.

"I want to show you the real New York," he said and grabbed her hand. "Come on."

"Where is this real New York?"

"It's Greenwich Village. That's where I live."

They walked past the steady sea of tourists and headed to the subway station.

"It will be faster if we take the train there. I know of a great pizzeria. After that, I'll show you where I live. We can walk there."

Nicholas purchased two tokens. Music echoed through the station, and Adelina stopped. "What's that?"

"Street musicians. Some are quite talented. Is this your first time in the subway?"

"Yes, my professor didn't think it was safe for us. He was afraid we'd get separated."

"Well, then. You're in for a treat."

The music grew louder, pulsing to a beat. It vibrated the dingy white tunnel walls.

"My apartment is only two blocks from here," he said when they exited the station.

Although she thought his apartment was small, it had charm.

"I think I could live in New York," she said, but I'd need a bigger place."

"Most apartments in Manhattan are small, but there are older buildings with railroad apartments."

"Railroad? Are they close to the trains?"

"No, silly. Railroad apartments have rooms in a line, one after another. Thus, the name."

"I'm getting kind of hungry."

"Let's go then."

They walked to the Brooklyn Bridge, flirting and teasing each other. Suddenly, he stopped.

"What's wrong?" she asked.

"I think we made a wrong turn. I don't know where we are."

"I thought you were a New Yorker," she teased.

He smirked. "Don't worry. I'll get us back to the bridge."

After a few turns and many blocks, they were back on the east side.

"See, I told you."

Chapter 66

On the last night, Adelina felt excited to see the actual play but sad because she was leaving in the morning.

Searching the faces in the theater, she didn't see Nicholas. A dull ache filled her chest when the lights dimmed and the curtain went up. The music began, and the stage filled with players. Adelina's mouth dropped open.

Nicholas was one of four dancers in the middle of the stage. Bursting with pride, she smiled at his good fortune.

At last, the lights came up, and the cast gathered on stage to take their final bow. The applause filled the theater, drowning out the music. Adelina and her class stayed in their seats until the crowd thinned, but she was impatient to see Nicholas.

Finally, she went bounding into the lobby and through the side door to the back of the stage. The other players were gathered around Nicholas, slapping him on the back and thanking him for filling in.

Adelina threw her arms around him. "You were great!"

"It was incredible," he said. "At the last minute, one of the dancers called in sick. I knew all his moves. The producer said he'll find a permanent spot for me. I'm closer now than ever to achieving my dream."

"I'm so happy for you."

"Why do you look sad then?"

"I wish I could stay in the United States longer. My flight home is tomorrow."

"I'm going to miss you. I hope you can come back again."

She smiled. "Perhaps, but I have obligations. I'm not sure when or if I can...."

The producer came up behind them. "Nicholas, there's a cast party at the Plaza. I hope you're coming. Oh, and bring your girlfriend along."

Encouraged, he beamed at Adelina. "Do you think your professor will let you come along?"

"I can't see why not. He knows you well enough by now."

Adelina thought she was dreaming when she walked into the famous Plaza Hotel on Nicholas's arm. Her mouth dropped open. Her eyes remained on the glass ceiling as they followed the people into the banquet room. Another cathedral ceiling of stained glass above, and double-glass doors lined the walls. Gold-leaved chairs were pulled back from the smooth white linens on the tables, each with an uncorked bottle of champagne. Everything was white and gold.

Nicholas and Adelina quickly found their seats, and he held the chair out for her to sit on.

Adelina fingered the silver cutlery and gilt-trimmed plates. She wasn't used to such luxury and felt honored to be Nicholas's date.

Servers were already serving the food and pouring the champagne into fluted glasses. Thousands of tiny bubbles sparkled under the lights. She lifted the glass to her lips and took her first sip of champagne. The fragile bubbles raced across her tongue, and she hummed with pleasure. She emptied her glass and set it on the table. The waiter immediately refilled her glass.

Nicholas laughed. "Slow down. We have all evening, and they haven't even brought out the wine yet."

She smiled, her head already fizzing slightly.

The first course was placed before them, a cream soup.

"This smells wonderful," she said.

Sitting across from her, Nicholas seemed to relish her childlike excitement. "Now that I have a little experience, I think I'll be getting more shows," he said. "I feel it in my bones. This is the life I'm supposed to live."

"Thank you for allowing me to accompany you. This whole night feels like magic." She stared into his green eyes, the color of summer ivy.

His face changed, and he looked sad. "I almost forgot. This is your last night."

Suddenly the music started and lightened the mood. People were on the dance floor, and he took her hand. "Let's enjoy this evening. I want to remember it forever."

*****

The following day, they stood in the airport, not knowing if they would ever see each other again. With one last hug, she rested her head on his shoulder.

"I'll come to Florence as soon as I get time off from work," he whispered.

Adelina straightened and joined her class to board the plane. Before disappearing into the walkway to the plane, she turned and waved.

Adelina returned with fresh ideas, a funny New York accent, and the glow of love.

"Mama, I met someone special while I was in New York. I'm in love."

"Love? In love with who?"

"His name is Nicholas DeLuca. He works on Broadway. He promised to come to Florence as soon as he gets time off from work."

"I'm happy for you," Antoinette said, worried that Adelina would get her heart broken.

Chapter 67

Three months passed, and Adelina hadn't heard from Nick. Disappointed, she no longer had an interest in acting and would rather be a designer like her parents. Adelina renovated her mother's workshop. She created one-of-a-kind outfits with a dramatic flair.

After hiring five new seamstresses who could follow her direction, she designed five outfits worn by Broadway actresses.

Her designs attracted celebrities, and the demand increased. They sold so well that they could hire a woman to manage the factory, allowing her to take over the boutique shop for her mother.

Amid the commerce district of the working class near the old bridge, she came to the shop her mother had started almost ten years ago. Adelina paused outside the front door, noting the faded lace curtains in the window and other changes she would make to the décor. Taking out the key, she let herself in. A faint bell tinkled above her head. She flipped the sign on the door to *open* but changed her mind after looking around the shop. Mannequins stood like dancers displaying outdated fashions. Some were missing limbs. Starting with the rack of woman's dresses, she sorted the clothing. All outdated garments sat in a pile on the floor. She took a deep breath of contentment and went to the supply closet to get more dress forms.

The bell on the door tinkled.

"We're not open yet," she called out. "Come back at ten."

"But I've traveled a long way to see a beautiful woman."

She looked up. It was Nicholas. His smile made it easy to remember why she fell in love with him.

Adelina came into the house with a big smile.

"Mama, Mama."

"What is it?" Antoinette asked from the kitchen.

Adelina looked into her face, her cheeks flushed and the eyes of a child bursting with a secret.

"I want you to meet someone. He's in the living room."

Nicholas sat on the couch and stood up when Antoinette entered the room.

"Mom, this is Nicholas, the boy I told you about from New York."

Antoinette looked flustered and then remembered her manners.

"It's very nice to meet you," she said, extending her hand. Adelina has told me so much about you."

"I'm sorry. I should have come sooner, but the distance is great, and I don't get too much time off from work."

"What are your plans, Nicholas?" Antoinette asked.

"I'm not sure yet, but I'm considering moving to Italy."

"What about your job? What about your career?"

He looked at Adelina and then down at his lap. "I love your daughter more than the job, and my dance career hasn't gone anywhere. It's time to let that dream go and settle down."

"Where are you staying," Antoinette asked.

Nicholas looked at his lap. "I haven't secured a room yet. I wasn't sure if Adelina wanted to see me again."

"Well, you can stay in the guest room if you like. Adelina can bring some fresh linens."

"That's very generous of you."

Antoinette laughed. "It's not for you. It's for me to get to know you."

*****

At the end of the week, Nicholas packed to return to America.

Adelina waited outside with him on the porch for the driver to pick him up for the airport.

Antoinette wanted to give them privacy, so she said her goodbyes in the hallway.

Expecting to see a melancholy daughter, she was surprised when Adelina cheerfully bounced into the house.

"He seems like a very nice young man," Antoinette said.

Adelina looked at her with moonlight eyes. "We're engaged."

"That's wonderful." Antoinette hugged her.

"That's not all. A famous director has offered Nicholas a major part in a musical."

"That's lovely, dear."

"It's in New York City."

"New York? But that's in America."

"We've decided to live in the United States. It's a great opportunity for Nicholas. I'd never forgive myself if I denied him his chance to do what he loves. I can get work designing stage costumes."

"I don't want you to leave, Adelina. I'll miss you."

"I would miss you too, Mama. That's why I want you to come with us."

"Me? Oh, no. I can't leave Italy. I won't!"

Antoinette felt the blood rush to her head. Her heart thumped wildly. Feeling faint, she reached for a chair.

"I don't want to move to America. I love Florence."

"Mama, you can't live alone. You're getting older."

"I have friends," she argued. "This is my home."

Adelina breathed in deeply, trying to remain calm. "I have to leave, and you are coming with us."

"What about the shop? And the boutique?"

"We can sell the businesses. The competition from designers like Versace and Gucci is overwhelming. Besides, you always say you're getting too old to work."

"No! I refuse." She marched to her room and slammed the door.

Antoinette climbed into bed and lay there, thinking.

The following day, the house was quiet. Adelina had already left for work. She washed her face. Before Antoinette turned to go, she caught her reflection in the bathroom mirror. As if she were a portrait of someone else, she looked unfamiliar. The edge of a shadow threaded through her golden pupils. She blinked and forced herself to look away. Sighing, she put the kettle up for tea and took her cup out to the back porch Ethan had made so she could sit outside and watch the geese fly over the river. A few landed on the shore to nibble the grass. Consumed in their meal, they kept their heads down.

I'm an old lady who's already lived her life. It's Adelina's turn.

Chapter 68

Nicholas made all the arrangements to fly to America. Antoinette had never flown on a plane. Since Ethan's death, she had hardly left the house in the past ten years. Since Adelina took over the shop, she'd grown accustomed to life at a slower pace. Her life in Florence had been so insular. This was the place she called home—the place where she was born. Yet, she was leaving. Although uneasy about her future, oddly enough, she felt hopeful about leaving the memories behind. Once and for all, maybe she could make peace with her past.

Suddenly she felt apprehensive about getting on a plane to a place she had never been. Her bags were packed and waiting by the door. She wondered if she was making a mistake.

She had never spoken about her life before Ethan. Adelina knew her mother was married before but didn't know she had two brothers who died in the war. Although she wanted to, Antoinette convinced herself it didn't make sense to tell her she wasn't sure what to say. It was a blur.

Antoinette looked around at the accumulation of objects over the years. They were only things. She left everything behind except the box of photos she had found in the closet.

The sky was darkening with an oncoming storm. Antoinette thought it was fitting and matched her mood. She watched Nicholas load her suitcases into the trunk with a heavy sigh.

As she walked to the car, a sudden breeze swept over her, playing with the strands of her hair. The air was heavy with the scent of gardenias. It spurred a distant memory that slipped away before it came to consciousness. The ruffle of feathers caused her to look up as two geese made a pass. The migration of birds returning from the south had begun. She sighed. This time, she wouldn't be there to feed them.

Home—it was hard to let go, but nothing was left to bind her there. It was time to go.

Adelina opened the taxi's back door for Antoinette. Before getting in the back seat, she turned to the house and said a final goodbye.

Adelina slid in next to her mother while Nicholas sat in the front with the driver.

As the car picked up speed, the house vanished like a train around a bend. Swallowed up by the passing trees, it was gone. She closed her eyes. When she opened them, they were at the airport.

America lay ahead like a sleeping giant.

Chapter 69

Antoinette's heart quickened as she walked about the second-story apartment. It was sparsely furnished except for beds in each bedroom and a kitchen table and chairs. Living room furniture was scheduled for the end of the week. Until then, the polished wood floors caused the sounds to echo and bounce along the empty room.

She ran her finger along the dust accumulated on the windowsill in the kitchen, then looked out at the groups of similar apartment buildings with clotheslines hung across the courtyards. Outside was an iron fire escape. She opened the window and stepped onto the metal grating. The building shook as the subway train sped past underground. Looking down at the commuters hurrying to work, she felt lost in this strange new land. She'd left everything she'd ever known and was unsure where to put her feet.

Beyond the rooftops, the low-lying clouds blocked out the sun. Even though the neighborhood was primarily Italian, it felt alien. In Florence, she would be feeding the geese at this hour in the morning. So, this is America, she thought.

Across the courtyard, she noticed pigeons. Rummaging through the kitchen cabinet, she grabbed a few slices of bread and climbed the hall stairs to the roof. It took all her strength to push open the old, rusted door. The sounds of the city were reduced to ambient static. Clothing swung from the laundry post in the soft morning breeze, and a clean scent of freshly washed clothes filled the air. A kid's pool sat in the center. The water was dirty from the day before. She leaned against the low brick wall at the edge and marveled at the city, the way the light swept between the buildings. Car horns and sirens faded, making room for her to get lost in the weeds of her memories. Antoinette knew she would spend a lot of time on the roof. It was the only place she was able to breathe.

The metal door flung open with a bang. Three girls dressed in bathing suits spread their towels. Adelina had told her that the roof was where people lounged during the summer when they didn't want to go to the crowded shores. They called it *Tar Beach.*

Before she left, she looked at the girls lounging like cats. A snippet of a memory overcame her, and she saw herself at the water's edge of a lake, the sun baking into her skin. A handsome young man was by her side. She tried to hold onto the vision, but it was gone.

It was a long hot summer in the city. The roof became unbearable in the heat of the day. Antoinette waited until the sun went down to go onto the roof to look at the stars.

*****

By fall, the long stretch of Indian summer had faded away, replaced by the sudden cold snap turning the leaves a brilliant red, gold, and purple. The heat gave way, and the humidity decreased to an airy softness.

The windows fogged with frost told her it was a chilly morning. She rolled over and pulled the covers over her head. It took time for her to get used to the fickle weather in New York. Mornings were chilly, requiring warm clothing, but the sun fought its way through by the afternoon.

Nicholas had already left for work, and Adelina was rushing around the apartment to find her scarf.

"I'm sorry," Antoinette called out to her. "I borrowed it yesterday." She put on her robe and went into the living room.

Adelina pulled on a coat and wrapped the scarf around her neck.

"I should be home early today. It's a matinee."

"Would you like me to start dinner?"

"That would be great, Mama. Do you have any plans today?"

"Not really. Perhaps, I'll walk the avenue when it warms up."

Adelina kissed her cheek. "I'll see you this evening. Don't get lost." She laughed.

Antoinette made herself a small breakfast and then took a long hot shower. Before she dressed, she stuck her head out the window to gauge the temperature. The sun was in full blast, and there was a slight breeze.

Wearing pants and a short-sleeved shirt, she put on a light coat and set out onto the city streets. She walked along Broadway toward Midtown, browsing the department stores. Manhattan rose before her, block after block of tall buildings. At each street crossing, the wind picked up unhampered by the buildings. The scent of dumplings caught her attention as she passed a Chinese restaurant. Feeling hungry, she entered.

"What is good?" she asked.

The old man behind the counter looked at her with a tilted head. "Well, most people like Lo Mein."

"All right," she said. "Let me have that."

"What meat you want?" he said with an accent.

"Meat?"

"Yes. Chicken, beef, shrimp?"

"The chicken sounds good."

Taking her food to a nearby park, she sat on a bench and reached in her pocket for a handful of seeds to feed the birds.

Antoinette had grown to love pigeons and small sparrows. Surrounded by her feathered friends, she pushed the metal handle aside and plunged the wooden chopsticks into the white container. *This is good,* she thought, as she scooped the lo mein noodles into her mouth. She ate it all and dumped the empty carton into a trashcan at the corner. Then she continued her walk.

As she approached 84th Street, she ducked into a Lowes movie theater. Although it was late in the day, going to the movies was her favorite thing in New

York. Sometimes, romance and others comedy or adventure, depending on her mood.

Thomas Lamb, a Scottish-born American architect, had designed the opulent theater. The lights dimmed, and she sank into another world for a few hours.

When the credits rolled, she waited for the crowds to thin out. Antoinette stepped out of the theater just as the sun disappeared behind the buildings. There was a chill in the air. She thought about taking the subway, but the station was busy with commuters, so she shoved her hands in her pockets, pulled her coat closed, and rushed home. By the time she arrived, her cheeks were numb.

"Where were you, Mama? I've been so worried."

"I'm sorry. I ended up going to a movie. I forgot all about starting dinner." She rubbed her hands and warmed them near the radiator.

"Why didn't you wear the heavy coat I bought for you?" Adelina asked.

"It wasn't cold when I left. I thought my light jacket was enough."

"You need to layer," Adelina said.

"Layer?"

"Yes. Wear something light and cover it with a sweater, then a coat if you go outside. You can peel off the extra garments when the temperature rises."

Antoinette laughed. "It seems colder here in America. I'm not looking forward to winter."

"Cheer up. The holidays are coming." "That's all right. I'm just relieved that you're home. I'll call Nick and ask him to pick up some take-out."

*****

The first snowstorm was beautiful but caused an awful mess within a week. On a sunny day, the sun heated the streets just long enough to thaw the slushy snow. Then it was gone, sometimes turning to ice. The blowers piled it on the sides of the street, and within a week, as it melted became tinged with black soot.

Finally, the last of the snow melted under the sun's warmth. The promise of Spring was in the air. Feeling like a caged animal all winter, she grabbed a sweater and a bag of seeds for the birds and left the apartment. At first, she didn't know where she was going, but her feet had a mind of their own. Antoinette walked through the Bowery and found herself at Washington Square Park.

Chapter 70

Domenico rolled out of bed and smoothed the covers, trying to shake off the ache in his old bones. Vittorio had married a local Irish girl. They gave him three beautiful blonde-headed grandchildren, two boys and one girl, who was the apple of his eye.

Vittorio and his wife bought a cozy four-bedroom house in Prospect Park. They insisted his father move in a few years after he retired.

After a light breakfast of coffee and a slice of toast, he walked down 18th Avenue to Washington Square Park, where he played cards with his Italian friends under the shade of the oak trees. It had been his daily routine since he retired.

While playing cards with his friends, he gazed at the woman sitting alone on the next bench. There was something familiar about her.

"Does anyone know who that lady is?" he asked.

"She lives in my building," Charlie said. "Moved in six months ago with her children. I once met her daughter in the hall, picking up the mail. She said they were from Florence."

"My wife was from Florence," Domenico said. "She was the most beautiful woman. Her eyes were amber."

"We know," Paul said. "You have told us about it every day for the past twenty years."

Domenico dealt the cards, but something about her kept him stealing another glance at the woman.

"Are we going to play cards or what?" Charlie asked impatiently.

*****

The mysterious woman returned every day. She was lovely. Her hair was brushed back and clipped with a barrette—a lily. Her delicate hand reached inside a brown paper bag and scattered a handful of seeds onto the grass for the birds. She looked sad. For the first time in years, something stirred in Domenico. He wanted to take her in his arms and comfort her. Domenico couldn't help staring. He thought about approaching her, but she left before he mustered the courage.

The next day, he went to the park early, hoping to see her again, but she wasn't there. He crossed the street to buy a cup of coffee. When he returned, she was sitting on the same bench. He walked past her and studied her face, which had lost the softness of youth. There was something in her eyes. He would know them anywhere.

Antoinette? How can this be?

He felt as if he was struck by a thunderbolt. There was no mistaking Antoinette for anyone else. The lines of her cheek, the bow of her lips, and those eyes. Standing there with his heart pounding in a flurry of rapid beats, he felt dizzy. The blood surged through his body from the tips of his fingers to the ends of his toes. He had so many questions. Where had she been all these years? Why hadn't she tried to find him? His questions built up until he couldn't hold them in any longer.

"Antoinette?"

Startled, she looked up at him. Her heart lurched at the sight of this stranger. "How do you know my name?"

"It's me, Domenico?"

Domenico—a name that ached like a bruise in her heart. Anguish washed over her face as if she had retrieved a deep and long-forgotten memory. Her eyelids fluttered. For a moment, the world fell away, and everything quieted around her. The years rolled by in her mind until she saw the man she had fallen in love with so many years ago.

"Domenico?" Antoinette was transfixed.

"Si, Piccola," he whispered.

Held in his gaze and unable to look away, the light of recognition shined in her eyes like diamonds. She stepped out of the darkness and reclaimed her memories. "I remember you. I remember." She was trembling. "I thought you were dead."

Memories filled her mind like puzzle pieces falling into place. The first day she saw him peering over his camera in Milan. Lying next to him on a blanket by the lake. The warmth of his arms when he held her. The images flashed by, melting the empty years away. Their wedding… their honeymoon… and the birth of their sons. A feeling of love washed over her, followed by the heat of anger. She remembered his last words at the train station. He promised that no one would put them asunder.

"You didn't keep your promise," she said.

"Forgive me." His voice thickened.

"Where have you been?" she asked.

"I thought you were…." His eyes brimmed with tears. "I was heartsick and couldn't remain in Italy."

Her anger dissolved. "I understand."

He reached for her, and Antoinette returned his embrace.

"Antoinette," he whispered into her ear, repeating her name.

"What are you doing in America?"

"I moved here a few months ago. I didn't want to leave Italy, but after my husband died, I was so alone."

"Husband? What are you saying? I'm your husband."

"You are my husband, but so was Ethan."

"Ethan! The fashion designer from Milan?"

"Yes. Ethan found me. When I woke up in the hospital, but couldn't remember what had happened. He tried to help me regain my memory, but all I had were flashbacks and nightmares." She took a deep breath and turned away. I traveled to Naples and searched through many ships' manifests, but…."

"It's not your fault. You couldn't find me on the manifest because I changed our names."

"We were married after I thought you were gone forever."

"I was devastated when I lost you, so I left Italy to be with my uncle in America."

A tidal wave of memories flooded back to her.

"I remember now. The Germans invaded Florence. There were bombs. We were running over the Ponte Vecchio. We made it to the other side to the shops—then. "Where are my sons? Where are Dom and Vittorio?"

"I'm sorry...."

Antoinette felt a sense of dread. She guessed what he would say but didn't want it confirmed.

"Dom perished during the bombings." He threw his arms around her and felt her wet cheek against his. They cried over the loss of their son.

"But Vittorio is alive! He's here in Manhattan. We have three beautiful grandchildren, two boys and a girl."

"Take me to them," she said, trying to compose herself. Her face brightened and then dimmed. "Ethan and I had a daughter."

"A daughter?"

"Yes, her name is Adelina. I live with her and her husband."

"I'm sure she is lovely, just like her mother."

Antoinette stopped walking. "Do you have a wife?"

"No, I never remarried."

"Why?"

"You are the only woman I could ever love. You have remained in my heart."

Antoinette couldn't stop trembling. Her eyes fixed on him, and she stood up and touched his unshaven jaw. "Are you still a photographer?"

"I was, but not in fashion. I worked on Broadway. I'm retired now."

"My daughter, Adelina, loves Broadway. It's where she met her husband. He's a dancer. He's the reason we left Italy."

"Performing on stage is a nice dream, but it doesn't pay the bills."

"No, but they do all right. Nicholas is also a lighting technician. My daughter makes costumes for the shows."

"Just like her mother. You were a magnifico with a needle and thread."

"Ethan inherited a textile factory, and I worked with him. I took over after he died."

"That's good to hear. You had so much talent."

Tears filled her eyes. "I remember that sunny day at the station like it was yesterday. You left us to join the partisans and vowed you would return to me. It was the last time I saw you."

"Leaving you and the boys was wrong. I've regretted it ever since."

"We have the rest of our lives."

He wiped away the last of her tears, steadying her as she stood. "Let's go see our son."

Chapter 71

Domenico led Antoinette into his house and followed the voices to the living room, where their grandchildren were playing.

They stared at the strange woman. Antoinette ran over and hugged them.

"This is your grandmother," he said.

"Antoinette, this is Anthony and his brother Paul. And this," he said, scooping up the little girl. "This is Rosa."

"I'm so happy to meet you," she said with tears in her eyes.

Hearing the commotion, their mother, Katie, came in from the kitchen.

"Are you two boys fighting again?" she said and stopped.

"Katie," Domenico said. "This is my wife, Antoinette."

Her mouth dropped open. "I don't understand. How can this be? You said she died in the war."

"It's a long story, but... where is Vittorio?"

"He'll be home soon. I sent him to the bakery for bread."

They sat on the couch and explained what had happened to Antoinette while the children returned to their games.

"Would you like to see my Dollie?" Rosa asked.

"Yes, I would love to," Antoinette said.

The little girl ran to her bedroom and returned with her doll. "Her name is Annie."

"That's a lovely name."

"She can drink a bottle. Want to see?"

Antoinette nodded.

Rosa lovingly fed her baby doll a bottle and then put her over her shoulder to burp.

The front door opened, and Vittorio entered.

Antoinette recognized him at once, even though he was older than her memories.

"Daddy, Daddy, Rosa shouted and ran into his arms. "Grandma's here."

Stunned, he stared at Antoinette. "Mama?"

"My son," she said. Another recollection flashed through her head. She was shielding her boys from the falling debris after the bombing.

Vittorio ran to Antoinette and buried his head in her shoulder. "I don't understand. I thought you were dead."

"I was… in a way. During the bombing, I sustained a head injury that made me forget who I was. But my memory has returned."

"It's nothing less than a miracle," Domenico said.

"So many people died that day," Vittorio said. "I thought you were one of them.

Tears welled up again when she saw the scar on his forehead.

"Vittorio," she whispered his name. "Your brother. . . he's—"

"I miss him every day of my life."

"I'm so sorry, Vittorio."

"What are you sorry about, Mama?"

"For not protecting you."

"No. There was nothing you could have done."

She embraced him. Even though she hadn't been there to raise him, the connection was strong. Her maternal emotions thrilled her. He was her boy.

"You have a half-sister. Her name is Adelina. I'm sure she'll want to meet you as soon as she hears about you. Her husband is an actor. He performs on Broadway."

"Do they have other children?" Vittorio asked. "I mean, do I have any nieces or nephews?"

"No, Adelina and her husband Nicholas haven't started a family yet."

"Where is she? What does she think of this wonderful news?"

"We haven't told her yet. I don't know how she'll take all this."

"Invite Adelina and her husband for dinner tomorrow evening. We can get to know each other."

"I will," she said and hugged Vittorio.

"Why don't we break the news to your daughter," Domenico said.

The children gathered around her before she left, and Antoinette promised to come back again with a surprise for them.

The breeze blew sycamore leaves across the sky, carrying autumn's faint aroma. Domenico reached for her hand. It felt odd but comforting.

"What will you tell your daughter?"

"Adelina knows that I had a life before her father. We never discussed it because I couldn't remember. It was frustrating. The memories came in waves but didn't make sense. I was always on the edge of recollection, but then they would disappear. Then Ethan died, and the loss was unbearable."

"How did he die?"

"Cancer. He only had six weeks to live by the time he was diagnosed. It was so sudden."

"I'm sorry," he said softly.

"I hid him and his sister from the Nazis, but they were discovered and sent to the camps. Ethan survived. After the war, he returned to Florence. The new resident in my house told him where I was. He cared for me until I was strong enough to leave the hospital."

"Did you love him?"

"Yes, but not in the same way I loved you," she said.

"I'm glad you had Ethan. He was a good man."

"I was afraid Ethan's memory would fade over time. I wanted to hold onto every second of our lives together.": She wondered if she'd said too much.

Domenico gently held her face. "You don't have to feel guilty. I'm glad he made you happy."

"Do you like it here in America?" she asked, changing the subject.

"I've adjusted to this country, but my roots are in Italy. Sometimes I feel like a plant ripped from the ground."

"Adelina wanted to move to America and begged me to join her. At first, I refused. But then, I realized that life goes on, so I agreed to come."

"I left Italy to escape my memories." The words lodged in his throat. "It felt as if I'd died along with you. If I had any idea you were alive, I wouldn't have left. I'm so sorry."

"Don't be. Ethan was good to me. I don't know where I would have ended up if it weren't for him."

He nodded, and the two walked in silence for a few blocks. The sun glowed in the distance through the trees.

As they reached the brownstone where her daughter lived, she stopped.

"I need to tell her by myself. It would be a shock if we did it together."

"I understand. I'll wait outside."

Chapter 72

Adelina was in the kitchen cooking dinner. She was startled when she turned around and saw her mother.

"Are you alright, Mama? You look different. Has something happened?"

"Yes, something wonderful. Please, sit down. I need to talk to you."

Adelina wiped her hands on the dishtowel and sat at the kitchen table. "What is it?"

"Do you remember when I told you something terrible happened to me in the past?"

"You never really wanted to talk about it. Even as a child, I sensed it was not a good subject to bring up."

"That's because there was nothing to say. I had lost my memories of a life before your father."

"Mama, you don't have to explain."

"Adelina, I remember."

"Remember what?"

"Everything! Please, listen and let me finish."

Antoinette paused to gather her thoughts. "First, I was married to someone else before your father."

"You mean you were married?"

"Yes, but I didn't know what had happened to him."

"Your husband, you mean."

Antoinette shook her head, perturbed. "Yes."

"Did Papa know?"

Adelina leaned forward, trying to understand. "I already have a father. I don't need another."

"I'm not trying to replace your father, but he would be the first to embrace Domenico. Your father tried to help me find him. Please, give him a chance."

"All right, Mama. I haven't seen you this happy in a long time. I'll do it for you."

"Thank you, sweetheart.

"So, you thought he was dead?"

"I'm trying to explain, but my memory isn't complete."

"I'm sorry. I won't interrupt again. Please go on."

"I was much younger than you are now. Domenico was the love of my life." She smiled briefly, enjoying the pleasure of saying his name.

"We married and had twin boys.

"I have brothers?"

"Well, you have one brother."

"But you said, twins?"

"Yes, one died during the war when we were caught in the bombing. Domenico thought I was dead, but I was in a coma. The hospital transported me to a special unit. When I awoke months later, I had no memory of the bombing."

"Is that when you met Papa?"

"No, I knew your father before I married Domenico. When he was released from the concentration camps, he searched for me. Ethan showed up in Florence and discovered I was alive."

"How did he know?"

"Your father was a very influential man before the war. He knew people, who knew people, and found me."

"Did you recognize him?"

"No. I pushed Ethan away, but he was persistent. He told me that we dated before the war. I couldn't remember, but I felt that he cared about me. We grew closer every day until he was the only person I trusted. My love for him grew stronger. I agreed to marry him, but not before we turned over every stone to find my first husband."

"He knew about your children?"

"Yes. Ethan told me about things I couldn't remember. I was hungry for the details, but I couldn't connect them. It made me feel terrible. Somehow, I felt like it was my fault."

Adelina shook her head and said nothing for a few moments. "Why are you telling me all this now?"

Antoinette hesitated, unsure how to proceed. She closed her eyes and found the words.

She took her hand. "I was in the park today, and a man came up to me. The minute I saw him, I knew.... He was Domenico."

Adelina pulled her hand away.

"Domenico? He's alive?"

"Yes, he's been here in Manhattan all these years with our son, Vittorio."

"How do you know it's really him?"

"Do you know what it's like to look into someone's eyes and know without a doubt that the person is your soulmate?"

"If he was alive all this time, why didn't he look for you?"

"He thought I died when the Germans bombed Florence."

"What does he look like?"

Antoinette went to her dresser and pulled out the photo album.

"This is all I had left. After Papa died, I found it in a box with a key."

"I remember seeing that box and wondering why it had a lock."

"Your father hid it in the back of the closet. It was too painful for me to look at the faces of my family without having nightmares of the bombing. But now, it's time to share this with you."

Adelina opened the book and stared at the pictures of her mother and first husband. Years of holidays and celebrations—their wedding, the birth of their sons.

Adelina's eyes opened wide. "I know this man."

"What? How can that be?"

"I met him in New York during my class trip. He was taking pictures of the actors for the billboards."

"He's waiting outside."

"Outside? Now?"

"Yes, I wanted to break the news to you myself."

"Well, tell him to come in."

Antoinette hurried outside and returned with Domenico. He was surprisingly good-looking for his age and had a youthful appearance except for the gray streaks in his hair.

"Adelina, I'd like you to meet someone special."

"Buona Sera," he said "I'm Domenico. You're mother and I, eh...." His eyes lit with recognition. "I know you."

"It seems our paths were meant to cross. My mother told me about you, and I recognized you from the photos."

She looked flustered for a moment but found her manners.

"I'm making dinner. Would you like to join us?"

"I'd love to," he said.

"Can I help?" Antoinette asked.

"No, I can handle the cooking. You relax. I'll open a bottle of wine to celebrate." Adelina reached into the cabinet, pushing aside a few open bottles.

"This should do nicely. It was my father's favorite. He... oh, I'm sorry."

"No need to be," Domenico said. "Your mother told me all about Ethan. He was one of my best friends when we lived in Milan. I was sorry to hear of his passing."

"Thank you." She looked at the clock. "Nicholas will be home soon. Boy, is he going to be surprised."

"How is Nicholas? I haven't seen him since I retired."

"He's auditioned for many plays and musicals and has gotten the lead in a few. He's even had his name listed on a billboard."

"I remember he was always very talented."

"Yes, I can't wait for him to see you."

"Is there a bathroom I could use?" Domenico asked.

"It's down the hall," Adelina said. "Second door on the left."

Antoinette smelled Domenico's familiar scent as he passed, triggering another rush of memories.

"What do you think, Adelina?"

"He's very handsome. But the main thing is... what do you think?"

"I don't know what to think. My memories of life with him are returning, but mostly, I remember the love."

Chapter 73

Nicholas came through the door.

"I'm so glad you came home in time for dinner," Adelina said. "We have a guest."

Nicholas looked amazed. "Domenico! I haven't seen you since you retired."

"Nicholas!" Domenico jumped up to hug him. "I see you took my advice and found the woman you love. I, too, have found my true love."

Nicholas looked confused.

"I'm Antoinette's first husband."

"First husband?" He shook his head and looked at Antoinette. "You're that, Domenico? I thought you were dead!"

"It's a true miracle," Adelina said.

Nicholas poured himself a glass of wine. "I'll need plenty of this. I have so many questions."

Adelina served the pasta, and Nicholas poured more wine. She covered her glass with her hand when he tried to fill hers.

"I'd like to add to this happy occasion," she said. "I'm having a baby."

"I'm going to be a grandmother?"

"Yes. I'm about four months along. I've known for a while but wanted to wait until the baby grew."

Antoinette burst into laughter. "My family is growing faster than I can keep up."

They clinked their glasses and made a toast to famiglia.

After dinner, Nicholas helped Adelina with the dishes.

It's a beautiful evening," Adelina said. "Why don't the two of you go for a walk while we clean up."

"Yes, that would be nice," Antoinette said. "I'll grab a sweater."

"Thank you for dinner, Adelina. Your brother, Vittorio, wants you and Nicholas to come to their house tomorrow evening."

"I can't wait to meet him."

"This was quite a surprise," Nicholas said. "I guess this makes us family."

Antoinette came back, and Domenico helped her with her sweater, and they went outside.

"Your daughter is beautiful. She has your eyes."

Antoinette smiled. "I don't know what I would have done if I didn't have her. She was my rock when Ethan died."

"From now on, I want to be your rock."

"Let's go up to the roof," she said. "The moon is full."

Domenico smiled. "That sounds like the perfect place."

"I'll grab some blankets," she said, "and tell Adelina where I'll be, so she doesn't worry."

They climbed the stairs and pushed through the metal door. The sky was filled with stars, and they stood at the roof's edge, gazing upward.

"This is where I spend a lot of time," she said.

The soft breeze gave Antoinette a chill. With a trembling breath, she moved closer to him to keep warm.

It was strange having Antoinette so close. His heart felt complete. They were no longer strangers but knew little of each other.

"Do you remember the fashion show in Milan?" he asked.

Antoinette nodded. "I remember everything in detail, like a movie playing before me."

"The first time we met, I knew you were the woman I'd be with for the rest of my life. I was devastated when I thought I had lost you. You were in my dreams."

"You were in my dreams, too, although I didn't know it was you."

Domenico could see the promise and desire in her eyes. He tilted her head to his and kissed her, and she melted into his embrace.

"I've dreamt of kissing you so many times. I can hardly believe this is real."

They spread out the blankets and lay down to look at the stars. Whispering to each other all evening, they reminisced about the past.

"We should go back to Italy," Domenico said.

"Yes, I miss Florence."

"I've promised my family I'd come back for a visit," he said.

"Family? Yes, I have an aunt who still lives there."

"I remember. We spent our honeymoon at your aunt's farm. You're as pretty as you were then."

Moving one step further along the road between the unknown and the familiar, they learned about each other.

She took a sleepy breath, trying to hold the moment—connecting the past to the present, eager to discover whatever waited beyond.

"I don't want to let you out of my sight," she said. "What if I wake up and this is all a dream?"

Domenico reached out, swept a lock of hair from her cheek, and wrapped the blanket around her.

"It's not a dream."

The city went silent as she rested her head on his chest and fell asleep to the drum of his heart.

*****

They woke in the morning to watch the sunrise as light reflected on the buildings. The air was cool, and Antoinette snuggled into his side for warmth.

"I hope my family wasn't worried about us," she said.

"Then let's assure them."

They entered the apartment to the scent of bacon sizzling in the skillet.

"Good morning, you two lovebirds," Adelina said. "You're just in time for breakfast."

"Coffee?" Nicholas asked and poured a cup for Domenico. He turned to Antoinette. Would you like me to make you some tea?"

"No. I think I'll have coffee today."

Domenico rested his hand on hers, and they ate fresh buttered rolls.

Days ago, he was a stranger to her; now, he was not. They waited until the whole family gathered in Vittorio's house to break the news they were going back to Italy to visit the family they left behind.

Chapter 74

Even thirty years after the war, Florence seemed deserted – nothing like the lively commercial place she had known before the war. The church still stood, along with the bridges and the town square, but some shops were boarded up. It was as if the energy had been sucked out of the city. Even the people looked different. They went about their business in a subdued routine without a smile. Still, it was a sunny day, and the Arno River sparkled as it flowed downstream. The sky was a perfect blue.

They walked past the piazza toward the Porte Sante Cimitero. It didn't seem right that they were going to the cemetery on such a beautiful day, but Antoinette felt an urgency to see their son's grave. As they neared the family plot, she remembered her father's funeral. At the time, she'd been distraught and had to hold her emotions in to help her mother. Antoinette held her head high, even in the face of those who condemned her family for their political beliefs.

She traced Gaetano's name etched into the tombstone and noticed her mother's name.

"Before I left for America, I added your mother, Josephina's name to his tombstone, but I'm sorry. I couldn't retrieve her body."

"Mama," she cried, tears spilling on the hot stone. "All my life, I thought my mother was weak because she never stood up to my father and his fascist ideology. But during the war, no one was braver or more vocal." She looked over at the small wooden cross beside her parents. It read, "Domenico Defino Jr."

The Cypress tree Domenico had planted loomed over his son's resting place. Antoinette threw herself onto the patch of grass with the heavy weight of sadness. "My boy!" she cried.

Domenico held her as she sobbed over the loss of their son. When her tears were spent, she looked up to see a handful of birds take flight.

"There's one more grave I need to visit," she said. "I must pay my respects to Ethan."

"I understand," he said and helped her onto her feet. They walked the dirt path until they came to Ethan's grave. The plants she had attended to when she lived there were overgrown with weeds. Her memories of Ethan didn't seem as real. He was all spirit now, not flesh and bone.

"I should have sent his body to his family mausoleum in Milan when he died, but I selfishly decided to keep him close. I sent a placard to the Shoah Memorial constructed below the city's central station's main tracks. It is where deportees had been loaded onto livestock cars. The last time I was, there was when you sent the boys and me away. Remember the men in gray uniforms? At the time, I didn't know who they were."

*****

On their way to Campania, they made a stop in Montepulciano. Zia Anna was still there. She took one look at Domenico and put her hand to her heart.

"Oh, dear. I think I feel faint. How is it possible? I thought you were...."

"Isn't it wonderful?" Antoinette said.

"Antoinette? I thought you moved to America with Adelina."

"Yes, I would never have found him if I hadn't moved to America. He was there the whole time."

"I miss my dear sister-in-law, Josephina. You look more like your mother every time I see you." Tears filled Anna's eyes.

"I wasn't there when she needed me most," Antoinette said.

What about your sons? Where are they?"

"They were caught up in the bombing of Florence. Dom perished, but Vittorio survived. He's a grown man now with children of his own. He lives in Manhattan."

"I'm sorry," Anna said. "It's always hard to lose a child."

"The war took a toll on all of us up North. I'm glad it passed you by."

"Oh no. The war didn't pass us by. Hundreds of Italians, mostly women, and children, were driven out of their homes. By the time they came to these parts, they were beyond hungry. They searched for any edible plants. The grape vines were stripped bare along with the vegetable patches."

"Couldn't anyone stop them from trespassing?"

"It was much too dangerous. People were angry that they had to leave their homes and their children were hungry. It was easier to let them have what they needed. After that, the Germans came and took whatever wine they could carry. Finally, the Allies came and took the rest."

"Oh, that's horrible."

"Yes, I'm afraid that war sometimes does that to the best of us."

"Where's Zio?"

"Your uncle Calogero lost his life nine years ago in a tractor accident. After the war, it was hard to find workers. He had to till the groves alone. Exhaustion clouded his mind. He overturned the tractor into a trench."

"Who's helping you run the farm? The trees are heavy with lemons, and the ripe tomato crop is ready to be plucked."

"Most of my workers have left, but my daughters and their husbands are moving into houses on the land. There's plenty of room for them to raise their families. The men will take over the business of the farm." Anna smiled at Domenico.

"Your honeymoon suite is still here. You're welcome to stay as long as you like."

"Thank you, Auntie, but we can only spend one night. We must go to Domenico's family in Campania."

Anna retrieved the key and pressed it into Antoinette's hand. "If there is anything you need, let me know."

The guest villa was dusty and neglected, but the view was still stunning. Fields of red poppies stretched as far as they could see.

Her memories multiplied as her past rose into the present. They regained the bond of intimacy they had once shared.

"I remember the first time we made love," she giggled.

Domenico smiled and put his arm around her. "Let's remember together," he said, kissing her passionately.

There was a catch in her chest at the idea of what would come next. Then she recalled how tender their lovemaking had been.

She awoke with Domenico by her side, the lemon-colored sun shining into the window. She thought she was dreaming but realized the man beside her was real.

Domenico smiled and planted kisses on her cheek. One bloomed on her lips, and she pressed herself to him, relishing the warmth of his body. Desperately yearning for his touch.

"Antoinette," he whispered against her throat. Arching her back, she moaned with pleasure as time blurred out of focus.

When it was over, she put her head on his chest and listened to the sound of his heart.

"We fit together perfectly," she said, her heart returning to a slower rhythm.

"This is how it should be," Domenico said.

For Antoinette, it was almost like before, except Domenico was gentler and more tender. She found making love to Domenico, even after years of separation, as natural as if they had never been apart.

*****

On the third day, they traveled to Uncle Sonny's farm. The vines wrapped around the yard like an emerald necklace.

Aunt Geneva cooked a feast for the cousins and their families. They sat around a large concrete table on the terrazzo with an abundance of wine, fresh fish, and pasta.

There was freshly baked bread with Aunt Geneva's exceptional olive oil for dipping. The bread was infused with fresh herbs from her garden with lemon juice.

They sat in the cool evening breeze, drinking wine and watching the sunset over the distant mountain ranges of Gaeta. Uncle Sonny filled Domenico in on the events after he left Campania.

"Before they left, German demolition squads blew up anything of value. Bomb craters were everywhere, and cars couldn't drive on the streets. For a while, we didn't even have water. The city smelled of charred wood."

"I'm afraid to see how Sorrento has fared after the 1944 eruption of Mt. Vesuvius," Domenico said.

"Most of the damage was in Salerno. The area sustained heavy ashfall that collapsed roofs. Sorrento wasn't affected. I don't think you have too much to worry about."

"We'll find out tomorrow, Uncle Sonny. We'll be living first thing in the morning. Marco is anxious for us to arrive."

Chapter 75

Domenico's parents had passed on, but he visited his brother Marco who had taken over the olive grove.

Marco and his wife, Teresa, had seven children. Their youngest girl lived on the property with her four children.

When they arrived, Teresa and her daughter were preparing dinner in the kitchen. Antoinette jumped in to help and peeled potatoes. She enjoyed belonging to a large family but had difficulty keeping track of everyone's names.

As the evening grew long, the children nodded off, and their parents carried them to the living room, where the young cousins camped out on blankets.

Returning to the terrazzo, the adults drank and played cards. Soon, Antoinette's eyes drooped, and she excused herself for bed, leaving Domenico to continue visiting his family.

*****

Antoinette woke and followed voices to the terrazzo, where Domenico sipped espresso with his brother. Marco was discussing his ideas about staring an olive oil export business. Antoinette stood off to the side of the door to listen.

Domenico agreed there was money to be made by bottling and exporting refined oil. "I think our father would approve."

"I could use a partner," Marco said. "I want you to come home, Domenico. We can work together. Two brothers in the olive oil business."

"The idea is intriguing. I've missed Sorrento, but things have changed. I found Antoinette. We have a life in America."

"The groves have been in our family for over four generations," Marco said. We have to keep it going for our father's sake."

"I want to help, but…."

Marco's expression hardened. "Listen, Domenico. I stayed silent when you took off for Milan years ago. Papa needed you then, but you turned your back. He forgave you, as did I, but I won't let you off so easy this time. We are your family! You owe it to our parents and grandparents."

"You're right, Marco. If this is what you want, I will talk to Antoinette."

Antoinette entered the terrazzo, interrupting their conversation. She noticed tears in Domenico's eyes.

"Good morning," she said.

"Buongiorno, Darling." Domenico kissed her on the cheek. "Come. Sit with us." He poured her a cup of coffee from the Moka. It was still hot, and Antoinette wrapped her fingers around the cup to feel the warmth.

She turned her attention to Teresa, who came out with a plate of brioche and a pot of homemade fig jam.

"Buongiorno, Antoinette."

"Buongiorno. Those look delicious."

"It's an old family recipe. I hope you enjoy them."

"We eat a lot of figs in Tuscany. My aunt has a few trees, but they're not easy to grow in the north."

"Figs need constant sun and well-drained soil. Some of the sweetest fruit grows in Sicily, where I'm from."

"I've never been to Sicily. What's it like?"

"I come from a fishing village in Sciacca. The men in my family come from a long line of fishermen."

"Do you go back to visit?"

"Yes, especially during Easter and for Carnivale."

Antoinette glanced at her husband, who was intently talking with Marco.

"It looks like it's going to be a beautiful day," she said.

"Yes. What are you two lovebirds doing today?"

"I'm not sure. It's up to Domenico."

"Have you ever been to Pompeii?"

"No, but I studied about the town in school," Antoinette said. "It's an ancient city buried under volcanic ash when Mt. Vesuvius erupted long ago."

"It sounds interesting, but I'd like to go to the beach."

"Sorrento has a beach, but it's shady most of the day this time of year. The sun only shines from mid-afternoon to dusk."

Antoinette looked disappointed.

"The Amalfi Coast is only forty minutes from here," Domenico said. "If you like, we can spend a few days there."

"Yes, I would love that."

"Wonderful. First, my brother and I have some business to attend to. Why don't you pack a few things after breakfast?"

Marco and Domenico excused themselves and walked toward the groves.

"Marco is so happy to have his brother visiting," Teresa said. "They were very close growing up."

"I don't recall Domenico talking about him very much."

"That's because they had a falling out when Domenico left for Milan, but they are brothers. They make up as quickly as they fight."

Antoinette looked over at Domenico and Marco, who were in deep conversation. She stood and began clearing the dishes.

"Don't bother with that," Teresa said. "Sofia will help me. You pack for your trip."

"Thank you. Breakfast was delicious."

"I'm glad you enjoyed it. Oh, and make sure to take a sweater. The evenings can get cooler in the hills.

*****

Domenico's car wove along the narrow, winding coastline that overlooked the Tyrrhenian Sea. Antoinette worried the car would go off the cliff around the hairpin curves. She held on tight as the car leaned to the right and then leaned to the left. Domenico, comfortable with the terrain, laughed as she gripped the dashboard.

They caught sight of the beach from the hillside village of Positano, where Domenico had rented a villa at the edge of town. The scent of lemons enveloped them through the open windows.

"Oh, that smells heavenly," she said.

The small fishing village was constructed on the side of a mountain, with shops and restaurants along the two-lane street. The streets were narrow, and they had to park the car at the villa.

As they walked hand in hand to the other side of the village, she wondered when he would tell her about his promise to Marco.

Domenico stopped as they passed a small restaurant at the edge of town. "We should stop here for lunch."

"Yes, it looks lovely, and I am a little hungry."

They sat outside at one of the small tables with sandwiches and limoncello. No one seemed to mind the stray cats who came up to beg. The feral felines didn't look underfed, but Antoinette couldn't resist sharing her fish with them. After lunch, they delighted in pistachio gelato.

In the distance, they saw the dome of Santa Maria Asunder and headed toward the church. Inside, Domenico bent to one knee and took her hand.

"Antoinette, will you marry me?"

She giggled. "We are married, silly."

"I know, but since we are here in a sacred place, I think we should renew our vows."

She smiled. "Yes, we should."

They walked to the white marble altar and stood facing each other, whispering promises they had made long ago. When they finished, loud applause came from the back of the church as witnesses to their love shared in their happiness. With their vows renewed, they exited the dark church and blinked in the sun.

"How do we get to the beach?" she asked.

Domenico pointed to a sign. **La Spiaggia.** "There's only one road that leads to the beach."

Antoinette heard the rumble of the waves below as they descended to the shore. Her excitement rose.

Laying their towels on the small pebbles, they wriggled out of their street clothes and ran into the water wearing their swimsuits. The clean and refreshing water brought Antoinette back to her memories of Lake Como. Only this wasn't a lake. It was alive with sea creatures.

"Are there any crabs in the water?" she asked nervously.

"Only one," he said, pinching her butt under the water.

"She screeched, and they burst into laughter. Then Domenico kissed her, tasting the saltiness of the sea.

Chapter 76

After spending two days on the beaches of the Amalfi Coast, Antoinette purred contentment like a cat. She listened to the waves thrashing the rock-strewn beach and savored every moment. Still, her mind was heavy with the conversation she'd overheard between Domenico and his brother. Hoping to get him to admit his intentions, she sighed.

"It's so nice here. I never want to leave."

"We could stay in Italy, you know. We could block out the rest of the world as if it doesn't exist."

"I love Campania," she said, "but I'm not sure there is a place for us here."

"Sure, there is. We can build a house on the border of the olive groves."

"What about our family in America?"

"They can visit us," he said. "We belong here in Italy."

She looked at him with thoughtful eyes. "They say that home is where the heart is."

Domenico put her hand on his chest. "My heart is here."

"Yes, but there are hearts in America too."

"Well, I … um." He fell silent.

"What's wrong?"

"I promised my brother I would return to Italy and help him with the business."

"How is that possible? We have a life in America."

"Yes. I realize that, but it's long overdue. Years ago, I left Sorrento to pursue my dream in Milan. If I don't help, we could lose everything. Marco had to deal with the family business alone after our parents died. I owe him."

"I understand your obligations, but I'm not sure I can move back."

"I thought you were homesick for Italy."

"For a long time, I've dreamed of returning home. The Italian neighborhoods of New York have everything the old country has, but it wasn't home."

"It still isn't."

"You weren't happy in America," he said without judgment. "You told me so."

Although feeling pressured, Antoinette smiled wistfully.

"I'll have to think about it." Until that moment, she had never considered leaving America for good.

Back at the villa, they made love. "We can talk about it tomorrow," he said through the drowsy aftermath of passion and drifted off to sleep.

"Tomorrow," she breathed. The word hung between them in the dark. Somewhere between one step and the next, they had come to a divide. Her heart was breaking. Maybe there was no tomorrow. Only tonight.

Antoinette fell back against the pillow and stared at the ceiling. *How can I stay in Italy? My daughter is on the other side of the world, about to have my grandchild.*

Yet, the Bible says a wife should cleave to her husband.

*****

The ride back to Sorrento was quiet, heavy with their thoughts. Glimpses of doubt escaped from her eyes, and Domenico patted her hand.

"When you smile, my world is brighter."

Antoinette tried to hide her sadness.

Teresa and her daughter had been cooking all day and invited the entire family to join them. Antoinette remained quiet as the voices around the table rose and fell with lively conversation. Her husband looked happy to be with his family. After opening the fourth bottle of wine, no one noticed her leave.

What began as a breeze earlier that evening picked up intensity, tearing through the olive grove with a wail. Torn between her love for Domenico and her family, Antoinette tossed and turned in bed, listening to the wind rattle branches against the windows. She sensed Domenico getting into bed but kept her eyes closed.

Antoinette waited until she heard his heavy breathing and slipped out of bed. She stared at her husband, sleeping soundly.

"Goodbye, my love," she whispered. Even in the twilight of his life, he was handsome.

Quietly, not to wake anyone in the house, she went downstairs with her suitcase. Her limbs felt leaden as if she weighed twice her size. Reaching for the phone in the hall, she called a cab and walked along the dirt driveway to wait outside the gate. The hour taxi ride to Napoli Airport was somber. Antoinette stared out at the rising sun. The cab driver didn't speak. Lost in her thoughts, that was fine with her. She'd thrown away the one thing she'd always loved. The sudden weight of it pressed on her chest.

The driver pulled in front of the terminal and helped her carry her suitcase to the curb. She paid him more than the fare, which made him finally smile.

"Grazie, Seniora," he said and jumped back into his vehicle.

Her heart ached at losing Domenico again. This time, it would be more painful because she carried his memory. It was easier when she couldn't remember.

Reluctant for the last thread joining them to snap, she walked slowly to the reservation counter to buy her ticket. The agent informed her that the next flight to New York was leaving in forty-five minutes, and she needed to get to the gate as soon as possible.

Chapter 77

When Domenico woke up, Antoinette wasn't by his side. He put on his robe and searched for her. It wasn't until he returned that the note on the desk caught his eye.

Dear Domenico,

This has been the most wonderful week. My love for you has brought me back to life, but I can't move back to Italy. Now that I have found Vittorio, I must make up for all the years I was absent in his life. I can't do that unless I am in New York. Also, my daughter is there. I can't turn my back on her, especially now that she's having a baby. I want to be part of their lives. Your brother needs you, and I will not make you choose. Apologies cloud my mind. I've decided, but if I look into your eyes, I will bend to your wishes. It's with a heavy heart that I must leave you. I'm sorry for leaving you this way. It's the only way I can bear it. Please forgive me.

All my love forever, Antoinette.

Domenico gazed east as his eyes misted. He sat silently for a moment before springing into action.

Waking his brother, he explained that Antoinette had gone.

Marco shook the sleep from his eyes and saw Domenico's panic. "I understand a love like yours," he said. "Maybe we can catch her before she leaves. I'll drive you to the airport."

*****

They approached the crowded terminal, and Marco pulled up to the curb.

"You go in," he said. "I'll park the car."

Domenico rushed into the terminal. An agent raised her arm to stop him.

"I'm sorry, sir. The plane is boarding. I can't let you through."

"But I must catch my wife before she leaves on that flight."

"Sorry. I can't let you through."

Domenico watched as people exited the terminal to board the plane.

Marco rushed up to him.

"We're too late," Domenico said. "The flight is leaving."

"Go!" Marco said. "Before they close the doors."

Domenico pushed past the agent and sprinted down the walkway.

Halfway down, he looked over his shoulder and saw two armed *poliziotte* chasing him. His legs pumped harder, focusing on the gate. He was just in time to see the doors close. Domenico stopped. Breathing heavily, he sank to his knees and cried.

"I've lost her again." He covered his face and sobbed.

"No, you haven't."

He looked up to see Antoinette, eyes shining with tears. His grief turned to joy, and he climbed to his feet. "I thought you were gone."

As Domenico reached to embrace her, one of the guards put his hand on his shoulder.

"Fermare," the other guard said and held him back. His partner gave him a puzzled expression.

"Amore," he said and shrugged his shoulders.

They backed off and let the couple have their moment.

"I couldn't leave," she said. "I don't want to live without you."

"I thought about what you said, and you were right. Italy is an important part of our past, but our future is with our children. As generations go on, they'll surely get busy and lose the connection to their roots. We must remind them of their heritage, lest they forget. That's why I'm coming home with you."

"Back to New York?"

"Yes. My life is meaningless without you. I lost you once. I will not lose you again."

"What about your brother?" What about the business?"

"Marco and I discussed it on the way to the airport. We'll open an import company in New York and have the olive oil shipped there for distribution. I can manage operations from America and travel back to Italy as needed."

"So, we can go home to America?"

"Yes." Domenico pulled her into his arms.

"Never let me go from your embrace," she whispered.

"I promise," he said. "Nothing will ever again pull us asunder."

Thank you for reading Asunder.
Please post a review on Amazon.com

Other Books by Janet Sierzant

Gemini Joe
Sauce on Sunday
Brooklyn Love Story
The Green Room

Author Bio

Janet Sierzant was born in Brooklyn, New York. After moving to Georgia, she graduated from Kennesaw State University with a bachelor's degree. She now lives in Vero Beach, Florida, and coordinates the Writers Window Pane critic group.

She is a member of the Florida Writers Association, the Indian River Chamber of Commerce, the Indian River Cultural Council, Main Street Vero Beach, and the Vero Beach Chamber of Commerce.

You can contact the author at
jsierzant@gmail.com

Acknowledgment

Thank you to the Writer's Windowpane, who endured countless readings and offered a valuable critique. Jorget Harper, Gage Irving, Walter Ledwith and Chaz.

Thank you to my Beta Readers, Ellen Contreras, Jeanie Gustafson, Jane Hancock, and Susan Quinn.